IN THE EMBRACE OF A DILEMMA

Elizabeth felt the Earl's lips, warm and soft, lightly touch upon her own. And a moment later, there she was in his arms, and, to her surprise, overjoyed to be there.

At last, it was he who ended the embrace. She was too shaken by emotion to see his expression clearly. If she had, Elizabeth would have seen that it was not lover-like in the least, but rather a look of chillingly cold appraisal. Would she, the Earl wondered, say with shy confusion, "No, we must not!" as his faithless first wife, Kitty, had? Or, "How lovely," as all his light ladies did?

Elizabeth had no way of knowing that either answer, from either pole, would damn her forever in his heart. And she had no way of knowing that she would have to give him the one answer that no female ever had. . . .

The
Mysterious Heir

The Mysterious Heir

by

Edith Layton

A SIGNET BOOK

NEW AMERICAN LIBRARY

A DIVISION OF PENGUIN BOOKS USA INC.

SIGNET TRADEMARK REG. U.S. PAT. OFF. AND FOREIGN COUNTRIES
REGISTERED TRADEMARK—MARCA REGISTRADA
HECHO EN DRESDEN, TN.

SIGNET, SIGNET CLASSIC, MENTOR, ONYX, PLUME, MERIDIAN AND
NAL BOOKS are published by New American Library,
a division of Penguin Books USA Inc.,
1633 Broadway, New York, New York 10019

First Printing, January, 1984

3   4   5   6   7   8   9   10   11

PRINTED IN THE UNITED STATES OF AMERICA

For Susie and her merry heart

— 1 —

There are those who champion a rainy day. Those who find a spring zephyr not half so delightful as a deluge, a sun-struck Sunday not nearly so fine as a steadily dripping Tuesday, and a brisk autumn breeze never as exhilarating as the prospect of windblown sheets of rain covering the town. For those select few who delighted in precipitation, it was an excellent day in London. For the majority of others, it was one of the most wretched days of the season.

But London being the sort of town it was, there were a good many miserable souls about, courting pleurisy at every step. These were men and women who had a living to see to. Merchants and food vendors, shopgirls and tradesmen, lower servants and hackney drivers, they swam through the drowning streets as though the sun were shining with all its might, though they cursed, to a man, and a woman, as they did. They were not of the select number who sighed, as they sat before a toasting fire, that there was something so romantic about a rainy day.

It was rich men's weather. They were the only ones who could enjoy the gusts of wind and shatter of rain on their windowpanes in the proper poetical spirit.

But one gentleman who was wealthy enough to order up a month of rain if he so chose, instead stood by his window and let out an involuntary muttered curse as he tried to see through the streaming pane. Then he sighed, turned, and gripping the head of his heavy molacca cane, made his difficult halt way to a high-backed chair by his fire. He sat slowly, placing the cane at his right side, and stretched one long glossy booted leg out straight in front of him, and absently massaged his leg as he stared into the fire. Though he had wealth enough to commission a parcel of poets to extol the virtues of rain, still he cursed the day as roundly as any of the vegetable mongers who stood shuddering and sodden behind their barrows in the marketplace. For rich or poor, rain is the enemy of old wounds, since old wounds wake to recount their sad stories on rainy days.

He sat and rubbed his leg the way a man might stroke the head of a faithful dog, absently and steadily, not stopping lest he give offense to the recipient of his attentions, lost in thoughts beyond the rain until a soft knock came upon the door. He looked up swiftly to see his butler, stiffly correct, bearing cards upon his silver tray, and startled a look of fleeting sympathy on the old man's usually correct countenance.

"Visitors, your lordship," the butler said, all traces of emotion vanished the moment his employer's eyes met his. "It is Lord Beverly and your solicitor, Mr. Tompkins. Are you . . . will you receive them?"

"Aye, Weathering." The tall man laughed softly from his chair. "Yes, the leg is giving me the devil of a time, but it will whether I have company or no, you old nursemaid. If sitting alone would cure it, why, I'd be ready to dance a quadrille now. No, this rain is only another installment of Bonaparte's revenge, and I'm well used to it by now, so don't send young Tom off for the sawbones, for there's nothing he can do. Unless he can conjure out the sun for me. And, yes, do show Bev and Mr. Tompkins in, but you'd best give them a towel apiece before you let them in, poor chaps."

The tall man straightened in the chair and removed his hand from his leg. He gripped the cane tightly in his right hand, so tightly that his knuckles showed white, and had hauled himself to stand as his two guests were shown in.

"Oh, bother, Morgan, sit down, sit down," the slight young man cried as he entered, still dashing raindrops from his light curls. "There's no need to stand on ceremony, that is, to stand at all with me."

"Lord Beverly is quite right," the neat middle-aged man who entered next said censoriously. "Do sit, your lordship, please do."

"I'm not quite ready for a bath chair, gentlemen," the taller man said with some amusement in his rich soft voice, and so saying, he came forward, limping only slightly, but leaning heavily on his cane, to shake hands with them both.

"Why, you'll do, Morgan, you'll do!" Lord Beverly said in delight. "Just look at you, fine as fivepence."

"But please do sit, your lordship," the other gentleman said, noting, as his younger companion did not, the white lines of stress that bracketed the taller man's mouth as he walked toward them, "for I've business to discuss, business that called me through this wretched storm to come here, and we may as well get on with it."

A look of amused understanding passed through the tall man's deep-set eyes, and he turned to his chair again.

"All business, eh, Mr. Tompkins? Quite right, of course. But not so urgent as all that, is it? For I confess I hadn't expected you on such a day as this. Such a day would have daunted all but the sternest of men on the most desperate of errands."

"Oh, Lord, Morgan"—Lord Beverly laughed, as he unceremoniously hauled a delicately fashioned chair up close to where the taller gentleman was stiffly lowering himself into his high wing-backed chair—"it's only a bit of rain, after all. We're not cripples, you know."

The tall gentleman continued to seat himself and arrange his cane near his right hand again, but Mr. Tompkins stopped abruptly in his efforts to settle himself and his briefcase of papers near a table by the fire and looked up in stunned horror at the younger gentleman's words.

Lord Beverly looked around in confusion in the silence that had settled, and said hastily, "Dash it, not what I meant to say. I meant that we're both hardy souls, Tompkins and I, no reason for us to shy at a spot of rain like milksops. That is, only a bit of rain, you know."

The taller man waved his hand dismissively and smiled. "Get used to Lord Beverly's way with words, Tompkins, and pay no heed. He doesn't mean half the things he says, and the half he does mean, he gets turned about.''

"Unfair," Lord Beverly said sulkily, completing the drying of his exquisite coiffure by running his fingers through it and ruining it entirely.

"Yes it is," the taller man said, "for he is the best of fellows and a staunch friend. However, his own tongue is no friend to him, and he's been tripping over it in his haste to get away from it for years.''

"That's true," Lord Beverly said brightly. "Remember back at school, Morgan? When I vowed not to say a word to get myself into trouble again, and then I got sent down for explaining my silence to the headmaster?''

The tall man laughed. "Yes, especially the part where you explained how you were holding your tongue so as not to comment on his speech impediment, among other things. But, Bev, my dear, Mr. Tompkins did not emerge from his snug chambers on such a day to have you regale him with our school reminiscences. I believe you said something in your note about legal action, Mr. Tompkins, and you, Bev, wrote about an impostor. I assure you, Bev, you would have been welcome to come to Lyonshall to swap school stories with me for hours. In fact, you did come and do so not a few months past. But I only posted to London on the strength of your summons about this impostor. That alone. It sounds incredible to me.''

"Unfortunately, it is not. It is all true, your lordship," Mr. Tompkins said briskly, looking up from the papers he had arranged to his satisfaction. "I have the notes here. A considerable sum to the proprietors of Wilson's, another due Mr. Jensen, a chit from Barrison's, and this one, only recently received, from Matlock's. And these are only the larger ones.''

"Bills from the worst gaming hells in town," Lord Beverly said knowingly. "And that one from Jensen—why, I couldn't even get an appointment with the fellow. And he came out of nowhere. One moment, it's all the crack to have your hessians made by Hobley, and the next, it's Jensen or nothing. He has a way with tassels, you see, that no one else can get the knack of.''

Mr. Tompkins interrupted Lord Beverly's musings, leaving him to study his boots, brooding at them through his quizzing glass as he turned his feet this way and that, by saying portentously, ''And all the bills run up by one James Everett Courtney, by all accounts a well-set-up-looking gentleman, fair-haired and light-eyed, and most importantly: heir presumptive of the seventh Earl of Auden, who is yourself, of course, your lordship.''

''At your service.'' The tall man smiled, and went on, ''And of course, I have no heir presumptive—or none that I know of. And looking through the family Bible, I find there is no James Everett Courtney, and never was.''

''Just so,'' Mr. Tompkins said, quietly triumphant, and sat back.

''Your lordship,'' the butler said softly, entering with a laden tray, ''I took the liberty of bringing some refreshments, against the chill of the weather.''

''How uncivil I've become. Quite right, Weathering,'' the Earl said, watching the butler place the tray upon a table. ''Bev, you pour something fortifying for Mr. Tompkins and yourself.''

''Of course,'' Lord Beverly said, leaping up to find some occupation and promptly pouring three large measures of brandy. Then he noted what else there was on the tray and gave a crow of joy. ''Gingersnaps!'' he cried with delight to the butler's retreating back, ''Tell Mrs. Turner thank you, Weathering. Only fancy,'' he said to the Earl, handing him his glass, ''she remembered after all these years. From when we were both boys, Morgan.''

''And therein lies the problem, your lordship,'' Mr. Tompkins said, ignoring the glass Lord Beverly was urging on him.

Lord Beverly paused to look inquiringly at the solicitor.

''There's no problem with you, Bev,'' the Earl said softly. ''Mr. Tompkins was still talking about the bogus heir presumptive I seem to have acquired.''

''Just so,'' Mr. Tompkins said, accepting the glass from a relieved Lord Beverly.

"Heir presumptuous, more like, Morgan. Imagine the crust of the fellow, purporting to be your successor and getting all that credit all over town—in the best places, too."

"Not the best of places, your lordship." Mr. Tompkins frowned. "For there he would have to have some entrée. He would have to be accompanied by someone known to you. But he frequents the more raffish sorts of gaming hells, and the less respectable sort of establishments, and there, his knowledge of you and his familiarity with your life-style, combined with his affect of a gentleman, have been sufficient to carry it off. And then, of course, the fellow doesn't pay up and the bills are beginning to find their way to me, as your man of business. It is in the capacity of your man of law that I urge you to remain here in London for a space. Whilst you are here, there can be no question of anyone pretending to be your relative. It is your . . . ah, propensity for remaining at Lyonshall, far from London, or traveling on the Continent, which allows him free rein in London. You haven't shown your face here, your lordship," Mr. Tompkins said, leaning forward with a serious intent, "in years. Years. That is what the fellow is making his fortune on. And since, you . . . ah, have led such a secluded life, there are certain misapprehensions about you in society. So the fellow is able to impersonate your heir with impunity. The best way to squelch him is to remain here and take your rightful place in society. That will put him to rout. Otherwise, we will eventually have to begin to pay some of these bills. We will be unable to withstand all the creditors. And their claims will reflect upon your own reputation, not only socially but also financially. But if you set up here for the season, he will have to fade away."

"You'll catch cold at that," Lord Beverly said through a mouthful of gingersnaps, "for Morgan here won't stir stump. Hates London. I practically begged him to come down with me for the season. No, he said, and no."

'And no again," the Earl said, leaning his head back against his chair. "I have no intention of remaining in London. As soon as our business is finished, I'm going back to Lyonshall. London is not for me."

"But, your lordship," Mr. Tompkins said earnestly, "you have absented yourself from London for so long that there are few here in town that have the honor of your acquaintance. Lord Beverly is perhaps the only man in the ton who knows you well at all. And he alone cannot put down the pretensions of this impostor. And to put Bow Street onto the impersonator's traces will only give rise to more rumors."

"For ten impostors I will not take up residence here," the Earl said softly and with finality. Such was his air of command that Mr. Tompkins sat back with a sigh.

"Then you will have to produce an heir who will stay in London," he said.

"That's simple stuff, Morgan," Lord Beverly said happily. "Just who is your heir, anyway?"

"I haven't the least idea," the Earl said wearily. "I gave it some thought when I got your message. I have few living relatives and none male. And since my Aunt Clara is unmarried, and one uncle left no living issue, and one other left only a girl still in the schoolroom, I have no idea of who the lucky chap is. I wrote to that effect, Mr. Tompkins."

"Yes, and I have been busy these last days," Mr. Tompkins said with another slight frown, "with both your Aunt Clara, who while bedridden is still sensible, and with your family genealogy. As well as I am able to tell, your rightful heir would have to come from your two granduncles' lines. As it is a direct male succession unless you yourself produce an heir, your estate in Sussex, the one in the North, and Lyonshall itself, as well as a good deal of your funds, will all go to one of three male third cousins now living. None of whom, I venture to say, you have ever met. Really, your lordship, in these circumstances, rather than searching out these far-flung relatives, it would be much simpler for you to simply marry and settle the matter in that time-honored fashion."

Lord Beverly stopped chewing his gingersnap and glanced hurriedly over to the Earl, who was staring impassively into the fire. It was impossible to see the expression in his hooded eyes. The thin strong face was a study in planes in the leaping firelight. The Earl's face, with its high forehead, long straight nose, and high cheekbones, remained set and expressionless. He sat with his head back against the chair, his thick dark auburn hair almost black in the shadows.

"No," the Earl finally drawled softly, "I think not. Not simpler, not feasible, my dear Tompkins. Not for me."

And then, in a lighter tone, he said, "I do not think I am ready to limp down the aisle with some lucky girl again."

"Oh, that cursed limp," Lord Beverly cried, much agitated. "As if that mattered! You make too much of it, Morgan, I vow you do. Why, the right sort of female wouldn't notice you limp in bed at all!"

Mr. Tompkins' face grew rigid with embarrassment and the Earl gave way to a rare peal of true rich laughter; then he drew one slender hand across his eyes to wipe them.

"I hope not, Bev. But just what sort of a wife would such a female make if she didn't notice? No, no don't try to puzzle it out, it was delightful just as it came, unbidden from your lips. But that is not the problem. I don't care to seek out the right sort of girl right now, however observant she may or may not be. I'm sorry, Mr. Tompkins, but I am a widower, and the marriage was without issue. I do not choose to race to the altar with some unlucky female and hasten her to the sheets to produce the eighth Earl of Auden just to discourage this impostor. At some time I may, I may," the Earl mused, "but not now. I believe, then," he went on, as though the matter now bored him, but Mr. Tompkins could see him unconsciously begin to knead his leg with his hand, "you will just have to trot out those three chaps and we'll choose one. Third cousins, you said?"

"But you can't just name one without meeting him, without assessing his worth," Mr. Tompkins said, aghast.

"No, really you can't, Morgan." Lord Beverly frowned.

"I'm not exactly at my last prayers," the Earl said with asperity; and then more softly he added, "My left leg may think it is, but the rest of my poor corporal self is in fine fettle."

"That's true," Lord Beverly said happily. "You look leagues better than you did a few months ago. Look better every time I see you, as a matter of fact."

"Unpleasant though it may be," Mr. Tompkins said sternly, "everyone of us must accept the fact of life's impermanence. Even the youngest of us in the bloom of youth may be struck down. You are yet in both youth and health, but it is both improvident and unwise to leave the fate of your fortune to chance. At the moment, all three men have equal claim as your heir. Would you wish to see the entail broken and Lyonshall sold? Or go to a stranger who would gamble it away?"

"No," the Earl said thoughtfully, "never that."

"Ah, well, then, it is perhaps fortunate that this situation, however presently unpleasant it is, has arisen. For I was appalled, your lordship, to discover that you had not designated an heir. A man of your title and substance should have seen to it years ago."

"No, really, Morgan," Lord Beverly said sadly, "it wasn't right of you."

"And who is your heir, Bev?" the Earl asked pleasantly.

"M' sister's boy Randall. A lad with more teeth than wit. I mean it, Morgan, he's got more teeth than a shark. And they're crosswise. It's terrible to sit down to dinner with him. Every time I see him, I resolve to marry on the instant, just to keep him out of the direct line. But fortunately," Lord Beverly said seriously, "I don't see him often. And you know I've got no concentration. But, Morgan, it's shocking how you never saw to the succession, for you've got more wit than I, and even I have an heir."

"My family was not large, you know. My brother was the rightful heir and I his," the Earl said softly. "And then when I married I believed . . . I believed all sorts of things. And then, I confess, I never gave it another thought. No, you're right as usual, Mr. Tompkins."

"Then," the older man said briskly, "might I suggest that you send off an invitation to each of them. Meet with them. And then at leisure make up your mind. Mind, I think it only fair that you should inform them that they are only temporarily to be considered as heir, but that if worse should come to worst, at least you will have provision for the future of your name and your dignities."

"Have them all here, Morgan," Lord Beverly said with enthusiasm, "so I can cast an eye over them. I'm no mean judge of character, you know."

"No," the Earl said slowly. "I shall have them to Lyonshall and you can come too, Bev. Since it was your idea, you can lighten the load for me. Should you like to accompany us, Mr. Tompkins?"

"It would be a pleasure, your lordship," the older man said, arranging his papers. "However, the press of business, you know. But I shall come when you have decided as to which of them you choose. And I shall draw up the necessary papers. That will not only stop the impostor in his tracks, but I believe it will make you easier in your own mind."

"That blasted impostor's done you a good turn, Morgan," Lord Beverly commented from the table where he was refilling his glass. "See if he hasn't."

"Doubtless he's my benefactor." The Earl smiled. "Well, fill us all up again, you selfish lout, Bev, and we'll toast my three kinsmen. What are their names, then, Mr. Tompkins?"

"There's Owen Courtney, Richard Courtney, and Anthony Courtney, in all, your lordship."

"Well, then," the Earl said, "let us drink to my new family, my loving hopeful relations. Let us drink to . . ." He paused and listened to the rain slash against the window. ". . . Owen, Richard, and Anthony, the eighth Earl, the eighth Earl, and the eighth Earl. And of course to the perfect wife." He smiled wickedly at Lord Beverly. "An unobservant girl. And to my benefactor, James Everett Courtney . . . the man who never was."

"You're a generous fellow." Lord Beverly grimaced.

"My heart," the Earl said mockingly, "is as deep as my wine cellar. Drink up, old friend, to the next heir of Auden, a fellow who might like me while I live, but who will doubtless appreciate me more when I am dead. A fellow who will hang upon my every word, but will be most interested in my last breath."

"Ghoulish Morgan"—Lord Beverly shook his head—"must be the rain's got you in the sullens."

"The rain . . ." The Earl smiled, dashing off the brandy. "The interminable rain. Doubtless."

— 2 —

Although the first letter to be delivered was addressed to "Master Owen Courtney," it lay upon a tray just outside the door to a lady's bedroom. It had the honor of being first delivered only because the house to which it had been addressed was only a few short blocks from the Earl of Auden's London residence. Though the letter shared its space upon the tray with three other missives, it was placed foremost. The butler of the lady's establishment, having an unerring eye to quality, had placed it over what to his way of thinking were inferior correspondence.

It was an advanced hour of the day when the door finally cracked open and two little white hands, with a quantity of white lace frothing over delicate wrists, picked up the tray and bore it into the bedroom. Although the tray also held a silver pot of chocolate, two porcelain cups, napery, a dish of sweet biscuits, and flowery plates to put them on, it was the letter that immediately caught the bearer's eye as surely as it had dazzled her butler's.

"Lud," the lady breathed, sitting down upon her bed in a whisper of silks, and gazing blankly at the letter. Her blue eyes were opened wider than they usually were at that hour of the morning. She tossed her blond curls back over her white shoulders, took in a deep breath which caused the front of her negligee to gape becomingly, and slowly, reverently slit the envelope open.

She read the letter through once, and once again. But it was after the third reading that she gave out a little crow of delight. "Owen!" she cried, and then again, wonderingly, "Owen!"

A deep groan came from the other side of the bed and a muffled voice complained, "Again? Snooping little wretch. Get him out of here."

"No, no," the lady exclaimed, still gazing raptly at the letter in her hand, "He's not here, he knows not to come in here. He's with his nurse. But only see, only look!"

Another groan came from the gentleman, and slowly he sat up in bed, rising like some great Roman statuary, all un-draped muscle and sinew, from beneath the covers. After a gaping yawn he unceremoniously took the letter from the lady's hands and read it. And then, after rubbing his eyes, read it again.

"Auden," he breathed. "You never mentioned how closely you were related!"

"I did," the lady protested, "but you never listened. We're not, in fact, closely related. He scarcely knows me. In fact, when he was on the Town, he barely acknowledged my presence. But that must have been because he had his hands full with Kitty," she amended, preening herself. "But John was his distant cousin, just as it says in the letter. John had something of the look of him, too," she mused, "although Morgan got the best of everything in that family, money and looks."

"And now," the gentleman said, sitting up straighter, "Owen is going to be named his heir."

"No, no," the lady said, doing some rapid thinking. "Read it again. It says that Owen is to be considered for the title. There are two others as well. My God, that must mean that Morgan is at death's door," she gasped.

"Put away your handkerchief." The gentleman frowned. "It means nothing of the sort. I hear he's in London even now, and apart from his game leg, he's healthy as a horse. What it means," he said consideringly, "is that he's in no hurry to marry again, but that he has decided to name an heir."

"I, for one," the lady said indignantly, "cannot blame

him for not wanting to marry, not after the dance Kitty led him. Shocking stuff.''

The gentleman gave an amused laugh and stretched luxuriously. Then he began to run one large suntanned hand across the lady's silken back.

''So proper, then, Isabel? I suppose you never played dear John false?''

''Don't speak ill of the dead,'' the Lady Isabel said, pokering up and hoping he would not sense how her flesh rejoiced in his touch.

''I was speaking ill of the living, vixen, and you know it. So,'' he said, making larger circles with his hand, ''you are going to dress up little Owen and drill him in manners and trot off to Lyonshall in hopes that Morgan picks him as heir?''

''Of course,'' Isabel sniffed. ''What better fate for my poor fatherless little boy? What sort of a mother would not make a push to have her son named heir to Morgan's fortune?''

''And what sort of female would not make a push to have herself named Morgan's consort? Don't try to deceive me, Isabel.'' He laughed, hauling her down to the bed and gazing into her eyes. ''We rub on well together because we are so very much alike. It would make a neat package, wouldn't it? Owen as heir, and dear Isabel as lady-wife. For while Morgan's sworn off marriage, he's not sworn off women. And you are such a compelling little baggage,'' he said, placing his lips upon her throat.

''You say nothing?'' He laughed into her neck. ''Too busy thinking, no doubt. Well, rest easy. For I wouldn't mind.''

He felt the sigh of relief as it swelled in her chest. But then he felt a new tension in her, saw it begin to cord her smooth neck.

''But, my dear,'' she said softly, ''then that would be the end of . . . us, wouldn't it? And wouldn't you mind that?''

He laughed again and lowered himself to her. ''I never said that, now, did I? Now, that I would mind.''

''Still,'' she said before she gave herself up to his morning ritual of awakening for them both, ''it seems unfair to Morgan, doesn't it? I mean, after Kitty, especially.''

The gentleman drew away from her and looked at her steadily. She returned his gaze openly.

"Morgan, is it, eh?" he said with a little rise of anger. "He is a catch, isn't he? What did you say, 'He got the funds and the looks'?"

Seeing his anger, the lady put out one little hand and placed it on his lips to prevent him saying another thing.

"Truly," she said playfully, "you are a bear in the morning. You know, it is all you, you, you. How could anyone ever take your place in my heart? I would only do what I must do for my future. You know that," she said wistfully, dropping her gaze and pouting.

"Never forget the rules," the gentleman said, as he relaxed. "You may play your husband false whenever you choose, but you must remain constant to your lover . . . especially if you wish your lover to remain discreet . . . about many things."

"Why are you saying this to me?" the lady sniffed, allowing a tear to well artfully in one blue eye. "When have I ever given you cause for complaint? Now"—she smiled through the tear, which amazingly had already begun to retract—"are you going to spend the morning berating me? Or delighting me?"

"Witch," he said, dropping to whisper into her left ear. "Bitch," he said into her right ear. "That is what I like about you. Your single-mindedness."

But she did not hear what he whispered then or later, and he did not see that through most of his ministrations that morning, she kept her eyes closed so that he would not see her rapid calculating as she weighed her options.

The second letter to be delivered lay outside yet another door. This letter could not be delivered till late afternoon, as the address was a locale on the unfashionable outskirts of Town. This one did not lie upon rich carpeting, but rather upon a cold, somewhat grimy floor. And a floor, moreover, that was three stories up and in a public hallway. So that by the time the recipient saw it lying there, a glowing white rectangle in the dim hall, it already bore a heel print.

But the gentleman scooped it up and peered at the crest,

and made sure of the name it was addressed to, for he did not at first believe that it was for him at all. But it read clearly "Richard Courtney." Then he carried it into his room and closed the door tightly, as if against intruders, before he settled himself in a somewhat threadbare chair near the window to read it before the last light left the afternoon sky.

He, too, read it through several times before he rose and paced the room. It was a small room, badly furnished with what looked like castoffs from someone's attic. An iron bed, a few dispirited chairs, and a table that looked as though it might swoon if it held a large meal, comprised the decor. A small bundle of wood lay ready to be lit in the grate, but it would not be lit until the temperature truly tumbled, for the price of fuel was prohibitive for the occupant. The gentleman who paced the floor looked no more able to hold a substantial repast than his mean table did. He was tall, but bone thin. His shoulders were wide, but wide with the raw look of adolescence, though he appeared to be a man in his second decade of life.

His was not a handsome visage—it was too stark for that; each feature seemed too large for the background it was placed upon: the nose too long, the chin too long, only the long brown eyes seemed to complement the thick brown hair. But as he paced, the long mournful face began to take on light and life, lending animation to the whole.

Finally the gentleman stopped in his tracks, then went swiftly to a large book that stood almost alone in the one bookshelf in the room. He scanned the back pages of the old Bible, tracing names that had been written so long ago that the black ink was growing rusty with age. Then, and only then, did he allow a wide grin to form upon his wide mouth. He rose and inspected himself in the mirror above the fireplace. His clothes were clean and his brown jacket and biscuit pantaloons fit well and seemed newer and more rich than any other objects in the room. He scanned his shining boots for dust, and finding none, he smiled again and went hurriedly toward the door, still clutching the letter.

He looked at the letter once more before putting it carefully into his pocket. For it was the letter that he would bring to his ladylove. And it was the letter he knew that would mean more to her than candy, than flowers—more, perhaps, he thought, halting only for a moment in sorrow, than himself.

The third letter had a long and weary journey and finally arrived limp after more than a week's travails. It bore upon its formerly pristine surface the fingerprint of a coachman in Leicester, a small warp from a rainstorm over Nottingham, and the scars from a drubbing it had received when it fell from the pouch near Mansfield. But now it lay safe and snug next to the beating breast of a tall, stout gentleman as he stood outside a shop window in Tuxford.

The gentleman was engaged in tapping a coin upon the window to attract the attention of those within. But after a few moments, when, from what he could see looking into the shop from behind a quantity of bonnets and feathers that impeded his view, no one turned to see him, he sighed, dropped the coin back into his pocket, and went in through the door. Three elderly women were debating the correctness of having a purple feather upon a mourning bonnet and a young girl and her overbearing mother were debating about the merits of a chip straw against the wisdom of a rather more dashing white satin bonnet with what the young girl tearfully maintained were the sweetest blue flowers. No wonder, the stout gentleman thought, grimacing, no one had heard his steady tapping.

The elderly parties were being waited on by a weary elderly woman, who nodded like a metronone at their every opposing comment. And the girl and her mother were being served by a slender young woman dressed serviceably in brown. When she looked up for a moment and saw the stout gentleman, her wide light brown eyes grew wider in dismay and the faint blush on her white cheeks fled. She began to step toward him, but he shook his head and smiled back at her to alleviate her distress. He took out his watch and pointed to it, nodded, and went out of the shop again. At that the young woman relaxed and went back to the transaction she had been overseeing, which was beginning to end in a flood of tears on the girl's part and a tight-lipped nod on the mother's side.

The stout man stood sighing and rocking back and forth on his heels in impatience outside the shop. He did not like to go into the shop where Elizabeth worked. It always filled him with dismay and a feeling of incompetence when he saw the way she actually had to go out and earn the money she contributed to the household every week. Deuce take it, he thought savagely, she ought to be making the rounds picking out bonnets to adorn herself with, rather than creating and selling them like a common shopgirl. His niece, working as a shopgirl. His niece, still on the vine, and such a fine-looking girl too, but with no husband and no prospects of one and no dowry and no prospect of one. He felt the familiar guilt and sorrow he always experienced when he thought of Elizabeth, but this time he pushed the thoughts away with the force of the rising excitement he felt about the letter he now bore, beating wildly with every wild beat of his heart.

It was only after the girl and her mother left, the girl sniveling, the mother looking triumphant, that Elizabeth herself came flying out the door. She had thrown her pelisse over her dress, her light brown hair glinted like satin where the westering sun touched it, and her fine topaz eyes were bright and wide with excitement. Her uncle thought again, with a pang, of roses born to blush unseen, and so with none of the preamble he had been rehearsing, he pulled the letter from his coat and thrust it at her.

"What is it, Uncle?" Elizabeth breathed, unable to take in the fact of the letter till her eyes had scanned his face. "You never come to the shop. Is it Mother? Or Aunt? Or Anthony? Miss Scott let me out early, for even she knows it is not your habit to come to the shop. Oh, please, what is it?"

"Nothing dire. Nothing amiss with anyone at home. It's only that I've such exciting news, it couldn't wait until you got home," he said with truth. For it was of prime importance that Elizabeth read and absorb the contents of the letter before she got home, and more importantly, before she spoke with her cousin Anthony.

"This letter?" Elizabeth asked, puzzled.

"Yes, the letter," her uncle said impatiently. "Read it. Read it and then ask questions."

Elizabeth stood in the center of the street and rapidly scanned the letter. Halfway through it, she looked up at her uncle, her speaking face lit with radiance. But her uncle shook his head and urged her, "Read on, read on."

"Oh, Uncle," Elizabeth gasped when she had finished, "it is too incredible! Anthony has a chance to become the heir presumptive to the Earl of Auden. It seems unbelievable."

"Incredible and unbelievable," her uncle said slowly, "but quite true. Your aunt babbled on for so many years about how her dear Howard had expectations but died too young, it became a joke. We none of us believed her. But we've checked the Bible and the peerage and there it is. And now she's sitting at home like a cat after a bowl of cream. It's true, all right. Anthony's in the direct line. Do you know what it would mean for us, Elizabeth? No more working in a shop for you. We could give up that slum of a house we're dwelling in and get a proper home. And for you, my dear, there would be a chance to shine as you were meant to do in the society where you belong. Above all this," he said, dismissing the entire town with a wave of his hand, "for with such expectations my credit would rise. I could do everything I've always wanted to do for our little family."

"Uncle," Elizabeth said with a small, happy sigh, "it's beyond everything wonderful. What did Anthony say?"

"Ah, well," her uncle said wretchedly, "I didn't tell him yet. I couldn't. Not yet. Not till you and I had a chance to talk about it. Well," he said, not meeting her eyes, "you know what he would say."

"Oh, yes," Elizabeth said, shaking her head sadly and then seeming to let out all the radiance with a long sigh. Her face grew still. "Well, then, so much for your dreams, Uncle. Let's go home," and she turned and began to walk again.

Her uncle caught at her arm. "No, we can't let it go like that, Elizabeth, we can't. Think of the opportunity."

"Yes, and think of Anthony," Elizabeth said grimly.

"I am thinking of Anthony," her uncle retorted in an

undertone, pausing to touch his hat to a neighbor, "and I cannot in all conscience let him pass up such an opportunity. There will come a day," he went on sweepingly, like an orator upon the stump, "when he will put all this childishness behind him. And then he will regret his lost chance. *We*," her uncle said, gazing at Elizabeth, "cannot let him pass up such a chance."

"You know," Elizabeth said as she paced on toward home, "that I will do the best that I can. But even so, I think you refine too much upon it. There are so many ifs in the case. There is no cause to believe Anthony would be chosen as heir above the others; rather the opposite, I should think. And even if he were, why, even in that unlikely eventuality, it might be years before the Earl passed on and Anthony came into the inheritance."

"I know for a fact," her uncle said eagerly, "that the Earl is quite an old chap. I met him years ago when I was in clover. He had two sons, I recall. I know the elder died young, and the other, last I heard, was in the wars. Pity, he must have been killed. And so Anthony stands a very good chance at the succession. One man's misfortune is the making of another's; no one lives forever."

Seeing Elizabeth's shocked, barely concealed expression of distaste, her uncle hurried on, "But even if the old chap lives to be Methuselah, Elizabeth—and of course I hope he will— think of what it would mean for Anthony to be designated heir! It would mean," he said, staring wonderingly at his niece, "that as his uncle, my credit would be restored. That I could bring our fortune back."

"I'll do my best," Elizabeth repeated earnestly. "I'll prime him like a pump, I'll find a way to convince him of the rightness of it, if it takes me days on end. And then we'll dress him up and send him off to the Earl as a prime candidate for the office. I promise, Uncle," she said firmly. "Will that suit?"

"Not quite," her uncle said slowly. "That won't be quite enough. You know Anthony, Elizabeth. That won't be quite enough."

Elizabeth tensed. She knew, with a terrible certainty, what was coming.

"You must accompany him," her uncle said with finality, as she stopped again and stared at him aghast. "There it is. Think about it. There is no other way. Someone must be there to see he minds his manners. His mother can't. I can't. You are the only one who can oversee him, the only one who can handle him at all. Now, you know that."

"Ah, Uncle," Elizabeth began, "I don't wish to—"

"Elizabeth," her uncle said sternly, "what do you think will happen if you don't?"

She paused, and he knew the battle was won by the arrested look in her eyes. But still she went on falteringly, "Oh, Uncle. What do I know of Earls? And the society they travel in? I'd make just as much of a cake of myself as Anthony would. And I haven't been invited. And I haven't the clothes for such a venture," she said desperately. "And what of my position with Miss Scott? One shouldn't cast off dirty water till one has clean."

Her uncle smiled benignly, and her spirits sank.

"You have common sense, Elizabeth, and good breeding and birth, much beauty, and beautiful manners. That will serve. And it is unexceptional for a young man of Anthony's age to travel with an older female relative. And I can raise enough funds to see you and Anthony dressed in style."

Her uncle took her arm as they walked the last street toward home.

"Your Miss Scott is such a toadeater, she would be delighted to tell all and sundry that her assistant is off for a visit with an Earl. Even if it all worked out badly—which it won't, my dear, which it won't—she'll snap you up again as helper, for you're the only one who knows how to make her poky bonnets look stylish. It will serve, Elizabeth, it will serve. It must serve," he said forcefully, tightening his grip on her arm. "I must have a chance to recoup our fortune. Elizabeth," he said, swinging her round to face him and looking directly into her clear light brown eyes, "let me have at least just that one last chance, once more before I die."

Elizabeth looked at the pleading expression upon her uncle's flushed face and closed her eyes. She owed him so much, she thought wearily. So be it, she thought with resignation, and nodded. "Yes, Uncle."

"And don't look so forlorn," her uncle replied happily, his spirits restored miraculously, for Elizabeth was the brightest in his household and he had never really doubted her support. He knew he could rely upon her, even as he had known that with her natural shyness the scheme would terrify her, "First you'll talk Anthony round," he continued blithely, "and then we'll tog you out in the style you should have had years ago. And then you're off to the Earl's."

"To the Earl's," Elizabeth echoed dully.

"Not just to the Earl's," her uncle amended lovingly with a distant look growing in his eyes; he raised his head to the sky and let each syllable roll off his tongue like a sweet: "But to Lyonshall, principal seat of the Earl of Auden, Viscount Louth and Baron Kitteredge. That's all one man, y'know," he finished helpfully.

"I was afraid it was," Elizabeth said sadly.

— 3 —

The sun was the palest of yellows, and a little nippish breeze warned wise men that spring was in its early days yet. But as Elizabeth sat and watched the clouds go by as tearaway as spring-struck lambs, she was filled with gratitude to whatever powers were that it was at least not raining. For she would have gone on a picnic today even in the teeth of a gale. Picnics were, after all, among Anthony's favorite diversions. As she had to speak with him alone and apart from the rest of the family, and speak with him when he was at ease and content, a tranquil picnic party was the ideal circumstance for their conversation.

Anthony stood apart from her, looking out over the countryside. Elizabeth sat upon a blanket hugging her warm woolen cloak about her, wishing she had had the foresight to bring at least two more blankets, for the earth was cold beneath her. She and Anthony had happily demolished the contents of the wicker basket they had brought, so lovingly and hopefully packed up by Elizabeth's mother and Aunt Emily. "For if he's had enough chicken, the way I make it," Aunt Emily had said contentedly, "he will agree to anything." "And my biscuits," Elizabeth's mother had reminded them, "are Anthony's idea of heaven."

Elizabeth sighed. But if only biscuits were Anthony's idea of heaven, this whole subterfuge would not have been necessary. She well knew what Anthony's idea of bliss really was; that was the crux of his problem. But as she had known Anthony from the moment he had teethed upon his first biscuit, she had to believe she also knew what exactly to say to him to make the scheme that she, her uncle, her mother, and her aunt had sat up nights hatching, palatable to him. For now, upon Anthony's narrow young shoulders, the entire family fortunes rested.

She gazed at Anthony with a mixture of fondness and consternation, as he stood watching the quiet spring Sunday afternoon peacefully tick by. Her feelings toward her young cousin had always come in twos: pride and shame, amusement and anger, impatience and guilt. For Anthony was, in the words of his uncle, "a rare terror." One wouldn't think it to look at him. For he was an ordinary enough lad. Just a slender seventeen-year-old of medium height and dark eyes and hair. Still beardless, still enough of a boy to have a fishhook or two in his pocket, yet old enough to take on the affect of a man. And bright, ferociously bright, the vicar who instructed him in Latin and languages had said. But he had also said kindly, "A bit misguided."

A bit! Elizabeth thought, biting back a groan. If it were only a bit, she would not have to sit up on a damp hillock and secretly plot and scheme. But should anyone say right out to Anthony that he had a chance to be named heir presumptive to an Earl, he would in all probability say right out in response that they might take themselves away and do something vulgar to their own persons. For Anthony did not believe in Earls, or Kings either, for that matter. Anthony, for reasons no one in his family had ever been able to fathom, though Lord knows they had cudgeled their brains about it often enough, was a flaming revolutionary.

Where other boys were lost in hero worship to Nelson or Wellington, Anthony was far gone in absolute adoration of Bonaparte. Through the course of the war, in fact, since he was tall enough to reach the top of the map he had pinned to his bedroom wall, he had charted the course of his hero with gaily colored pins. It was in vain that the family talked to him of patriotism, loyalty, and the glories of being an Englishman. Anthony would agree to all that, and then say he awaited the day when he could be an Englishman under the rule of the greatest man of his century: Napoleon Bonaparte. As he grew he had begun to lounge about the commons and the green, extolling his hero's virtues. Since everyone in town had known him since he could toddle, he had been greeted at first with amused condescension. And since everyone knew what an upstanding family he came from, he was said to be "going through a phase" and ignored.

But when the war had begun to heat up and when Mr. McArdle, the grocer, had lost his Willie in Spain and the Wilsons grieved for Johnny in an unmarked watery grave somewhere near Nelson's fleet, their amused tolerance vanished. When Anthony had come home twice with blackened eyes, the family decided to call the town off limits for him. And he was left to follow the course of his own star from the confines of his own house.

It was not only his being entranced with the Little General; it went across the board. Anthony championed a multitude of people he had never seen: chimney-boys, child prostitutes, weavers, miners, impressed seamen. And he railed against an equal number he had never clapped an eye upon: Dukes, Kings, Duchesses, all those who flew in high society. If Anthony had his way, the tumbrils would be rolling through the heart of London. He buried himself in books and incendiary pamphlets and for hours discoursed on the inequality of life as he knew it. Not discoursed, Elizabeth corrected herself, harangued. Till his uncle grew flamed-faced and slammed out of their little house, till his mother wept, till his aunt called him ingrate, or until Elizabeth herself came down from where she had sought refuge from the battle in her own small room, to quiet him and lead his thoughts in other directions.

For only Elizabeth could handle him at all. From the first, when his mother, newly widowed and deep in mourning, had come home to her brother's house for succor, Elizabeth, then only a shy seven-year-old, had looked down upon the sleeping year-old babe in his cot and had inexplicably taken him to her heart. Perhaps it was because she herself, fatherless and bereft, had come to her uncle's house only a year earlier and had sympathized with the mite. Or perhaps it was because no one else, neither her mother, busily working as housekeeper for the brother kind enough to shelter her, nor his own grieving mother, nor her uncle himself, busily trying to repair his finances, had then had time for the babe. But Elizabeth had taken to him and it was she who had helped him with his lessons, drilled him in table manners, and soothed his hurts. It was she who had at the age of seven appointed herself as his mother.

And like a good mother, she now sat on the hillside and tried to arrange matters so that he could advance in the world. So that the family could advance in the world. For at that moment Elizabeth definitely felt the invisible breathing anxiety of her whole family behind her. She let out a long sigh.

"Why, what's the problem, Coz?" Anthony asked, turning and seeing her lost in thought.

"Why, nothing." Elizabeth laughed, turning a bright countenance toward him. "What could possibly be troubling anyone on such a delightful day?"

"Delightful?" Anthony frowned. "Yes. I suppose it is for those with money and leisure enough to sit and occupy themselves with pleasure."

He was forgetting, Elizabeth thought, her anger boiling up, that they had little money and she had only leisure today because it was a Sunday and Miss Scott's establishment was closed for the Sabbath. But then, Anthony did not think much of material things. Nor of the Sabbath either, she remembered.

"Come sit down with me," she said placidly enough.

He flung himself down and plucked at a new stalk of spring grass.

"Anthony," she began, "wouldn't you delight in being able to help those who are too poor and too wretched to enjoy such a day, to help them to be able to disport themselves as happily as we are doing?"

"You know that is my aim in life," he retorted, "but little chance at it I get here in Tuxford."

"But if," Elizabeth guided him, "for today is a lovely spring day, and such days were meant for air-dreaming. *If* you could, wouldn't that be the best of all worlds?"

"I think," Anthony said, "of little else. But how, Elizabeth? I cannot join the army, you know. Mother won't hear of it."

Elizabeth refrained from commenting that was because the

only army he had wanted to join was the French one, and merely nodded.

"Uncle hasn't the funds to send me to a proper school where I could make political connections. The church is out of the question, for they would only try to teach me how to preach forbearance, and I'll have none of that. What opportunities are there for me? A position in Mr. Eldrige's shop? He wanted me to be clerk, Elizabeth. I, Anthony Courtney, a clerk in a sundries shop!"

Elizabeth bit her tongue to keep from reminding him that he was conversing with Elizabeth DeLisle, a lowly clerk. Pasting another vapid smile upon her face, she stretched and went on, "Just think, Anthony, if you were born a Duke, or a Marquess, or, say, an Earl, of what you could do."

"A Duke or an Earl?" Anthony snarled. "Have your wits gone begging, Elizabeth? Those parasites born to money and title? All men should be equal. It is just those sorts of titled leeches who hold the world in thrall!"

"But if," Elizabeth put in hastily, seeing another tirade beginning, "you had such a title, such a position, what you could accomplish!"

"It is not necessary to be born to fortune," Anthony said morosely. "Just think of Bonaparte himself. He wasn't born to greatness, he made it for himself." But here his voice dropped a bit in confidence, for his hero was presently kicking his heels in a snugger sanctuary than the one he had burst forth from last year in 1815.

"But think, Anthony," Elizabeth said with enthusiasm, "if he had been born to wealth and fortune, how much easier it would have been for him. Why, if a man were born to a dignity and to a fortune, and then he decided to change the world, he would have the leverage to do so, wouldn't he?"

"Of course," Anthony said, flopping down full length upon the blanket, "but not one of them does. They are content to just sit and revel in luxury. Without a care for the workingman, without a—"

"Anthony!" Elizabeth put in quickly, seizing her chance before Anthony, who had never turned his hand to a day's labor, began again about the travails of the working class. "I have news for you. News that could change not only your life but also the lives of countless others. Workingmen, and . . . chimney climbers and . . . perhaps even Napoleon himself,'' she added wildly.

Anthony looked at her as though she had run mad. The cool wind had stirred her light tresses into silken streamers, her usually pale white oval of a face was flushed with high color, her eyes sparkled like water in a brook.

"Are you ill, Coz?'' Anthony said, fearfully edging away, for he was wary of infection, his own father having succumbed to an influenza.

"No, dear nit,'' she said affectionately, "but I have news. That's why I lured you here today. Anthony, what would you say if I told you that you may at last have your chance to change the world? But that you'd have to be very, very sly to go about it?''

His interest caught, for the thought of being clandestine tickled him immensely, as Elizabeth had known it would, Anthony leaned forward to catch her next whisper. For now she spoke rapidly and in low tones, though there was not a soul to hear them within miles, save for a few sheep, who could not care less about the future of the suffering hordes of mankind.

Elizabeth talked herself dry as the afternoon grew old. And while the air grew chill after its brief exercise in spring, her words became warmer, and Anthony's face became positively overheated with the force of his emotions. At last, with the sounds of her own voice ringing still in her ears, Elizabeth stopped, parched and exhausted. But Anthony seemed in transports of delight.

"What a capital scheme,'' he crowed at last, rocking back on his heels as he rose from kneeling beside her. "I have only to cozen the old chap and I inherit the title. Then beard the lions in their own dens,'' he went on jubilantly. "I'd have the power, and the position. You're right, Elizabeth. And then see how I'd change the world!''

"But mind,'' Elizabeth croaked as she began to gather up their picnic things, "if the old Earl knew what you were about, he would likely leave the whole to some idle ornament

of society. You'd have to be very, very careful not to divulge
your true intent. It would take some . . . I hesitate to say this,
Anthony,'' she said, packing up the last napkin from their
luncheon. "Subterfuge."

"I could do that," Anthony cried, "knowing what a chance
I'd have in future. I could, Elizabeth," he said, watching her
struggle to her feet with the basket. "I know I could."

"Still," she said through dry lips as they went down the
hill together, "the old gentleman likely lost a son to Bonaparte,
and if you so much as breathed one word of praise about him
in front of the Earl, all would be lost. It would take forbearance.
You did say that wasn't your long suit, and excessive tact,"
she warned, glancing at him sidewise through her long lashes.

"I don't like to do it," Anthony said thoughtfully, "but
knowing what has to come, I could. I would, Elizabeth," he
promised, tagging after her like a hesitant puppy. "I know I
would. Truly."

"Well, then," Elizabeth said, thinking of how her throat
would need a nice draught of honey and tea after this
afternoon's exertions, and refusing to think of the depth and
consequences of her own deception just then, "we'll begin."

And begin it did, with a rapidity and thoroughness that
startled Elizabeth, for once Uncle had gotten the word of
Anthony's compliance, he had begun, joyously, to set his
scheme in motion.

Orders for the latest in fashions for herself and Anthony
had gone out at once to the one fashionable store Tuxford
boasted. Elizabeth's aunt and mother bent their heads over
fashion plates for days, deciding on what exactly a young
woman of means should have in her traveling case. Uncle had
taken a secretly smiling, strangly acquiescent Anthony in tow
to all the fittings to assemble a wardrobe suitable to a young
gent of leisure. Every step of their itinerary was planned as if
it were a day of invasion. And in a sense, Elizabeth thought,
it was. An invasion of a poor young man and his equally
impoverished female cousin, upon the sacred territory of the
privileged.

Only Elizabeth knew how her uncle had schemed and sold
family treasures to finance their mission. In a way, she

thought one day, seeing, by not seeing, the Dresden shepherdess in her accustomed spot in the china cabinet, Uncle is
making this his final gamble. But, she worried, as she tossed
at night unable to sleep, in the past it was his own judgment
that lost his small fortune in bad investments. This time it is I
who will have to do the gambling. And Anthony will be a
poor unknowing pawn. For if Anthony thinks by going along
with the scheme he is hoodwinking the privileged, Uncle
believes he will become one of the privileged again by this
ploy. On such nights, Elizabeth had to close her eyes and
forcibly shut out her thoughts in order to sleep.

Only a scant two weeks had passed since Elizabeth had
gotten Anthony's approval, and now she stood in the parlor
as her mother took the pins from the last dress that had been
deemed necessary for her new wardrobe. Elizabeth stood and
gazed at herself in the mirror.

"No," she said at length, in horror, "absolutely not.
Never!"

Her reflection glittered back at her. She seemed as out of
place in the cramped little parlor as a Duchess taking tea in
their work-worn kitchen might have been. The new gown was
the exact shade of coffee shot with cream. Its bodice was low
and the little puffed sleeves exposed her creamy shoulders to
her audience's rapt gaze. The frock was sashed beneath her
rounded breasts, showing her slender figure to advantage.
Her tresses had been done up with a ribbon of the same shot
silk, only a shade darker than her own gleaming tresses and
light brown eyes. She shimmered and glistened as she took a
step to crane her neck to see the soft folds of drapery at her
back. And the sibilant silk sighed almost as softly as her
mother did as she saw it.

"Oh, Elizabeth," her mother said in an uncharacteristi-
cally trembling tone, "I had no idea you had grown so
lovely. All these years, hiding your light 'neath a bushel."

"Never too late." Her uncle coughed with embarrassment
from where he sat in his armchair. "Twirl about for us,
Elizabeth, that's the girl."

But Elizabeth did not exactly twirl, she spun about and said
in her soft sad voice, "Oh, no, Uncle, it is too much. I have

five new frocks now. Five! Just think. And this would make
it six. Which I do not need, indeed not. Why," she went on
indignantly, willing herself not to gaze into the mirror to see
herself again, lest she lose her resolve, "with the three good
ones I already own, that would make nine! I'll take this back
to Miss Cook, for I don't need such fine feathers."

"Indeed you do," her uncle answered. "In those circles,
you'll need four a day at least. I know, for I lived life in such
style once."

"And your other three dresses, Elizabeth," her mother
chided, "are not so fine."

"But it seems so extravagant, Uncle," Elizabeth protested,
at last allowing herself another glance in the mirror at this
elegant stranger in the shining silks, so unlike the everyday
vision of herself in plain, serviceable stuff gowns.

"You can't look like a beggar girl," her uncle said promptly.
"You must look as though you belonged. No point in sending
you off dressed up for defeat. You must dress the part to
make the point." Her uncle put his hand in his pocket to
withdraw his watch to check the time, as was his habit, only
remembering once his fingers had touched the empty fob
pocket that he had sold it to help defray the expenses of this
and the other frocks. He coughed and pretended to be patting
his stomach, but Elizabeth's quick eye caught the motion.
She knew the reason for it and mourned the loss of his
timepiece, even as she found herself hating her fine raiment
because of it. But she smiled and dipped into a low curtsy.

"Delighted, your lordship," she breathed, and the look of
gratification on her uncle's face absolved her and the dress.

Elizabeth gave herself one long, last measuring look in the
glass.

"Uncle," she tried again, "I am only Anthony's cousin. Is
it truly necessary for me to be gotten up in such style?"

"It will never do for them to guess at our present financial
status," her uncle said again. "If you look in need, you will
remain in need. Money goes to money," he said sagely. "It's
the way of the world. Look like a thousand pounds and you
shall receive a thousand pounds. Such is life," he sighed.

Elizabeth dropped a light kiss upon her uncle's brow, and

was about to go upstairs to her room when Anthony sauntered by the door of the sitting room where Elizabeth had been showing off her new dress. Both she and her uncle gaped when they saw him. It was hard to believe it was their Anthony resplendent before them. He wore a tight-fitting jacket of blue with padded shoulders and an immaculate cravat in an intricate fold. His waistcoat was white with red trim and his legs were encased in tight knit buff pantaloons. A pair of shining hessian boots completed his outfit.

"Only look at you, Coz." He grinned. "Done up to the nines. Very nice," he commented before he sauntered away.

Elizabeth was as shocked by his comment as by his appearance. For he never noticed what she looked like, only occasionally stirring himself to comment if she had a smudge on her cheek or had thrown a spot on her brow. But he had looked and sounded so unexceptional that Elizabeth and her uncle exchanged one long conspiratorial look before they both laughed aloud with relief.

"We'll pull it off, b'God!" her uncle exclaimed.

But late that night when all the household slept, Elizabeth sat up in her narrow bed and worried. She had packed and done with counting and recounting her possessions hours ago. Now, at last, she worried about the task before her.

The entire responsibility of the venture was upon her shoulders. Uncle had reassured her that no more was required of her than to see Anthony minded his manners and kept his mouth shut about his ideologies. But Elizabeth worried least about that part of her duties. She wondered whether she herself might prove an embarrassment. For she was all of three-and-twenty and had never mixed in such exalted company as she believed awaited her at Lyonshall. Even if it was to be only the old Earl, his servants, and the other aspirants for the honor of being chosen heir, it would be enough to keep her awake this night.

Three-and-twenty, she thought, roaming her room, almost blindly finding her way about in the dark, and nervous as a schoolchild of going out into the world alone. But wasn't that just what she had been secretly praying for all these years?

She had never complained about her lot. How could she

when Uncle had been kind enough to take her and her widowed
mother in after Father had been lost in the wars? For though
an officer gave his life for King and Country, his country
seldom gave his family more than a lovely written commenda-
tion to be taken out and wept over by his survivors on the
anniversary of his death. Uncle had unhesitatingly taken in
his other widowed sister and her infant son as well. Elizabeth
often wondered if the burden of living with his widowed
sisters prevented Uncle from marriage, even though he always laughed and declared that with three females at his beck
and call he had little need of another as wife. She often
consoled herself with the thought that he had been a case-
hardened bachelor long before tragedy had befallen his family.

But by then he had also lost what remained of his funds, all
but this meager holding of the house and enough to keep their
bodies and souls together. So how could an ungrateful chit of
a girl quibble about her lost opportunities for a social life?

Nor had she complained about being unable to join the
other girls at their play. She had been told often enough that
she was a lady born, and as such could not mix with common
village girls. But all these common, laughing girls of her
youth were wed now, and most with babes of their own. And
only she, Elizabeth DeLisle, lady born, had no more to show
for her years than a tenuous position in a millinery shop—of
the better sort, of course.

How many nights had she sat by her window, hugging
herself against the night wind, wondering if life would ever
touch her? How many nights when a roving gypsy moon
would cause panic to well in her as she wondered how many
more years would go by as she sat by a window and waited.
Twenty-three, thirty-three, forty-three . . . On those nights
she would think in despair how long it would be till she
became exactly as her mother and her aunt, waiting on Uncle
and Anthony, watching the years creep by.

For there was no money for a come-out at eighteen, no
funds for a dowry at twenty, and no hope for anything at
twenty-three. There had been young men—the world is filled
with young men—but none for her. The smith's son, Edmond
Priestly, had eyed her when she was nineteen and then quite

properly proposed to young Elsie Fairchild when he was twenty, as both their families expected. Robert Mason, the hard-drinking squire's son, had walked out with her when she was twenty and stolen hasty whiskey-scented kisses. But then he, too, had turned with many a backward sigh to wed the young Litchfield heiress as his family had ordained. Elizabeth too had sighed, but with relief. Even for Uncle's sake, she could not have made a match with Robert. Now James Wattle, owner of the only apothecary shop in town, was casting glances her way, but when she thought of her reaction to his perennial sniff and condescending manner, she knew he would soon turn away and make a match with some other, more obliging lady.

Now her wish had been unwittingly granted by some ancient, ailing member of the aristocracy. She was to have an adventure. She was, at last, to leave Tuxford, if only for a space. But as in all fairy tales, there was a condition attached. She must pretend to be wealthy. She must help to convince a poor old man that Anthony was an upstanding young fellow, well able to shoulder the burdens of title and fortune. And she, she who had never spoken to a more exalted personality than the squire, was to pretend that she was used to hobnobbing with the Quality.

It would be a grand adventure, she told herself, as she tucked herself up into her own bed for the last time in the knowable future. Uncle had said she could hold her head high, for her own birth and bearing were of the finest. And she had a case of new clothes and a mission to carry out. Why, then, she thought sleepily, with all those riches and all that opportunity, did she feel so very frightened and so very guilt-stricken?

— 4 —

Elizabeth examined Anthony covertly in the available lurch-
ing light that shone through the travel-stained windows of the
coach. Yes, she thought finally, he'll do. His hair, his jacket,
even his boots were correct to the last and least degree. There
was no fault, she sighed, at least none that could be seen by
the eye. Aye, that's the problem, she sighed again, leaning
her weary head back and closing her own eyes. But then, that
was in the hands of fate fully as much as in her own two
neatly gloved members.

Anthony had been in excellent spirits throughout the long
journey. While Elizabeth was nominally his keeper, in charge
of both his baggage and his behavior, oddly enough it was
Anthony who had taken charge at the White Hart in Derby
and demanded more commodious rooms, and Anthony who
had grown angry with the innkeeper at Stourbridge when he
had discovered an overcharge on their luncheon bill. While
Elizabeth knew more of the world than he did, by dint of her
reading and her six years' majority, she had never traveled a
mile farther than her junior cousin. She was by far the more
reticent of the pair as well, for Anthony, having been absently indulged by three females since birth, was never one to
let a slight go by. That prickliness of his served them well on
their trip. All who encountered the impatient young gentleman and his attractive companion thought the pair Quality.
Uncle's every shilling had been spent to create just that
illusion.

Uncle's pocketbook had stretched to provide them clothes,

but even a magician could not have ferreted out one more coin after the cost of wayside accommodations for both the going and return journey had been calculated. Their fare cost nothing, as the local squire, with visions of Anthony as Earl of Auden, and with the omnipresent vision of his own unmarried daughter fixed firmly in his mind, gladly gave them the use of his coach and his cattle for the trip.

But for supposed scions of a fashionable family there was still a great deal they did not have. Thus what they did not have they were fully armed with excuses for. Elizabeth's fictitious maid was to be explained away as suffering from both coachsickness and homesickness to such a degree that she never made the journey past the town limits of Tuxford. Anthony's valet, that sentimental and imaginary fellow, had, of course, to be back in London seeing to his aunt's decent interment. Elizabeth, it was decided after a long night's conference, had never made her come-out in London, as her mother had been ailing and she had feared to leave her delicate mama for so long a time. And when Aunt Emily had protested that it was an unlucky sort of excuse, Elizabeth's mother had shushed her firmly by stating that if Anthony let a fortune slip through his fingers for superstition's sake they would all be a great deal unhealthier in future.

Elizabeth's head was so filled with admonitions, excuses, and outright lies that she feared to open her mouth lest the whole budget spill out unbidden. Anthony, although equally primed by Uncle, had an unusually devil-may-care attitude about him from the very moment of agreeing to the scheme. In fact, Elizabeth noted with dismay, he seemed to be wearing a perpetual smirk of self-satisfaction. It was that very sunny air of compliance that disturbed her even more. For she knew Anthony well, and it was not at all in his style.

But now she had no further time to worry, for the coach was at last turning in through a pair of iron gates and even Anthony sat up straighter as they proceeded down the long and stately drive toward Lyonshall. Elizabeth gave not one more thought to Anthony as her gaze took in the full splendor of the Earl's principal seat. There was a wide and well-manicured greensward where no one blade of grass dared presume to lift its head higher than its fellows at one turn; masses of purple rhododendrons that were so riotously profuse in their spring flowering that they colored the very air about them with an aura of lavender at another; and then finally, after passing what appeared to be a detachment of gardeners engaged in drilling a display of tulips and lilies to stand properly and not slouch as inferior blooms might tend to do, they caught sight of the great house itself.

Seeing its vast outline, its tall white form dominating the landscape, Elizabeth caught in her breath and frankly goggled. It was as well that she did not catch a glimpse of her cousin's face as he took his first look at the stately pile that might, if the fates were kind, someday be his. For she would have seen his lips form the words "disgraceful" and "parasite."

By the time Anthony had aided her in descending from the coach and Elizabeth's legs were used again to firm unmoving ground beneath her, they had to ascend the marble steps. Before they could pause, they were shown into the great house itself. Breathless from the climb, and struck speechless by the vault of a front hall, scarcely able to register the beauty of her surroundings in the light flooding in through high stained-glass windows, Elizabeth could only mutely follow the butler who led them farther into what seemed to her to be the Earl's treasure cave of a mansion.

So it was that by the time she had given her bonnet and wrap to a footman and the polished oaken doors to the withdrawing room had swung open, Elizabeth was reduced to merely attempting to keep her composure so as not to present a picture of a gawking peasant to whoever awaited her within. Thus when the butler stentorianly announced "Mr. Anthony Courtney and Miss Elizabeth DeLisle," the assembled company saw an unremarkable young man saunter in followed by a very attractive but very dazed-looking young woman. Indeed, the first feature of hers that anyone noticed was a pair of remarkable hazel eyes, as wide, but unfortunately also as blank, as saucers.

Anthony moved into the room as if he were indeed to the manner born. And as she followed, Elizabeth was aware of a group of people posed as if in tableau, in various indolent

positions in various parts of the room. They looked, she
thought with despair, as intimidating and as unreal as figures
from a fashion plate. The brightest spot of color in the room
came from a grouping on an elegantly curved gold settee.
There sat an exquisite little Dresden figure of a woman,
looking in all her gold-and-pink splendor much like the very
figurine poor Uncle had sold in order to purchase the stylish
tea-colored walking dress Elizabeth now wore. Next to that
blond vision of a female sat a small, plump boy, all done up
to match the lady, even down to his golden ringlets and lacy
cuffs. A tall gentleman sat in a maroon chair to the fair-haired
couple's left; another exquisitely stylish-looking fellow with
buff pantaloons and boots so shined they twinkled in the
afternoon light stood near him, seemingly interrupted in mid-
sentence by their arrival. And a tall, imposing man stood
easily by the fireplace mantel, one hand upon a gold-tipped
walking stick, the other cradling a tall snifter of brandy.
Caught in that one frozen moment of interruption, they were
all gazing at Anthony and Elizabeth with the liveliest curiosity.
And for that one moment, Elizabeth had the mad impulse to
simply drop a curtsy, pick up her skirts, and flee out the
door, back to the coach, and back to her home again.

It was the tall man by the fireplace who first spoke in a
slow, deep, rich voice. "Welcome, Cousin," he said smoothly
as Anthony came toward him. "You come in good time. We
were just having some refreshment and conversation. Surely
you will join us, and then you will have time enough to rest
and shake off the dust of your journey before dinner."

"We'd be happy to," Anthony replied with what to Elizabeth seemed to be supernatural aplomb, and bowing slightly,
he went on, "Sorry to arrive so late in the day, but there was
some misunderstanding with the innkeeper at our last stop,
and that delayed us. The fellow toted up a bill for us fit for a
regimental banquet and then expected us to pay up without a
whimper."

Elizabeth winced inwardly at any mention of money and
feared Anthony had instantly put a foot wrong, but in a
moment the curly-haired exquisite with the miraculous boots
spoke up eagerly. "Dashed impertinence," he cried. "Those

fellows all seem to think that if you're dressed as a gentleman you're so well larded you'll pay anything without a blink. I hope you gave him a piece of your mind.''

"Oh, I did," Anthony said, "and that's why we are so late.''

"Well, then, Cousin Anthony," the tall man said, "come sit and tell us all about it, and, Cousin Elizabeth, come have a chair here as well, you must be weary from your journey. All the way from . . . Tuxford, wasn't it?''

As Elizabeth speechlessly sank into the chair the gentleman had indicated, Anthony accepted a glass from the curly-haired fellow, who seemed incapable of retaining one position for more than a few moments, and said carelessly, "Aye, Tuxford. But you've got it wrong. Elizabeth ain't your cousin, she's my cousin.''

"Well, never you mind, m'dear," the curly-haired young man said as he handed Elizabeth a glass of some red liquid, which she grasped on to as though it were a lifeline, "for I ain't a cousin of anybody's at all. But, Morgan, if she's young Anthony's coz, surely she's got to be yours?''

"It would be an inestimable honor if she were indeed mine, Bev, but I don't think that's what you meant." The tall man laughed. "Rest easy, Miss Elizabeth," he added with an intent look toward her. "It's genealogy Bev's discussing.''

Seeing Elizabeth's faint blush, the fair-haired woman gave a tinkling laugh. "Oh, Morgan, you are a one. See how you've discomposed poor Miss Elizabeth. No need to color up, my dear, it's only Cousin Morgan's way of joshing. Come, Morgan, Miss Elizabeth's clearly not used to such raillery.''

Since the other woman's tone seemed to imply, "See how you've upset the poor rustic, she's not used to more than the conversation of cows," Elizabeth, to her further embarrassment, felt the more color flooding to her cheeks. She searched for an answer to turn the attention from herself, but before she could think of one, the tall gentleman seemed to take pity upon her and said swiftly, "But my wits have gone begging. We've pitchforked you both into a roomful of strangers. I'll remedy that in a moment. Cousin Anthony and non-Cousin

Elizabeth, allow me to introduce Lady Isabel Courtney and her son, Owen, from London.''

Lady Isabel smiled and placed her arm about her son, creating yet another ''mother-and-child'' set piece.

Gesturing toward the silent thin gentleman in the maroon chair, the speaker went on, ''And this is Cousin Richard Courtney, also from London, and the noisy fellow with all the brandy at his elbow is, you'll be relieved to discover, just as he claimed, no cousin at all, but only a dear friend of the family, Sir Reginald Beverly, called 'Bev' for friendship's sake. And I,'' the tall gentleman concluded, with the merest tilt of his head, suggesting a bow, ''am Charles Morgan Courtney, called 'Morgan,' as there was once a surfeit of Charleses in our family.''

''Delighted to meet you,'' Elizabeth murmured inadequately, but her answer was lost in a welter of ''Delighteds'' and ''Charmeds'' from all parts of the room.

Lord Beverly immediately began to engage Anthony in conversation, and Elizabeth relaxed as soon as she overheard they were discussing no more than the wicked way that local innkeepers sought to cheat travelers on room-and-board rates. Since Anthony stood staunchly against any kind of criminal behavior, save for the radical sort, Elizabeth felt it was a safe enough topic and allowed her attention to wander toward the other assembled guests. The tall morose gentleman in the maroon chair who had been introduced as Richard Courtney was giving monosyllabic answers to Morgan Courtney, who still stood at the fireplace near him. Lady Isabel, after giving Elizabeth's dress, hair, and face a long searching look, seemed uninterested in starting a conversation with her and instead turned to the plump little boy at her side and began to talk with him in light, happy accents.

Left completely alone, Elizabeth sipped at her glass, stopping with sudden disgust as she realized it contained only ratafia, dull watered-down sweetened stuff that her uncle had warned her ladies were supposed to prefer. For herself, Elizabeth much preferred good wine, for Uncle had at least a decent palate left over from the days of his high fortune, and had taught her the nose for a fine wine. So she merely nursed her glass and watched the others with interest.

Although Lord Beverly was certainly the most fashionable gentleman in the room, and Lady Isabel the most beautiful female Elizabeth had ever seen outside of a picture book, Elizabeth's gaze kept straying to the tall gentleman by the fireside. He was the most imposing, virile-looking man she had ever laid eyes upon. For a certainty, Tuxford had never held such a gentleman. His simple presence diminished the others, making their attempts at fashion into mere foppery. He had a commanding air of certitude and a slow smile of inner amusement. Not above five-and-thirty, she guessed, he was tall, and while slender, by no means as gaunt and rawboned as Cousin Richard, with whom he was chatting. Rather, he had the graceful, easy look of an athlete, from his lightly tanned, strongly planed face, with its high cheekbones and strong jaw, to his wide shoulders and trim waist, to his long, well-muscled legs. His hair was a dark auburn, worn slightly longer than was fashionable, and his eyes were so deep-set they seemed hooded. But when he turned, as though her glance had compelled him to, Elizabeth saw, in the one moment before she dropped her gaze in embarrassment, that his eyes were long and clear and the color of blue and green intermixed.

"But we have neglected you," he said with an easy smile. "Perhaps because we don't know how to call you. As you are not our cousin, may we then name you only 'Elizabeth' and still remain in your good graces? For this is a family gathering, and we do not stand upon ceremony here."

Elizabeth, with the full weight of his attention upon her, was so intimidated that she could only blurt out a graceless, "Yes, of course."

"And," he persisted, still looking at her, with Richard Courtney and Lady Isabel both now doing the same, "I see you have not touched your ratafia. Would you care for something a bit more full-blooded? I have an excellent claret, or at least I did before Bev arrived on the scene."

Now, with all conversation stopped, for Lord Beverly had turned at the mention of his name, Elizabeth found herself the

focal point of attention again. Remembering Uncle's admonitions as to manners that prevailed in the highest circles, she
only dropped her head low and whispered a polite, "No,
thank you," adding rather weakly, "I do not drink," and as
the insipidness and dishonesty of the comment reached her
own ears, added softly again, "Before dinner."

"Well, then," Cousin Morgan said briskly, his smile rather
fixed, and his attention leaving her, "that's a fine idea at
that. Cook has been in ecstasies all day planning this family
reunion. Let us not disappoint her. We do keep country hours
here, so we must adjourn this pleasant gathering till later and
continue it at dinner."

As Lady Isabel began to gather up her possessions—her
fan, her shawl, and her little boy—Anthony broke in, "But
what of the Earl? Isn't he coming to meet us here? Or shall
we see him at dinner?"

Lady Isabel tittered, and even the long face of Richard
Courtney showed some animation.

"But surely you know—" Lord Beverly began, but the tall
man at the fireside cut him off with a wave of the hand.

"Cousin Anthony, what more would you have me do?
Before dinner at any rate?"

Anthony stared at Cousin Morgan blankly.

"Why, Morgan's the Earl, of course," Lord Beverly said in
consternation at the look upon Anthony's face.

Elizabeth, having already risen, turned to stare at the man
who had introduced himself as "Cousin Morgan" and blurted
before she had time to stop herself, "But you said you were
'Cousin Morgan.'"

"And so I am," he returned.

"But the Earl of Auden is old. Very old," Anthony
stammered.

"From your point of view, young Anthony, that's sadly
true." The Earl grinned.

Before Elizabeth could signal to him, Anthony went on in
tones of outrage, "Uncle said as how the Earl was at his last
prayers."

"So he was," the Earl said gently, "but the Earl your

uncle doubtless remembered was my father. And he has since passed from this mortal coil.''

"Then we missed the funeral?" Elizabeth asked, aghast at her social gaffe in not offering condolences when she entered the house, and then wondering why relatives who were mourning would be so gaily attired, so lacking in funeral sentiment.

"By about five years," the Earl answered.

"Then if you are Auden, why did you summon us?" Anthony demanded passionately. "How can it be that you need an heir? Do you indeed need an heir? Or is it all a hum?''

"Every man needs an heir, young Anthony, and, yes, I summoned you to that purpose," the Earl said abruptly. "You are my last living male relatives. And I welcome you. Now, I think we really must adjourn. Anthony, you may remain and hear me out if you wish, but the others will doubtless want to go and change for dinner."

"No," Anthony said petulantly, "no need for me to stay. I quite understand now."

Elizabeth knew that Anthony understood no more than she, but she knew of his pride and wondered if their misunderstanding of the situation would cause him to give up the whole enterprise.

Feeling three kinds of a fool, Elizabeth stood and let her teeth worry at her lower lip. Then, as the whole company rose, chatting lightly to dispel the air of outrage that Anthony had summoned up, the Earl came slowly across the room. Only then did Elizabeth see that the walking stick he carried was no mere fashionable ornament. Only then did she see how tightly clenched his hand was as he bent his weight upon it. And only then did she see how even his air of grace was hampered by the obviously painful halting manner in which he made his way to the door.

He turned once to say something to Lord Beverly and startled the look of dismay upon her face. His face set still and she could not see the expression in his eyes. But, she thought in chagrin, first I act like a dumbstruck rustic, then as a pokered-up teetotaler, then a fool, and now I gawk at a man's impediment as if it were a raree-show. And, she thought, wishing she would wake in a moment and discover the whole incident to have been a disturbed dream taking place on the coach somewhere between the inn at Stourbridge and Lyonshall, Uncle thought it was Anthony he had to worry about!

Dinner, from Elizabeth's point of view, was a disaster. Immersed in her confusion, she had no way of knowing that the Earl would have agreed with her appraisal of the meal completely. Indeed, no one else at the long table would have guessed his opinion either. For he was a most gracious, pleasant, conversant host to them all. Elizabeth sat on his right and Lady Isabel on his left, with the Earl at the head of the table. And he divided his time between them. Rather, he attempted to divide his time that way, but as every least comment made to Elizabeth was met with some subdued, noncommittal answer, it was impossible. As facile as he was, even the Earl would not poke a conversation out of her polite little "Of courses" and "Yes, quite sos" and "No . . . nevers," no matter how deftly he tried.

Elizabeth had known she was dressed correctly even though she had refused the services of Lady Isabel's maid. She had never used a lady's maid, and did not wish to start with an employee of a fine London lady. The look in the Earl's eyes as she sat down was frankly admiring and so settled her worries on that score. But in the clear light of so many candles and in such close physical proximity with such an overwhelming gentleman, she had soon found herself totally at a loss. It was not just that he was the most compelling man she had ever met. Under natural circumstances, her quick understanding and interest in the many challenging questions that were tossed up for her to catch at would have soon evaporated her shyness. For she would not have cared if it were Adonis himself conversing with her once she got a good conversation under way. It was her total misery at the way she and Anthony had misread the situation, coupled with her sense of failure at the start of her mission, compounded by her fears for her uncle's plans, that made her unable to participate in any of the Earl's gentle raillery. And the deadly knowledge that she was behaving like a simpleton only served to increase her state of unease, and thus, of course, her frightened air of silence.

When the Earl turned to Lady Isabel, he was greeted by such an air of concentration upon her part as to point up Elizabeth's reticence even further. Lady Isabel hung upon his every word, her great blue eyes fastened upon the Earl's lips as though she were a deaf person, only able to comprehend him by watching each utterance as it formed there. Lady Isabel's face was a mirror of the conversation, Elizabeth thought sadly, as she wondered whether to try the potted prawns even though she did not know which of the many silver implements that surrounded her plate like a shining army was fit for the purpose in this establishment. But then, one could speak only Greek and still be able to follow their conversation just by watching the lady's animated face. For she laughed becomingly at every witticism and batted the Earl's arm with a lace handkerchief at any comment she considered a trifle "warm" in a lady's company. And she listened with such concentrated efforts to his soft discourse, one would think he were telling her fortune.

Little Owen Courtney sat silently at his mama's side, eating with an intensity that equaled his mama's conversational performance. He said very little, and except for occasional grave requests for more of his favorite foods, seemed to wear the popular sampler motto, of children being seen and not heard, upon his very heart. He was already so rotund that even Elizabeth, used to the ways of small boys, had to pinch herself from leaning across the table and cautioning him against taking yet another helping of caramel pudding.

Richard Courtney sat at Elizabeth's right and mercifully paid her little attention. His concentration was not upon his meal as he ate automatically and without zest. But it was not upon anyone at the table either. That seemed to suit Lord Beverly and Anthony down to the ground, for the two were deep in their own conversation throughout the meal. By watching carefully through the side of her eyes and listening closely, Elizabeth was able to ascertain that the two had struck up an immediate friendship. Their talk never had a chance to turn to politics, they were so immersed in discussing topics which Anthony had always admired, though could little afford, such as horses, racing, and hunting.

When at last even young Owen had partaken of as many sweetmeats as he could hold, Lady Isabel, with a sweet smile, rose and said lightly, "I expect the gentlemen wish to be left to themselves for a while. Elizabeth, let us have a pleasant coze by the fire."

And Elizabeth, feeling once again put firmly in her place, trailed after Lady Isabel as she made her way out of the room.

But Lady Isabel had scarcely time to settle herself artistically against the background of the beige settee which most complimented her pink gown, and scarcely time to ask Elizabeth how old she was, why she was as yet unmarried, and whether she had any prospects of matrimony, when the gentlemen came into the room.

"Scarcely any reason to leave this young gentleman to his port," the Earl said as he made his halt way in, "for his eyes are half-closed as it is. His next port of call, I believe, should rightly be his bed."

"Oh, no, Cousin Morgan," Owen said quickly in his sober little voice, opening his blue eyes wide, "for I am not a bit fatigued. Truly I am not."

"He had yards of rest on the trip here in the coach," his mother protested.

"I wish I could have," Lord Beverly said with a yawn, "for the deuced thing rattled my teeth out. And I just had it resprung."

"Children can sleep through anything," Lady Isabel persisted. "Why, it's only early evening."

"And early days yet," the Earl said softly. "Anthony and Elizabeth have traveled leagues today. We do keep country hours here, and," he added, smiling conspiratorially at Lady Isabel, "tomorrow is another day. I say we should all retire early this night, so that all our young things can have some rest without fear of being thought less than congenial company."

As Lord Beverly, barely suppressing gaping yawns, swiftly seconded the Earl's suggestion, Lady Isabel rose and with recovered good humor bade them all a good night. Elizabeth mounted the stair so fatigued and so troubled she did not even bother to mark where Anthony's room was located. Tomorrow, she thought, as she made her way to the elegant room the Earl had given her, is indeed another day.

"Thank you," the Earl said with a sigh as he raised a glass to his lips and sank back into his armchair. "I thought I'd never be rid of them."

"Least I could do," Lord Beverly replied, at ease before the fire in the Earl's study. "Is the leg bothering you so much today, then? For you looked in a state, Morgan, you looked drawn to pieces."

"No," the Earl said softly, for the house was quiet, and with all his guests abed, the night was still. "Actually, it's been a great deal better since I left the damp environs of the City. But what a cork-brain I've been! Why the devil I let you and Tompkins talk me into this mad start, I do not know. I think I should rather suffer the imprecations of a dozen impostors, yes, and foot their bills as well, rather than put up with this set of legal relations. I think I'll just pick one of their names from your hat, Bev, and bid them all good-bye tomorrow. First thing tomorrow," he said broodingly, staring into the fire.

"Wouldn't be right. You ought to pick a right one, so long as you're about it. Gone this far, ought to see the thing out," Lord Beverly chided him. "And I think you're being hard on them."

"Hard on your newfound friend Anthony, is what you mean, Bev. What you see in the fellow is beyond me." The Earl sighed.

"He's a good sort of lad," Lord Beverly protested.

"He may well be, but I wish he'd scrape some of the canary feathers from off his chin," the Earl interrupted, "for the boy goes about with a damnable smirk on his face all the time, as if he had the family silver in his back pocket already.

And that chit of a cousin of his watches him constantly as though she knows he does indeed have designs upon my silver cabinet.''

"Why, Morgan, where are your eyes? She's a beauty, pretty as a picture. Eyelashes a yard long," Lord Beverly defended, rising out of his chair in his gallantry.

"Yes, a picture. But a still life. The girl's got as much conversation as a bowl of fruit. And if you look at her sidewise, she colors up just like a pippin. She makes that other clam, Richard, seem as talkative as a parrot. And Lord knows all I've been able to get out of him thus far is his name.''

"True," his companion mused, "he is a dull dog.''

"A secretive one," the Earl amended.

"But there's little Owen. Nice little lad," Lord Beverly said valiantly.

The Earl barely repressed a shudder and drank off the rest of his claret. "Come fill the cup, old friend, and have done with championing that little article. I swear he gives me the chills. He looks an uncanny miniature of our dear Regent, curls, corpus, and all. A middle-aged child. I listen for the creak of stays every time he moves. Not that he moves much"—the Earl laughed, accepting another glass—"save to get himself another sweet.''

"But there's Isabel," Lord Beverly tried again, sinking back to his chair. "She's up to all the rigs. Gay as a linnet.''

"And about as constant as one, too," the Earl said with a tight smile. "And tonight, fastening on my every word, positively rapt with interest. I scarcely had a bite to eat, you know, she was watching my lips so closely. It's very difficult to eat properly when someone's watching your mouth as carefully as a cat watches a mouse hole," he complained, draining off the rest of his glass quickly.

"You're sousing yourself into the sullens," Lord Beverly complained, getting up nevertheless to refill the glass. "Isabel's only trying to let you know she's interested. Wouldn't be such a bad thing, either, a wife with a ready-made legal heir.''

"You forget," the Earl said softly, "that Isabel was a good friend of Kitty's. Yes, a very good friend. I know Isabel a great deal better than she thinks. And I often wonder why it is that little Owen looks so very unlike his late brave captain of a father."

A silence fell over the room, broken only by Lord Beverly's quiet comment: "You should not class Isabel with Kitty. That is all the past. It is over and done with."

"I don't usually," the Earl said, finishing his glass again, and now slurring his words only very slightly. "You of all people should know that. You, who was used to be constantly on about my talking it out. But all this ado about heirs and marriage . . . It's very natural for me to think about my own dear departed wife again."

"Kitty was . . . unique," his friend said seriously.

"Well I know it," the Earl answered, laying his head back. "And well you know it too, old friend. You were the only man in London to refuse her, I think. No, don't say a word. I know you too well, Bev. And know you never mentioned it for fear of giving me hurt. But she wouldn't have passed you by. Never. You are, after all, far comelier than most of the others. And more important, not to demean your manly graces, you were accessible. But do not worry. I knew you, at least, had turned her down."

"I did," Lord Beverly said simply, in quiet tones, fearing to break the strange mood that had come over his friend, for he never spoke of Kitty, and no friend ever dared to broach the subject to him. "And with a flea in her ear, too. I'm only glad that you knew it. Did she tell you?"

"Kitty?" The Earl laughed. "Oh, no. Never. She only said once, on the way to a ball, plucking the thought as though out of the ether, that she thought you preferred boys. It was her charming way of comprehending any rejection, so I knew. I had so many horns put upon my head, old dear, by that time, that it would have hardly mattered if she'd found room for one more antler. But I remember being glad then that you, at least, had said no."

"Morgan," Lord Beverly said after a quiet moment, rising

to see that his friend's eyes were slowly closing, and taking the glass from his unresisting hand, "you cannot judge all women by Kitty, you know."

"I don't," the Earl said in a barely audible voice. "I only wish I could. And then have done with them."

— 5 —

"Country hours" may well have been what their host had specified, but most of the Earl's guests had their minds and bodies firmly set to London time. And so it was that when a lovely spring morning dawned there were a great many people abustle at Lyonshall, but in the main they were servants who had never had the habit or opportunity to sleep the day away. Their life-style marked them firmly as provincials, but much the dairy maids cared as they felt the dewy grass beneath their feet. The housemaids felt no social stigmata settle on their shoulders as they worried at the dust that had settled in the night, and the stablemen were too busy whistling and joshing with each other to fear that their being abroad so early on such a fine morning put them firmly beyond the social pale.

For as the sun rose higher in the sky, Lady Isabel sighed and snuggled deeper into her feather pillow; Lord Beverly tossed in restless sleep as his valet labored over a worrisome smudge on the fine leather of his master's left boot; Richard Courtney slept as a dead man, for he did not often have such leisure and had a great deal of catching up to do; and Anthony Courtney slumbered on as only the heedless young may do until something more interesting tempts them from their beds. Owen Courtney, however, already had one large blue eye open, as hunger had begun to nudge him into the world of reality.

But Elizabeth DeLisle had been awake for hours and she sat by her window and waited for the morning to blossom into full day. She yearned to be up and about as was her wont to do at home. But Uncle had warned her that even if she were to whistle, or to scratch her buttock, no single act would point her out as a shopgirl more than if she rose before noon. But she was a shopgirl, she thought sadly. Yet obediently she sat pent in her room so as not to let the rest of the world know of her ignoble position and her charade. Elizabeth waited for the stroke of noon like a daylight Cinderella, so that she could spring up and be out at last.

She had settled herself in for a long morning and amused herself by watching the many servants of the house and grounds as they went cheerily about their business. But then her eyes widened as she spied the unmistakable figure of the Earl himself making his laborious way past her window toward the stables. Only moments later she saw the Earl, clearly this time, mounted upon a huge black horse, cantering into view upon the drive. She could clearly see that she had not been mistaken in thinking him an athlete. For the mount and rider were one, restless, graceful, and imperative. While she watched, the Earl looked toward the house, and seeing her at the window, raised his hand in slow salute before turning and galloping off in the direction of the near wood.

He had seen her awake and alert at this unfashionable hour, Elizabeth thought with dismay, turning too late from her window. She rose and walked with determination to her writing desk. For she had erred again, and Uncle must know, she vowed, as she reached for paper and ink. Uncle must know that I must go home, for Anthony is behaving just as he ought, all on his own. And it is I, she despaired, who will bring the whole scheme down around our ears.

Charles Morgan Courtney, seventh Earl of Auden, Viscount Louth and Baron Kitteredge, let his horse, Scimitar, of even more impressive pedigree, have his way and lost himself in the flow of motion and the steady rhythm of their passage. It was the mindless pleasure of speed and movement that he had sought this morning. So he neither smelled the cool spring scent of blossoms, nor noted the new green of his lands as the racing horse turned the forest to blur. Run, my friend, he urged soundlessly, as I cannot, and I will follow anywhere.

It was only when he felt the tightly muscled body beneath him begin to blow with effort that he at last reined in and allowed Scimitar to pick his way aimlessly through the fields and meadows beyond sight of Lyonshall. But though the horse had worked out all its restless energy, Morgan Courtney felt locked and blocked within himself. He patted his mount absently. The animal could do no more, he thought, indeed no creature he could have ridden could run fast enough this morning to leave his thoughts behind.

Bev had assisted him to bed last night, he remembered. He never could seem to drink enough to bring complete oblivion and had given up trying for that long ago. How many bottles had the surgeon primed him with, all that time ago, as he waited for unconsciousness to overtake his patient so that he could begin to remove the shell lodged in his leg? There had been other patients groaning, and new ones being brought from the battlefield by the moment, and still after each long swallow of bad spirits, he had kept smiling tightly up toward the harried surgeon. Till at last the surgeon had shaken his head and sighed. "You're a sponge, lad. Sorry, but I'll have to go ahead anyway."

And those days in London, in Scotland, and in Wales, all those glasses, those liters of fine aged liquors he had sought escape from Kitty in had no effect either. They were no more effective in sealing him off from the shrill pain of his life with her than the crude liquor had been in numbing him from the keen cutting of the surgeon's knife. In neither case had it even brought him the release of tears. "You're a brave lad," the surgeon had said when he had finished. "You're a strong man," Kitty's father had said when she was done. Neither was right, he thought as Scimitar now carried him even farther. It was only that he had never learned how to suffer correctly. For if he had, he thought, he would have wept and been done with it, gotten it out of his system. And then neither wound could still cause the pain that they did.

The leg was one thing he had learned to live with by living with it. The memory of Kitty was a thing he evaded and seldom allowed himself to recall. But when those years were brought back, as they now were by this travesty of a sudden search for an heir that he was embarked upon, her memory came back as fresh in its cruelty as though no time had elapsed since he had last laid eyes upon her living form. It had been seven years since the world had held her breathing presence. And seven years later, on a spring morning that he should have been celebrating as busily as the birds were, she yet lay like a shadow over his sun.

Scimitar paced his way slowly through a meadow as his master picked his way back through the thicket of years. Here, at Lyonshall, over a decade ago, there had been three male Courtneys. Each with a clear heritage to the title and a clear obligation to the land, not like the ill-assorted ragtag of males he had been forced by circumstances to invite to his home this year. His mama had died when he was an infant and his father, the sixth Earl, had been old since he had known him. But he was a capable and loving father to both his sons, Simon and Charles Morgan. Simon was the elder by twelve years and was to be the seventh in the long line of Earls that had held Lyonshall from time out of mind. But Simon was not a healthy man, for a fever as a child had damaged his heart. Father and elder son had both given young Morgan to understand that. Gently but firmly they had told him again and again that as his father was old and Simon not robust, there was every chance that he, the younger, would someday succeed to the title. But he had not wanted to hear it or know it. Simon was his loving brother and would live forever, and his father was immortal as the sun. He would not believe it.

When he was three-and-twenty they told him it was time to look about him for a wife, to ensure the succession. For Simon had taken none and never would, in the wisdom of his own treacherous body. So young Morgan agreed to be off to London for a season or two, not to find a wife as they asked, for he thought he needed none, but to find a taste of life. And he had, he thought now; he had found more than he bargained for.

In London, he had found Kitty.

Kitty Clairmont, the most beautiful creature to have ever met his roving eyes. She was not the toast of the season, nor even one of the leading incomparables. But she was a beauty and at eighteen had a following among the ardent young men in the ton. When he had seen her that night at Almack's, at first glance, she had driven him wild with the desire to make her his wife. He did not see it as his first taste of calf-love, for at three-and-twenty he had already lain with five women and thought himself an expert at love. No matter that three were females he had paid for and two were girls of the servant class, and none were relationships that lasted more than a night, or were expected to last beyond the rising of the sun. He was three-and-twenty and no one could have told him differently. His father and his brother were fast at Lyonshall and all his friends were of an age with him and knew no more of the true love for a woman than he. Indeed, some knew less and thought Morgan Courtney in his tall, straight, handsome form as worldly as he himself did.

When he saw her standing there, slender, slightly taller than average, with her clear pale olive skin and midnight hair and slow dark gypsy eyes, he thought she looked like a Madonna from one of the paintings that hung in the corridors of Lyonshall. When she danced with him and he felt her slim form against him and tried to look into those fathomless eyes, he felt she was some sort of seductive houri from his childhood books of *The Arabian Nights*. Though she spoke seldom and lowered her lashes when he gazed hungrily into her eyes, and never laughed or coquetted as more spectacular belles might do, he was lost to all reason. He would marry her, he must marry her, he could not live if he did not. And lost to all reason, he thought this was love.

She had no mother, but did have a strict father who had brought her to Town from their small holding in Wales. Her family was obscure, but of a good line, their fortune was established, and young Morgan Courtney could see no impediment. But he did see competition, and lived in a fever of anxiety each time he called at her town house and saw other young men awaiting an audience with her. She was strictly chaperoned and slow to speak, and though she seemed to look kindly upon him, he did not know her feelings and that drove him to new heights of acquisitive passion.

Once he had drawn her out to the garden at a ball, and that once, he had taken her in his arms, and that one time he had been allowed to kiss her briefly. In a moment she had gently pushed him away, turned her head in shame, and whispered, "We must not." And that gave him the fuel to continue courting her for weeks. Three times he made his offer to her father, and three times her father had evaded his eyes and said, "She is young yet, give her time." But Morgan Courtney knew that an older, twice-widowed Baronet was also courting her, and impatience gnawed at him. Then, at the end of the season, the Baronet veered off, and when Morgan Courtney made his fourth offer, her father had sighed and said, "So be it." And he had won her hand.

During their engagement, which lasted a summer, he spent every available moment with her. But she was still closely chaperoned and he was given to understand that this was the custom in her small part of the world. And he suffered it. Yet each time he finally got her alone and begged a kiss, she was flustered and withdrawn and made him feel a ravening beast. Though she never joked or held long conversation, he was so lost in love he saw no lack of humor or intellect in her, but only lack of confidence in herself. He knew there were worlds to discover in her deep dark eyes. The only real fear he had for their forthcoming marriage was as to how he would overcome that shyness and lead her to physical enjoyment of their union. But he was confident. He had been loved all his life and he was three-and-twenty and had lain with five women and knew he could win her to him, in both mind and body.

He did not attempt to make her his wife physically till they had been wed for more than two weeks. He waited till they had been together for a space, he waited till they had reached the solitude of their rooms in the estate he had rented in Scotland for their honeymoon. He would have wished to take her to some exotic clime to match her mood and style but had no desire to risk her safety, and travel abroad was out of the question due to the armed camp the Continent had become. But after two weeks in her constant company he could wait no longer. He could not wait till he had gotten to know her better, for in truth she was still slow of speech and shy and he could wait no longer.

After much whispering of assurance to her, after long starts and stops, after slow sweet extended embraces, he at last took her to him to complete their union. Suddenly from her armor of reticence she grasped at him, she came forth boldly and clutched him and writhed with him and overwhelmed him completely, making him feel as a child might who stepped into a still pool and found himself carried over a cataract of rushing waters. Later, his mind still whirling as he lay there exhausted, she spoke softly in the stillness of the room.

"You know, of course," she said, lying quiet now, and studying the lofty ceiling of their room.

"Yes," he said, wondering what it was he was supposed to know.

"It was only that once," she whispered.

And whispering, she told him of the stableboy that had overpowered her and taken her when she was only fifteen.

"Do you hate me for it?" she asked in a sad, flat voice.

"Hate you?" he cried, reaching for her again. "No, never, how can you say that? You are my wife. I love you."

And she smiled into his hair as they renewed their union, again and again.

The weeks that followed, while they rested at their honeymoon home, were a sensual blur to Morgan. If he had had time to think, if he were not so totally immersed in his senses, he might have wondered how it was that she knew so much more than he, how she knew so many ways to please him, how she could be, after that one brute encounter in a stable, so endlessly eager. But their only communication was through their bodies, and he had no time, no thought for thought, until even he, at three-and-twenty, was exhausted and wanted some surcease from the endless demands of her body and time for communion of a different sort.

But she yawned through the art galleries he took her to in nearby Edinburgh, and sat with sphinxlike smile as they toured the antique streets, and fanned herself with uninterest within medieval castles, and toyed with her fan at concerts. In the end she told him with a small smile that she would prefer he went on his sightseeing without her, as she needed her rest.

He had thought it might be a child on the way. So he left her to rest in her warm bed while he toured the vicinity. And on that one Wednesday afternoon, he had been standing in a great picture gallery when his gaze fell upon a portrait of the Madonna and Child that looked so like his dear Kitty and the babe of his fantasies that he slapped his hat against his knee, bit back a grin, and turned to hurry home to her. To surprise her with his early return and his reawakened desire.

Her maid flew at him from a shadowed part of the corridor and tried to call him away from their bedroom. She flapped at him like a great bat, but he only smiled and put her aside, for he knew Kitty would not mind this interruption of her daily nap. He opened the door and saw the ruddy, freckled young man's body like a pulsing growth upon the pale olive clarity of her unclothed form. He remembered the obscenity he saw when he pulled the man off his wife and remembered trying to beat that offending body into nothingness, to erase all signs of gender from the shrieking man he battered.

And then he felt her cool hand upon his shoulder and heard her slow soft voice, louder than cathedral chimes, "Let him be," she said, tugging at his arm. "Let him go. I asked him to. I asked him," she said.

Long after the young man had been restored to his senses, long after his wounds had been tended to and he had been given his clothes and dismissed from his job as footman and shown off the premises by the scandalized staff, Morgan sat, his head cradled in his hands, and listened to his wife's gentle litany, a long and slow telling of her tale, a longer conversation than she had ever had with him before, or would ever have again.

At the time he heard everything and heard nothing, his senses were still so disordered. Yet every word would stay with him till the end of his days.

Yes, she had told him, it did begin at fifteen for her. But it had been no attack, no more than today's episode had been.

She had been curious. The stableboy had been obliging. But her father had discovered them and reacted just as her husband had. There was mild amazement, Morgan remembered, in her voice as she related that. Her father had kept her under strict chaperonage, but she was endlessly inventive. There had been, in the years before she had caught his astonished eye in London, many such episodes. Many times. Few refused her, from stableboy to farm worker, from chance acquaintances of her father's to tradesmen from town.

She had been taken first to men of God. Her father had thought, in his strict Methodism, that it was unholiness that accounted for it. That she, poor motherless creature, had been drawn into the devil's net. Thus, she had been lectured, she had been sermonized, she had been beaten, she had spent hours upon her knees, only to arise and slip out to yet more encounters.

In her seventeenth year, her father had given up on God and taken her to a different set of holy men. He had brought her far from home to a round of physicians of all stripes. Her diet had been altered to whole grains and spring water. She had been denied spices and salt. And then sweets and savories, then red meats and hot foods. She had endured it, for her hunger was of a different sort. She continued to indulge that hunger whenever she could steal away. She had been immersed in steaming hot baths to draw out her sensual humors, and when that failed, steeped in icy waters to depress her heated passions. And no cure was effective.

At last her father was told of an operation, a surgical procedure that would remove that tiny wedge-shaped part of the female anatomy that was supposed to give the keenest pleasure and be the root of unseemly female desire. The surgery would thus effectively remove all her desire for future encounters. The Arabians, her father was told, regularly performed such mutilations upon their women in childhood to keep them content in their harems. "After all," the learned physician had joked, for he was a jovial fellow as well as a man of science and he was both perturbed and annoyed at the look of horror writ large upon his patient's father's face, "how else do you think the old sultans can keep one hundred wives happy?"

When her father, driven to despair after yet another fall from grace upon her part, had threatened her with that, she had only smiled and told him it would be to no avail. It was not pleasure she sought, she had explained, it was only a thing she must do.

Yet his distress was such that he was about to give his consent for it to be done, when the physician said in passing the one thing that stayed his hand.

"Of course," he had said, "you know that then marriage for her will be out of the question. For her husband would of course notice the alteration and would then have adequate grounds for divorce. There are some men," the physician said, with a sad shake of his head for those less scholarly and scientific, "that would find a woman thus scarred repugnant to them."

But if the physician had removed one possibility of escape, he had implanted the idea of another. She was yet young, her father reasoned. He could not, as some had urged, incarcerate her in Bedlam; she was his only child. Perhaps marriage would be the answer. Marriage would mean a man at her constant service. Marriage to a man stern enough to contain her might answer.

They went to London.

"Papa wanted me to marry the Baronet," she said at last, in the last hours of the night, "but I didn't like him. He was old and ugly. I liked you, Morgan. I do. I told Papa so. Truly. And you are the best I've found. But I cannot help myself. I cannot. I didn't mean to hurt you, you know. I will try harder in future. I will, Morgan, truly," she said, and then curled up in peaceful sleep, while he sat up through the dawn and tried to understand all he had been told.

They packed the next day and returned to London. Morgan could not bear to touch his wife; could not now bear the looks of admiration upon the faces of other men when they saw her glowing beauty, which had once pleased him; could not even speak with her. He paced and thought, went without sleep, and finally, his mind too full to bear it alone, left Kitty in London and rode back full tilt to Lyonshall.

His father and brother wondered at his leaving his new bride alone so soon. Morgan spun them a tale of her exhaustion after their travels on their honeymoon, and they smiled knowingly. Perhaps, his father suggested gently, they would be seeing her soon again, perhaps then with his grandson in tow? A new terror gripped Morgan at his words.

It was late night after dinner on the third day of his visit that Morgan decided to seek his father's counsel. They sat before the fire and let a companionable silence fill the room, and Morgan had just cleared his throat to speak the unspeakable problem when his father sighed with contentment and spoke first.

"Simon and I are pleased, Morgan, to see you so well settled. He would be here with us now, poor soul, if he felt sturdier. But the doctors have said he needs his rest, and so he does, so he does. And as for me, my boy, I suppose now that you have a wife and are about to start your own family, you can bear the news. For I have been told I have not much longer a race to run, either. It is my one solace, my dear son, to know that you are so fortunate in your life, and that you will ensure that Lyonshall remains as it is. You were a surprise to your poor mother, God rest her, and to me, coming so late in life. But the Lord is wise, and now I can know that when I leave and Simon must go, all will yet be well."

When Morgan Courtney returned to Town, he was a changed man. Marriage had matured him, his friends opined when they saw his set face, his new air of dignity, his sober aspect. He went to his clubs, he drove his curricle, he visited Gentleman Jim's, he lived his life as befit any young man of his rank and station. He confided in no one and none knew that he did not touch his wife.

"I cannot divorce you now," he told her, "as I yearn to, for the scandal would kill my father. But I shall kill you, my dear, if you present me with a babe. For I will know it is not mine."

"Have no fear on that score, Morgan," she had replied,

unfazed, "for I almost had one years ago, and when I lost it, I was told there was little chance of ever having another. I didn't lose it, precisely," she said, watching him closely, for he had so changed since she last saw him that she feared him a little now. "An old herb woman aided me. But, Morgan, I vow I shall make you forget those harsh words. For I promised I would try, did I not? And so I shall. But don't turn from me. For I need you."

Looking at her, seeing her soft and yielding, arms held out to him, he had stepped back and snarled, "All this you tell me now? Now when we are irrevocably wed? Perhaps I could forget all that went before, but why did you wait to tell me now?"

"Would you have wed me else?" she said with perfect mad logic.

And he had turned and left. He would not touch his wife, he could not seek other women, for in doing so he would give her license to pay him back in similar coin, and in truth now he wanted nothing to do with them. Those months they stayed in London, he fully believed he was slowly losing his senses.

Everywhere he went, he thought he heard hushed whispers. When he attended a ball with Kitty, he thought he caught sly nudges made by other gentlemen, and covert comment from the ladies. Conversations seemed to be cut off mid-sentence when he entered his club. And he thought he caught pitying looks from the older men he most admired. The world seemed filled with knowing eyes. He was a proud young man and could not believe what was happening to him. For when he taxed Kitty with it, she would protest he was imagining things and that she was faithful to him. And asked when he would come back to her arms.

Then the afternoon came when he returned to his house in London for a forgotten bit of paper and had seen again the mad recurrence of his waking nightmare. Only this time it had been the pudgy pale buttocks of Sir Belvedere that he saw trembling above his wedded wife. Sir Belvedere, a great useless, foppish fellow, had wept and pleaded and named five other fellows who had done the same thing and then left in a great haste, shrinking and sniveling, though Morgan had not even touched him.

"I did try," Kitty said, her dark eyes wide and frightened at her husband's great stillness where she had expected bluster and rage. But he only stared at her.

"Are you going to beat me?" she asked.

"Dogs are beaten," he said with deep sadness, "and if you beat a dog, you are left with a cringing cur who is afraid to do more than lick your boot. That is never what I wanted, Kitty. I only wanted a wife."

He left the house as silently as he had come.

When he returned a week later, he set Kitty's maid to packing, sent his servants scurrying to close the house, and called for his coach to be readied for a long journey the next morning. And it was not until they were long out of the City that he finally spoke to his wife. The words he then spoke were almost the last he ever had with her.

"I have joined the regiment," he said calmly, "and shall leave the country soon. I am returning you to your father. I have the legal right to lock you in a cellar in chains if I so choose, so do not think yourself ill-used by this turn of events. You shall stay with your father until one of two things occurs. You can gain your freedom in divorce if my father dies, or gain it as a widow if I do. But there you shall stay until either thing happens. And if you don't, I shall return and make myself a widower. I promise you."

He had gone from her father's house, riding like a fury loosed out into the world. Leaving her father weeping and begging forgiveness, and leaving her wearing her strange sad smile. He had gone to the battlefields and distinguished himself, since he courted death so assiduously. But death is a famously coy mistress, he discovered, and gave favor to other, less deserving men.

He was in hospital, waiting for his shattered leg to mend, when word came of Simon's death. He made his painful halt way back from funeral to funeral. For word came to him, even as he consoled his father, of his wife's last illness.

He was in time to stand over her bed and hear her last painful breaths. She lay, her inky hair witch-wild, scattered across her pillow, and breathed deeply as her father, twisting a Bible round and round in his hands, explained how difficult a birth it was.

"Don't despair, Morgan," she whispered, opening her eyes to focus on him, "for it died too. The physicians were wrong, you see. But I truly liked you, Morgan. And"—and here he had to bend to catch the last words—"you really were the best, you know. Truly."

"Enough!" the seventh Earl of Auden cried aloud, his hands tightening on the reins with the force of his thoughts, causing Scimitar to shy. Patting the great horse back to calm, the Earl wrenched his thoughts back to the present, back to the pale green spring morning. He turned Scimitar toward home. A mad start, this, he admonished himself, going back again over lost ground, a foolish unprofitable thing brought on by this ridiculous enterprise. Damn Bev and Tompkins, damn their eyes. I will pick them an heir and be done with it, and whoever I choose will be better than that sad blue babe my loving wife delivered herself of. At least whoever I pick will be my choice, and at least someone's legitimate son. But not his. He would not contemplate marriage again, not yet. Perhaps not ever. But he could not rid himself of women.

After Kitty, he had gone through a period of celibacy out of revulsion and, he admitted, out of fear of mockery or inadequacy. Then he had swung to excess, proving again and again that Kitty's wild need could not have arisen through any fault of his. Now he had come to terms with the entire female sex.

He still needed them, he liked them, and more damnably, he desired them. So he dealt with them on his travels on the Continent and he dallied with them only there. He would not return to London, where the echo of whispers still burned in his ears. Neither would he form alliances with local country lasses; the idea of practicing a sort of *droit du seigneur* revolted him. He had no wish to populate his district with farm and household help all bearing the same stamp of his face. He would not emulate old Lord Babcock down in the South, whose identically hawk-nosed footmen, maidservants, and tenant farmers were a joke through the land.

Instead he sated himself in far-off places, and only then did he return to his great love, Lyonshall. Here he stayed in his heart's home, until desire sent him ranging for surcease through the wide world again. He would settle the matter of the succession intelligently, he thought, as Scimitar moved on muffled hooves through the young grass to carry him unerringly home again. And he would be done with his regrets and inchoate wishes. He would choose an heir from this unpromising assortment of relatives and put an end to the impostor's plans. Then he would free himself to live out the rest of his life on his own diminished terms. This decided, as if to speed his own decision, he urged Scimitar to make haste homeward.

The Earl had reached the bottom of the long drive when he saw his friend Bev, neat as a pin and dressed to an inch, striding toward him and calling a hello to him.

"Where have you been, Morgan? It's almost luncheon and no one knew what you were about. Your guests are roving all over looking for you. You may have had a delightful time riding about, but I've had to placate them all and chat them up, and fiend take it, all they wanted to know is where you were."

"I was out, as you said, riding, and having a delightful time," the Earl said coldly.

"Don't look it," his friend said doubtfully. "Look worn to pieces."

"I shall assemble those pieces and go to greet my guests," the Earl said more amiably, seeing the concern on his friend's face.

"Anthony and I fancied a ride ourselves, but I didn't think it right to desert the ladies, don't you know," Bev complained. "They've been asking after you all morning."

"Now, Lady Isabel's wrath at finding me gone, I can imagine," the Earl said, thinking of blond, seductive Isabel, who had been one of Kitty's confidantes. "But how you managed to prize a question, much less a word, out of Anthony's great-eyed cousin, I do not know."

"She's a very nice sort of girl," Bev asserted stoutly. "You just frighten her, I think. She's just a bit shy."

And the Earl, walking Scimitar slowly back to the stables,

called over his shoulder, "Have a care, Bev, the shy ones are the very worst sort." As I, he thought with a grim nod, should well know.

"I ain't in the petticoat line, Morgan," Bev grumbled after him, "as you should know."

— 6 —

Although it was only a two-page letter she had finally penned to her uncle, begging permission to return home, Elizabeth spent the better part of two days reading and rereading it whenever she was at leisure in her room. Soon there was not a comma nor a period in her missive that she had not contemplated and corrected several times. And yet, it would not have been a great surprise to anyone who knew Elizabeth well to see her carefully tearing her earnest little letter into small shreds on the fourth day of her visit to Lyonshall.

It was not as if a single thing had changed since she had written it, nor that anyone had spoken with her and counseled her to destroy it. It was rather that Elizabeth had grown heartily disgusted with herself and her lack of enterprise. Her mornings were usually spent roaming her room waiting for the clock to chime noon. Her luncheons were spent in tongue-tied misery at the Earl's lavish table, her afternoons in solemn contemplation of her host's gardens and walks. After she dressed in solitary dignity, her evenings were used up first with the business of dining with the assembled company and then in retreating to a corner of the room while the other guests entertained each other. She had suffered through Lady Isabel and Lord Beverly's duets at the pianoforte, had watched Anthony or Richard and her host playing desultory games of chess, and had listened to Owen recite bits of tedious poetry for the company's edification.

As she had sat quiet as a clam she had also seen Lady Isabel making an unmistakably dead set at their host. She

made such generous play with her eyelashes that Elizabeth
wondered sourly that the Earl had not contracted a chill from
the breeze that was set up by them whenever he turned to
speak with his fair guest.

Although Lady Isabel was charming and effusive with all
the rest of the company, she had obviously early on discounted Elizabeth as either competition for herself or, indeed,
as a person of consequence at all, and scarcely addressed
any but the most inconsequential of remarks to her. Owen
followed his mother's lead, but then, Elizabeth thought in all
fairness, the child seldom spoke to anyone unless spoken to
first. Cousin Richard hadn't a syllable for anyone, he seemed
so intent upon some inner conflict.

It was not as if Elizabeth had no opportunity to speak. The
Earl had tried on some few occasions to coax some comment
from her, but he so overwhelmed her that she blushed to
recall her half-witted responses to him. But Lord Beverly was
an easy chap to speak with. Although he was more than a
decade older than her cousin and every inch the impeccable
man of fashion, Elizabeth soon found that she treated him
with the same easygoing maternal tolerance that she used in
dealings with Anthony. And that seemed to be the treatment
he was most pleased with.

Yet the person she most needed to have in conversation
was the one she found the most difficult to get alone. For
Anthony was busy every moment of his waking day. He slept
the mornings away, only to rise and go about some light-
hearted business with his new friend, Lord Beverly. If he was
not in that exquisite's company, he managed to steal off to
precincts unknown until mealtimes, and then he was up and
off again. It seemed to Elizabeth, who knew Anthony as well
as she knew herself, that he was deliberately avoiding her.
That was enough to firm up her resolve. So she tore her letter
into neat shreds and incinerated it at her hearth. Then, although it was the quiet time of day when all the guests were
dressing for dinner, she eased her door open, took in a deep
breath, and went off to beard Anthony in his den.

His room was far down the corridor and round a turn in the
hall. The Earl, Elizabeth thought as she walked quickly towards

Anthony's room, seemed to be a conservative gentleman and had housed his female guests far from the gentlemen's quarters. It was her own cousin she was going to visit, but as these were definitely masculine preserves she was entering, Elizabeth felt a bit nervous at invading them, so she rapped a bit more imperatively at Anthony's door than she had planned.

"H'lo, Liz," Anthony said as he opened the door. "Whatever are you doing here?"

Conscious that in some way she ought not to be there and momentarily a bit annoyed at Anthony's new breezy manner of speech, no doubt learned from Lord Beverly, Elizabeth entered his rooms and said snappishly, "We have got to talk, Anthony. You've been very expert at eluding me. But we've been here for some days and we haven't had a chance to speak. I had to discover how things were going with you."

"Don't know what's eating at you, Coz," Anthony said, going back to his mirror to arrange his neckcloth. "You've seen it all. Shouldn't have any complaints. Everything's going just as it ought."

"Anthony," Elizabeth said patiently, "the night we arrived, we were expecting to find an old gentleman on his deathbed. When we discovered the Earl to be otherwise, you seemed ready to fly into the boughs. Don't deny it. And now you appear to be pleased with the circumstances. If you would be so good as to leave off fiddling with that neckcloth for a moment, I would like you to enlighten me as to your sudden change of heart."

"Well, that just it," Anthony said, grimacing as he noticed the left side of his cravat was now an inch higher than the right. "Nothing's really changed, Coz. Nothing at all. The Earl still needs an heir. And I am here on the spot. What more do you want?"

"But the whole circumstance has changed, Anthony," Elizabeth said, turning to fidget with the fringe of a hanging of Anthony's bed. "Even if you were named heir, it would only be a temporary measure. For the Earl's a young man and might soon supplant you with a son of his own."

"No fear of that." Anthony grinned, seeing his toilette completed at last, and turning to his cousin. "You look very fine tonight, Elizabeth. But I don't know that it's proper for you to be here in my rooms.'' He frowned.

"Whatever are you talking about?'' Elizabeth said with some surprise.

"Well, it's true you're my cousin, but it's not at all the thing for you to be here, in secret, in my rooms. You're the one who lectured me on all the proprieties, you know.''

"Not that,'' Elizabeth said with consternation. "There's nothing wrong with my being here. How else would I be able to get you alone, when you're flying off in all directions all day? And I am more than your cousin, Anthony. I taught you your first word, if you recall,'' she said defensively, wondering all at once if he weren't right about how her visit might be construed by others, but trying to get in a few words before she left. "What was that you said about the Earl not supplanting you?''

"Oh, that,'' Anthony said. "Well, it's true. So you needn't worry, for nothing's changed at all.''

"That makes no sense,'' Elizabeth challenged him.

"Well, it does,'' Anthony said. "He's not going to have a son, and so whoever he names as heir shall stay as heir. That's what you and Uncle wanted, isn't it?''

"And I suppose he told you that?'' Elizabeth said on a sigh, thinking of the long effort she had ahead of her, trying to apprise Anthony of their new situation.

"No,'' Anthony said, a slow flush starting on his neck, "but deuce take it, Elizabeth, leave off. I just know it. That's the way it will be. Believe me.''

Elizabeth walked up to her cousin and gazed steadfastly at him as he tried to turn his head away from her.

"Anthony, you'll have to do better than that. Uncle beggared himself to send us here. And you must tell what it is that you know. Why, Anthony, you're red as a beet. Whatever is it?''

"There are some things,'' Anthony said staunchly, "that one just can't discuss with a female.''

"Anthony!'' Elizabeth said in shock. "Whatever has come over you? You are the one who read me all those pamphlets about the equality of the sexes. You are the one who vowed that if you had been in London, you would have marched side by side with the ladies for woman suffrage. And you are the one," she said with spirit, "who first told me about Mary Wollstonecraft! How comes this sudden reticence?"

"Well, that's all true," Anthony said sulkily, "but you ain't a woman precisely, Liz, you're my cousin."

"That beats all," Elizabeth said angrily, seeing for the first time how a man's lofty ideals may collide with his personal relationships. "I tell you, Anthony Courtney, that if you don't explain yourself, we will leave on the instant for home, where you can find Uncle's more fittingly masculine ears to pour your story into. Or you can stop blushing like a school-girl and treating me as one, and tell me what it is."

"Bev told me," Anthony said, looking fixedly at his dresser top, as he spoke in a low, quick monotone. "Didn't 'tell' me, precisely, but it's what popped out by the way. The Earl's been wounded in combat, you know. Well, anyone with eyes can see the way he hobbles about. But his leg's not all. He's looking for an heir now because some fellow's been running up debts in London claiming to be his rightful heir, and he needs to name one to stop the business. But he needs an heir anyhow, you see, because he won't be having any sons. Nor getting married either. He was married once, and he lost his wife and son in childbirth. But if he marries again, this time there wouldn't be any childbirth or any true marriage. He can't marry. You see?"

Elizabeth stood still and tried to take in Anthony's hurried speech.

"Not exactly," she said slowly.

"Don't be such a slow-top," Anthony cried. "He can't have one. It's a war wound. Devil take it, Elizabeth, you aren't usually so slow on the uptake."

"Lord Beverly told you this?" Elizabeth asked, aghast.

"Not exactly. But I can total one times one, you know. He said that between Morgan's marriage and his wounds, 'he's got more scars than any man can rightly be expected to bear.' And that he'll never marry again because of both scars. Now, devil take it, Coz, what else would it mean? Why else would a man the Earl's age be looking so desperately for an heir?

It's as plain as the nose on your face. Why should a lofty fellow such as Auden bother with poor relations like us if he could just go out and get an heir on some female? Not that he knows we're poor relations. Uncle was right enough in that. For the rich never give a care to those less fortunate. It's what will be their downfall. Even Bev, who is the best of fellows, don't know what I'm on about when I talk about the poor."

Elizabeth let this potentially enlightening slip of Anthony's tongue go by her, she was so startled by his revelations.

And Anthony, realizing that he had inadvertently let Elizabeth know that he had spoken forbidden words on his favorite subject, said hurriedly, "That's probably why Lady Isabel's so keen after him. She's got a brat already, and wouldn't mind being shackled to a fellow who can't do more."

Elizabeth even let that blindingly inaccurate summation of a female's expectations of the marriage union go by, as she stood and thought about the Earl and his grievous wounds.

"Both scars?" she only asked weakly.

"Yes, both, Bev said. Now I suppose you want me to take the Earl aside and ask him if I can have a quick look, to satisfy my cousin's curiosity?" Anthony said angrily.

Elizabeth, forgetting all her outrage at his previous reluctance to speak about such things with a mere woman, gave Anthony a withering look. "A fine sort of thing to say to a female, Anthony. I'm sure your mother would be proud of you."

"Fiend take it, Coz, there's no pleasing you," Anthony said in exasperation.

"I think," Elizabeth said loftily, to cover her inner confusion and her need to be alone with this new information, "that I ought to leave here and we can discuss this matter at another time when you are less excitable."

She gave him a brief haughty nod and slipped out the door. She flew back to her room down the long corridor as though there were wolves at her heels, although there was no more than the slow, soft closing of a door at the end of the hall as she passed, as the watcher silently took note of her flight from that quarter of the house.

It was a strangely subdued Elizabeth that came slowly to

dinner that night. Not that any of the assembled company
could tell the difference between an ebullient or enervated
Elizabeth, she had been so withdrawn since her arrival at
Lyonshall. But Elizabeth knew the difference, and she felt
subtly altered. She wore her hair back, letting a few curls
drift against her forehead, softening her look. She had chosen
a deep blue frock, which she felt exactly matched her mood,
not noticing or particularly caring about how the color ac-
cented the other worldly air about her tonight.

For her mind had been filled all afternoon with a great and
deep sorrow for the Earl. She had thought him the most
overpowering and virile man she had ever encountered. Her
new knowledge of his infirmity did not detract from his
attractiveness to her one whit; in fact, it enhanced it, and lent
him an air of desperate poetry. Elizabeth had no experience
of what went forth between a man and a woman beyond the
few embraces she had received in the course of her three-and-
twenty years, but knowing that the Earl could not further that
knowledge even in the unlikely chance that he might choose
to saddened her deeply.

She shied from trying to visualize the possible extent of
the wounds he must have suffered and thought instead of how
firmly apart his debility must have set him from the common
run of men. Then, in her thoughts, he had become not so
much unmanned as he had become a supremely unattainable
male. Her head being already filled with all the tales of
immortal chivalry and courtly love that she had read to pass
the time when most other young women her age were actually
experiencing life, the Earl now seemed to her to have become
a true figure of tragic romance.

Too shy to contemplate the possibility of actual dalliance
with the vital man she had first met, she was now easy prey
for infatuation with the romantic figure she envisioned. Especially since nothing could come from such a love. Although
basically a very honest sort of creature, Elizabeth could not
know that she was so unsure of herself as to be a perfect
victim for such an impossible sort of passion. Where she had
previously thought that an inexperienced nonentity like herself could have no place in such an exalted man's life, now

she thought only of how lonely he must be, and how, in that at least, she might be able to help him. Where the seven-year-old Elizabeth had once gazed down into a cradle and lost her heart to a helpless babe, the adult Elizabeth now saw before her a grown man who she perceived had need of a friend. And at that moment, alone in her room, she irrevocably gave her heart away again. And with it, felt a lightening of her whole person, as her fear and shyness fled. The Earl of Auden was a man in need of a friend, and Elizabeth knew she could and must be that friend..

And so the seventh Earl of Auden, seating himself at dinner with about as much enthusiasm as a man trudging to the scaffold, envisioning another evening of uphill conversation with, as he had confided to Lord Beverly, as rare a set of blockheads as he had yet encountered, found himself instead looking into the direct gaze of as fine a pair of topaz eyes as he had ever seen. And then found himself the bewildered recipient of as sweetly soft and welcoming a smile as he had ever experienced.

"Good evening, Elizabeth," the Earl said with awakened interest, for the girl was still bending a look upon him of such warmth as to make all his previous thoughts flee. "I see you are in high good looks this evening. The air of Lyonshall must agree with you."

For a wonder, the chit did not drop her gaze or color up, or stammer, as she previously had whenever he addressed her. She only smiled again and said in a delightful throaty voice, "Ah, but as the heir of Lyonshall is still a mystery, I cannot say if he does agree with me. But it is a fine evening."

Delighted with this new turn of events, the Earl laughed lightly and said, "But, Elizabeth, the pleasure of a mystery comes in the telling of it. Do not say that you are the sort of reader who cracks open the last page to see who the villain truly is before all the passages filled with mysterious clankings and apparitions have been gotten through? What joy could you have had with Mrs. Radcliffe, if you expected to be let in on all the secrets immediately you had begun her book?"

"Never say," Elizabeth countered with mock alarm, "that a gentleman admits to familiarity with such romances?"

"Heavens, Elizabeth," the Earl said, enjoying himself hugely now, "how long have you been sequestered in Tuxford? For the Regent himself, it is rumored, takes to his bed with a stack of such tomes and an equal pile of comfits, each night. Can a mere Earl do less that follow such an example?"

"Dear me," Elizabeth said with a pretty air of confusion, "why, in Tuxford we had heard he retired with more stimulating company of an evening. How very lowering to discover our error."

While the Earl laughed appreciatively and Lord Beverly called, "Have a care, Morgan. The chit's leading you into deep water. Ain't proper at all to talk about what Prinny takes to bed of an evening," Lady Isabel sat and gaped at Elizabeth. She could not have looked, Elizabeth noted, more shocked if her buttered crab had reached up out of its plate and pinched her.

But Elizabeth felt strangely giddy and unencumbered, free at last from her own self-consciously induced constraints. And she sat and bantered happily with the Earl.

Over the first course they pursued the topic of novels, and somehow, by the time dessert was brought out, Elizabeth was laughing helplessly as the Earl expounded on the personal habits of a poet of his acquaintance while Lord Beverly called impossible corrections to every detail related. There was no question that when she and the Earl had begun their odd, joking conversation, a thrill had passed along the table, and that by the time dinner was done, nearly everyone seated there had become part of a general raillery. Anthony and little Owen laughed immoderately. And even Richard Courtney allowed himself rare smiles. Lady Isabel, while still attempting every so often to add something to the conversation, occupied herself in the main by emitting little trills of laughter and patting at the Earl with her bejeweled white fingers when he said something she considered supremely amusing. But all the while she kept her eyes on Elizabeth, as though seeing her for the first time and disbelieving her eyes.

While the company waited patiently for Owen to finish his

second serving of sweets, for even laughter could not stay him from the enjoyment of his favorite course, the Earl smiled down at Elizabeth and then asked the others negligently, "Now, what's to do this evening? For I cannot think it right that we should all retire immediately with stacks of novels, as, I insist, our Regent does."

"Let's have a few hands of cards," Lord Beverly said. "I'm curst tired of having you clear the chessboard in an hour, Morgan, and Isabel and I have sung out our entire repertoire by now, I think."

While Lady Isabel began, quite prettily, to protest that she had only just begun and would not at all mind presenting a solo serenade, Anthony interrupted glumly, "Now, don't say cards while Elizabeth's in the room, for she'll skin you."

"What?" the Earl asked with a show of disappointment. "The lady does not approve of gambling? I had thought her more venturesome."

"It's not that," Anthony put in quickly. "It's that she beats everyone to flinders each time she plays. Uncle taught her, you see. And she has more of a head for it than I. It's not that she has such luck, you see," he told Lord Beverly. "It's her face. Why, she can look at the cards she holds with such a gloomy expression that you think your way is clear, and then a second later she has you in the net. Then, next hand, she looks so happy with them that you just know she can't be dissembling. But she is. She's a wizard at cards," Anthony said. "Now, don't color up, Elizabeth, I'm only stating facts."

But, for a wonder, Elizabeth did not flush. She only smiled and admitted that as Anthony was already in her debt for over a hundred pins, she did not think it fair that she played with him again.

They played cards till Owen nodded off his chair and his mother bade her maid bring him upstairs to bed. They played on till Richard Courtney excused himself and begged to retire, pleading a letter he must write. And they continued to play and laugh and say more outrageously silly things to each other till Elizabeth noted how far down the candles had burned, and then, over all their protestations, smiled and excused herself on the grounds that it grew so late she could no longer tell one suit from another. When she had left, Isabel, Anthony, Lord Beverly, and the Earl soldiered on, but much of the zest had left the party. It was not long then till Lady Isabel, with many winsome smiles, said she must see to dear Owen. And Anthony, seeing at last how advanced the hour was, and how disinclined his companions were to further play, yawned and set a time to ride into town on the morrow with Lord Beverly and took himself off to bed.

"There, I told you," Lord Beverly said with satisfaction as he had his customary late-evening drink with the Earl, "the chit needed a bit of getting accustomed to the place. That's all."

The Earl did not need to ask him what he was speaking of; Elizabeth's transformation from shrinking shadow to vivacious companion had been too complete and too obvious to comment on.

"Perhaps," the Earl commented softly.

"Perhaps?" Lord Beverly yelped. "That's coming it too strong, Morgan. It is. Why, you sound suspicious of her. I can't believe what a devious fellow you've become."

"It's merely," his friend said, smiling, and, Lord Beverly noted with relief, finishing his cordial and rising to leave without attempting to have another, "that the lady has a cousin. And a cousin she would most dearly love to see named heir. And she is excellent, as you know to your regret, at covering her hand at cards, at least."

"There's no talking sense with you, Morgan," Lord Beverly grumbled. "You see plots in every pretty pair of eyes. Well, as to that, I suppose you're going to have the interviews tomorrow. What time do you want me to have young Anthony back for a grilling?"

"What?" the Earl asked absently, pausing in his slow tread toward the door and leaning on his walking stick as he looked distractedly at his friend.

"You said you were going to get down to serious talk with each of the fellows. Don't you remember, it was just last night you said you were done with the lot of them and wanted to get the thing over with."

"Oh, as to that," the Earl said thoughtfully, remembering that he had indeed just last night scowled at his friend and said that he was through observing his company and disgusted with the lot of them. For he had learned nothing from their actions, he had said: Owen merely was a stout little boy who ate more than was good for him, Richard was disinclined to string three words together, and Anthony sauntered about as if he already owned the place and was wondering whether to change the color scheme in the morning parlor. So he had planned to call each of them into his study to interview them as though for the post of being Earl of Auden. Then, he had vowed, he would make his decision and send them all packing.

"As to that," the Earl said with a slight grin, "you were right, my dear. It is early days yet. And one doesn't interview for an heir as if one were choosing a parlormaid. I shall try to learn more of them while living with them, just as you suggested."

Lord Beverly looked after his friend in wonder as he made his halt way from the room and toward his own bedroom. But long moments later, as the Earl finally achieved his own door, and opened it silently, another door slowly closed. The watcher relaxed at last, seeing that the Earl had not stopped off at any other door, and that he had entered his room alone. Relieved but still anxious, the silent spectator paced for a while, and then sat to pen a letter, and only then the last wakeful guest blew out the candles and went off to sleep.

— 7 —

"I'm off to Town today," Lord Beverly said, mopping up the last of his egg with a bit of his muffin. "Don't suppose I can persuade you to come along?"

"Why, Bev, it was you," the Earl replied, "who lectured me about how boorish it was to leave my guests to their own devices. Never say you want me to desert them now?"

"Ha," Lord Beverly grunted, spotting a particularly appealing bit of pastry, and deciding his breakfast was not, after all, quite done. "Much they would care this morning. Anthony is a good lad, but he sleeps his mornings away. And Isabel don't stir till the sun is high. Little Owen spends his mornings in the kitchens, and as for that glum fellow Richard, it don't matter if he's abed or in the parlor, for all that a person can get out of him. There's no one would miss you, Morgan."

"Alas. Too true, but unkind of you to remind me," the Earl said gently.

"Not what I meant," Lord Beverly said through a mouthful of sticky bun, "but you're just being thorny again. Meant that you could slip out in the mornings, and no one would care."

But the Earl didn't seem to be listening to his friend; he was instead gazing out through the glass of the long leaded windows. Lord Beverly saw the object of his attention, a slight figure in green wandering far down the terrace, stopping every so often to bend over some bush or bloom.

"Aha," Lord Beverly said sagely, swallowing the last of his breakfast. "So it's Anthony's coz you're not willing to leave. Can't blame you. She's a delightful female, just as Anthony said. Caught your interest, has she? It wouldn't be a bad thing, Morgan. She's gently bred, the family's well-set-up, and she's a fine-looking girl.''

"Don't start posting the banns, Bev." The Earl smiled. "I was only wondering if her delightful mood of sociability extended to this morning or if she had merely dipped into the port too much last night. Such a turnabout might be due more to spirits than mere spirit. And a morning stroll through the gardens clears the head.''

"I wash my hands of you, Morgan, I do," Lord Beverly snorted, rising and brushing crumbs carefully off his waistcoat. "The poor girl shows a little enthusiasm and you have her deep in her cups. There's no pleasing you. I suppose you'd rather have had her sitting mumchance, instead of being the merry soul she was last night?"

"I would rather," the Earl said, rising with his friend, "know why a little shadow suddenly began to radiate light and charm."

"Why don't you just up and ask her while you're at it?" his friend said in disgust.

"An excellent idea," the Earl said, taking his walking stick from the side of his chair. "I shall."

While Lord Beverly stood and watched in amazement, the Earl bade him a good morning and made his slow way out the doors and into the gardens, toward Elizabeth's distant figure.

Elizabeth had seated herself upon a stone bench and had been contemplating a towering wall of riotous magenta rhododrendron blooms when she heard the Earl's approach. By the sound of his walking stick, as careful in its slow tap upon the flagstones of the garden walk as a third sure foot, she had known it was he before she had even turned her head. So she sprang up and said nervously, as soon as the Earl came abreast of her, "Good morning. I know it's a shockingly early hour to be up and about, but the sun was so bright and the day so fine, I simply could not stay abed.''

"No need to apologize," the Earl said with amusement. "My other guests are London born and bred, and I doubt Gabriel's trump could wake them before noon. The only way

they ever see the sun rise is from the other side of the day.''
The Earl stood and smiled down at her, and Elizabeth nervously sought a safe topic of conversation, for the fact that
she rose so early out of necessity, rather than habit, seemed
to her to be trembling on her tongue, awaiting one moment's
inattention to slip out.

"The flowers are so lovely . . . so pretty,'' she began,
only to see a slightly glazed look coming into her companion's
eye. The polite inclination of his head made her realize what
a ninny she was beginning to sound, so she paused and said
with rather more force, ''But actually, the sheer number of
them is rather intimidating. It makes one feel belittled. And
instead of admiring them, I get the nervous inclination to hide
from them. It's almost the way one feels on a starry night. I
begin to feel insignificant against the weight of their magnifi-
cence.''

''Would you like a pair of shears?'' The Earl laughed. ''I'm
sure that if we go at it with a will, we can get them down to
reasonable size in no time. Though,'' he said with a measuring look, ''I'm not at all sure my head gardener won't have to
be forcibly restrained from coming after you with shears as
well. For they are his pride. No, don't look so stricken. They
are overwhelming. I quite agree with you. So did my brother,
poor chap. He had no use for them at all, and was a bit of a
horticulturist himself. His garden is off to the back a bit.
Should you like to see it? I can't tell a radish from a rose, but
it was his consuming interest and I've kept it up for his
memory's sake. It's only a short walk away,'' he added,
seeing her hesitation.

''Oh, yes,'' she said, but added nervously, trying to broach
the subject of his lameness in some polite way, ''That is, if it
isn't too much trouble for you to go so far?''

''Oh, my hobble,'' he said with a grin. ''But it's a fine
clear morning. The thing has a will of its own, and is much
improved today. It's the way of these old wounds,'' he said,
beginning to walk with her, ''that they clear up for a spell so
that you think you've exaggerated the whole matter, before
they pounce upon you and remind you of their presence
again. Actually, the surgeons can't seem to see why the thing

persists, but it does. But I assure you," he added, puzzled at why she was coloring up so at the mention of his lameness, and trying to set her at ease, "other people make more of it than it deserves. It isn't life-threatening, you know, only an annoyance."

But he noticed that discussion of his impediment seemed to cause her to blush redder than the mass of flowers she had been discussing, so he left off the subject and engaged her in easy conversation about the history of Lyonshall as they strolled on, while privately he wondered why she thought lameness so embarrassing a subject.

She was, he noted, looking particularly fine this morning, her complexion clear, her hair shining in the morning light, her slim figure graceful and pleasing to look upon as they made their way down to the back of the grounds. Once off the subject of his health, she seemed at ease and was as charming a companion as she had been the night before, as he laughed and chatted lightly with her.

A slightly puzzled look came into her eyes when he paused and gestured with his walking stick.

"Here is my brother's garden," he said, watching her closely. "Now, as you've roundly insulted my famous blossoms, I'd like to know what you think of this bit of land."

He stood and watched as she walked slowly down the formal garden's path, peering at each shrub and vine. Here there were few flowers, and the garden was planted in neat concentric circles radiating out from a central sundial. Each plant and bush was tagged with a small marker. The overall effect was neat and spare, for while some trees and hedges lay at the outer edges, only one huge willow dominated the whole. Compared with the lavish bloom in other regions of Lyonshall's grounds, the garden was almost disappointingly sparse.

"Rue," Elizabeth said slowly, "and rosemary, fennel, pansies, and crowflower, and columbine, daisy, and common thistles . . . Oh, I see. How clever." She smiled. "It's a Shakespearean garden. Your brother must have been a scholar."

"He was," the Earl said, relaxing and watching her as she walked bemused through the paths. "And he would have been pleased that you caught on so quickly to his little conceit. Bev used to infuriate him by claiming that if Shakespeare had had enough funds, he would have put a few orchids or some more eye-catching blooms into his plays instead of 'such a lot of rubbishy shrub.' ''

The Earl settled himself upon a bench and watched as Elizabeth completed her tour of the little garden and came back to him.

"But it's a lovely idea," she exclaimed, taking his lead and sitting beside him, after looking to see that there was no other seat about. "And I wish we had such at home."

"Are you a great gardener, then?" he asked.

She dropped her gaze and began to pluck at a thread on her gown. "Why, no," she said weakly, thinking about the small utilitarian kitchen garden at the back of her house in Tuxford. "There just doesn't seem to be that much time in the day for such an occupation."

"How does a young lady fill her days in Tuxford, then?" he asked idly, and then noted with amazement that she dropped her head and began to inspect her slippered toes in momentary silence.

Elizabeth thought of her day, which consisted of rising early, trotting off to the shop, where she usually made herself busy taping and stitching feathers and flowers to the tops of ladies' bonnets, when she was not showing or selling them to assorted females, till sunset released her to go home and help prepare and serve the evening meal. She faltered and then in low tones, "Oh, you must know how it is. One never gets round to doing the things one ought. But," she said, raising her head at last and looking at him levelly, "how tiresome it is to speak of oneself. Your brother, I take it, was a scholar?"

"Oh, yes," the Earl said lightly, smiling a little as he noted how firmly she had led the conversation from herself, and perversely persisting in his inquiries. "You must have seen our library. It was all my brother's doing. Do you spend much time at home reading? Bev mentioned that your mother's been in poor health, which prevented your going to London. Surely you must be somewhat familiar with Master Shakespeare to have twigged to the secret of Simon's garden so

quickly? Or is it,'' he asked, seeing her bow her head again,
''so very shocking to be considered a bluestocking in Tuxford?
There are many ladies of Quality in Town who would rather be
drawn and quartered than admit to having a passing knowledge
of—dare I speak the word again in polite company?—Shakespeare.''

''It's not that.'' Elizabeth struggled, thinking of how dearly
she would love to have more time to read, were it not for her
work and her duties about the house. ''Or rather, it is. That is
to say,'' she went on with more determination, trying to get
off the forbidden topic of her life-style to firmer ground, ''I
do read. But I would dearly love to have been able to travel
more.'' And having hit upon a subject with which she could
converse with perfect truth, she raised her gaze to him once
more. ''I understand that you have traveled widely. How I
envy that.'' She sighed.

The Earl had a quizzical look in his eye, but he relented
and was soon telling her stories of all the fabled lands she had
ever wished to see. And while he sat and told her of Italy and
Spain, and of a particular treasure of a museum he had
discovered in Greece, she watched his face with fascination.

Though Elizabeth thought it might only be the effect of his
superior manners, the Earl seemed definitely pleased to be
with her. His strong features were relaxed and free of any
lines of pain, his auburn hair shone in the sunlight, and when
he glanced toward her, she could see his changeable blue-
green eyes alight with humor and interest.

Sitting next to him in the full clear light, she felt the
powerful tug of his personality and responded to it like one of
his prize blooms turning toward the sunlight. She asked
questions, laughed at his wit, and urged him to further
reminiscence.

He watched her too as he spoke, and then lightly added,
almost as an afterthought, ''But then, now that your mother is
feeling better, as your cousin said she was, you will have an
opportunity for travel yourself. Or is there a particular reason,
in the person of some persuasive gentleman from Tuxford,
that will prevent you?''

Elizabeth looked downward again. This constant need for

dissembling was making her very weary and heartsick. She had the wildest impulse to be done with the pretense and blurt out, "No, I cannot travel farther than Miss Scott's shop. I cannot afford a twopenny ticket to any place on earth. And even the clothes I stand up in were paid for by selling off all the family's china." And only by so saying, she thought, could she ever be able to look him fully in the face as an equal. Instead she said meekly, "No. There is no gentleman in Tuxford. It is not," she essayed weakly, "such a fast place as London."

"That puts me in my place." The Earl laughed, while Elizabeth sought to correct her statement. But he rose, and seeing her consternation, told her that it was only that they had talked the morning away and he was sure his guests would be now all awake and looking for their absent host.

"For," he said as they made their way back to the front of Lyonshall, "it will never do if they discover Simon's garden is my refuge. That shall be our secret," he assured her. This only served to make Elizabeth feel even worse about her deception, and she walked along with him in silence with her eyes downcast again.

Amazing, the Earl thought. Kitty used to look at me directly with her great dark eyes innocent and wide as she spewed out the most intricate lies. And this chit, he mused, does it the other way round. You have only to ask her a direct question about herself and she will look anywhere but at you and then tell what are probably the most appalling untruths. It is the lies which depress her spirit. For when she is being truthful, she is radiant. She is, he thought, looking down at her shining hair as she trudged beside him with bent head, obviously a very bad liar. But she is a liar. I seem to attract them, he thought on a sigh, both the good and bad ones, with uncanny ease.

Lady Isabel was waiting for them, standing poised prettily beneath her sunshade, as they turned toward the house.

"Oh, fie, Morgan," she pouted as he drew near. "You've gone for a lovely walk about the grounds, and left me to languish alone."

"But, Isabel, my dear," the Earl said, "it would be most

improper of me to roust you from your bed at dawn. Elizabeth here wakes with the sun, and we just happened to meet. But she, no doubt, would be glad of your company for another stroll. Alas, I've just been complaining to her that my poor limb has been acting up. It has been an abominable nuisance today and I must go inside for a brief rest. But,'' he said, holding up one hand, "don't let me detain you. We'll all meet again at luncheon.''

He smiled and bowed and gave Elizabeth one last long lingering smile. That, he thought, looking into her surprised eyes, is how one goes about lying, my dear. And vastly amused, he limped painfully up the stairs and left a puzzled Elizabeth and a fuming Isabel to their own devices.

The next few days dawned fair and balmy in a display of ideal spring weather that few had seen so temperate. The Earl's house guests amused themselves publicly and fretted privately about the impression they were making upon their host. Their noble host was subjected to a succession of daily flirts with Lady Isabel, coupled with interminable stories about what clever thing little Owen had lately said to his nurse. Richard Courtney addressed his daily three sentences to his host, and then, relieved, stumbled off to some deserted part of the house where he was thought to be variously brooding, writing, or sleeping. Anthony Courtney adopted a breezy camaraderie with the Earl, but spent the better part of his days with Lord Beverly. And Elizabeth DeLisle occupied herself each morning with a private chat with the Earl, secure and safe with him in his lost brother Simon's Shakespearean garden. Each morning they met as if by accident, and each morning they feigned surprise. And each morning they spoke of many things fluently and with delight. Elizabeth was careful never to mention a word of her existence previous to her appearance at Lyonshall, and the Earl took special care to watch her ill-concealed dismay whenever he attempted to bring the conversation to a more personal level.

But the fair weather could not last, and no one truly expected that it would.

When the rain came that Wednesday morning, the Earl had taken refuge in his study. He was poring over some papers having to do with a disgruntled tenant's demand for more grazing land when a soft tap came upon his door.

He noted with relief that it was only the butler. Peering past his shoulder, he could see no hovering relative, so he grinned and asked what it was that had caused the fellow to look so grim.

"Luncheon will be late today," the butler said in tones that signaled the end of the world as he knew it. "Unavoidably, your lordship, we shall have to set the hour back. We shall have to serve at two, rather than at one."

Looking at his master's puzzled face, the butler went on with distinct unease, "Cook's in a state, your lordship. She's been carrying on and tossing things about. She's in a rare taking and there's none of us can calm her down."

The Earl rose to his feet and took up his walking stick. "Mrs. Turner? But it must be cataclysmic. She's normally the most benign soul on earth. I'll just go and have a word with her."

"Oh, no!" the butler forgot himself so much as to cry in an agitated tone. "Never, your lordship. If you were to go down to the kitchens, she'd never forgive herself. Please, do wait here and I'll fetch her to you."

"Really, Weathering," the Earl sighed, "I am mobile. I can fetch myself the few steps to the kitchens. No need to summon her when I can just nip down and have a word—"

"No," the butler insisted, aghast at the sight of his master making his way toward the door. "Really, your lordship. Please, sir. She'll never get over it, your having to come to her. Please, just wait a moment."

And before the Earl could remonstrate with him again, the butler made his hurried way out.

The Earl sat heavily back into his chair. The way his staff cosseted him and regarded him, as though he were still an invalid, depressed him. So his expression was one of exasperation and grim tolerance when the butler showed an agitated Mrs. Turner into the study.

"Oh, sir . . ." Mrs. Turner quivered, her hands wrung against her ample chest. "Oh, sir," she breathed, her wide and shining face set in lines so dolorous she resembled a troubled basset hound. "To think that I've disturbed you. Why, I'd cut off my right arm, I would, before I'd set you at sixes and sevens. To think that you was coming down to the kitchens to see why luncheon was late. I'm that ashamed," she wept, "and I promise it won't happen again."

"Mrs. Turner," the Earl said softly, coming over to her and taking her hands in his, "I wasn't coming to see why luncheon was delayed. That didn't cross my mind at all. I only wondered what it was that had so overset you. Truly." He smiled at her, the way he had when he was a boy and begged some baked treats. "Now, come, sit and tell me what's untoward. For I won't have you so upset."

But Mrs. Turner, who had high standards for herself, refused to sit where the Earl had indicated. Instead, she tucked her hands beneath her apron and sniffed and nodded her head till her gray curls bobbed.

"It's only that boy. That lad has disturbed me something fierce, he has. And as I know my place, I can't be rude to him, as he's your guest. And your relative too. But I can't take it much more, your lordship. That I can't. I hold it in till it fair smothers me. And this morning just beat all," she said with misty eyes.

"Why, Owen, is it?" The Earl laughed. "The boy has a fierce appetite, I know, Mrs. Turner. But if he's in your way, just show him the door. We're not precisely starving him at table, and I'm sure he can somehow contrive to make it from meal to meal without coming down to the kitchens and cutting up your peace."

"Owen?" Mrs. Turner cried. "That dear little lamb? That sweet little poppet? No, it's not Owen. He's a lovely little fellow, and the way he chats and holds himself, just like a little man, he is." Mrs. Turner beamed, as the Earl repressed a grimace.

"No, it's not that dear little lamb. It's that Anthony lad. I know he's your cousin, your lordship. But I can't take it much more. That I can't," she protested.

"Out with it, Mrs. Turner," the Earl encouraged her, "for you'll feel much better once you've had it off your chest."

The Earl watched in fascination as Mrs. Turner took a deep

breath, inflating the aforementioned majestic portion of her anatomy, and then she began to unburden herself.

"It's the way he's been lounging about the kitchen, taking a snippet of this and a speck of that. Not 'cause he's hungry, 'cause I see he ain't. But as an excuse to talk me and the girls up. First, he was just asking questions all the time. Having to do with what was none of his business. About how much it cost to run the house. How much went to waste. How dear sugar was, and how pricey chocolate, like he was your lordship. But I put up with it. Then he began to ask about my wages. My wages! As if he paid them. And asking Millie and Jenny how much they gets per quarter."

Mrs. Turner panted in growing outrage, "Imagine asking that layabout wench Jenny how much her wages is, when she don't stir herself enough to earn the roof over her head. And then today, to top it all, he comes lounging in, all smarmy and friendly, and starts to tell, me—*me!*—about how I'm an exploited female. Me, who has as good a reputation as any female in the Kingdom. 'Exploited,' he says. And fairly soon he's got a crowd about him, Millie and Jenny and young William, and even Old Tom from the stables in for his tea, and he's going on about feudals and serfs and what-alls. But the way he was talking about you, sir, that I could not stomach."

"Me?" the Earl asked, an arrested look in his eye.

"Aye. Well, he didn't name you, sir, that he didn't have the gall to do, else he would not be about now to tell the tale, guest or not," Mrs. Turner said with a militant look. "But the Gentry, he said. He said as to how the whole lot was parasites and worse. I forget the words exactly, your lordship. But between ruining my reputation by calling me an exploited woman and nagging Jenny to unshackle herself, when she isn't even walking out with any fellow, and tossing about unhealthy words like 'parasite' and, yes, 'bloodsuckers,' it fair made my blood boil."

"I see," the Earl murmured, with a look of unholy amusement in his eyes that he quickly lowered his lashes over when he gazed with sincerity at his cook. "Do not worry, Mrs. Turner. I'll have a word with the fellow. And I promise you he'll not trouble you again. Now, take a little time to compose yourself, have a cup of tea, and forget the entire matter. Put it out of your mind. I'll have a word with him and he'll not trouble you again. That's a promise," he said.

"I am that ashamed of myself for bothering you, sir," Mrs. Turner said, "but it cannot go on. I have only so much control."

"No," the Earl agreed, "it cannot."

"It cannot go on," Elizabeth cried in vexation. "I tell you, Anthony, I am at my wits' end. It's no good."

"I don't see what you're making such a pother about," Anthony said, seated at his writing desk and watching Elizabeth prowl up and down his carpet.

"Well, of course you don't," Elizabeth said angrily, "for you're gone to heaven knows where half the day, or off with Lord Beverly the other. I don't think you've exchanged two words with the Earl. But I have. I speak with him most mornings. When the weather holds fair, I see him early out-of-doors, or if it's raining, I meet him at breakfast. And in the evenings, I play at cards with him or discuss the news of the day. And I tell you, I feel a fool every time he asks me about home. Or Mother, or Uncle, for that matter. What a tissue of lies I have been telling. And he is no fool, Anthony. Each time I spin some faradiddle about not riding because I never took to it, when in truth Uncle never had the funds for feeding a mouse, much less a horse, or simpering that I cannot play the piano well enough to make a guest endure it, when you well know we had to sell the pianoforte in order to repair the roof when I was ten, I feel like a cheat. It will not do."

"You don't have to see him in the morning," Anthony said reasonably. "You could sleep late, you know."

Elizabeth knew that, and also knew that the past few mornings had been the greatest delights of her young life, but she merely shrugged her shoulders and went on, "And, Anthony, just think. Nothing is as Uncle had thought. Auden is no doddering old recluse, and we are not here only to attend his last wishes. Heaven knows how long we shall have to stay on here, for no one has said a word about our leaving and it would not do for us just to take off without a word, before anything is decided. I could keep up such a deception for a few more days. But weeks? Never. I cannot."

"There's no need to," Anthony said. "I quite agree with you, Elizabeth. There are times when I'd like to make a clean breast of it with Bev, too. He's a good sort of fellow, and I know he wouldn't mind a jot. He's got no social conscience," Anthony mused, "but he's a fair-minded fellow."

"It's not Lord Beverly that's looking for an heir, Anthony," Elizabeth said in exasperation.

"I think you should tell him the truth, then," Anthony said calmly.

"And just think, I live in dread, Anthony, of the look in his eyes if he ever discovers our pretense. For I work at a rather public place, and one never knows who might have chanced by my shop. And Lady Isabel, I am sure she knows something of the truth, for she questions me so closely that . . ." Elizabeth broke off as Anthony's words finally registered with her. She turned to stare at him.

"It only makes sense. Use your head, Coz," Anthony said lightly. "The thing is plain to see. Our lack of money won't make as big a difference as Uncle thought. For whom else would Morgan name as heir? That Friday-faced fellow Richard? A man would sooner leave his fortune to an undertaker. Or that little stoat Owen? The little chap would eat up half the fortune before he reached his majority. No, it's plain that I shall be the one. Why," Anthony said to the disbelieving look on Elizabeth's face, "he even hinted that he might soon go over the accounts of the estate with me."

This was true, so far as it went, but what had actually been said in full, in an offhand but firm manner this very day, was that Anthony should not go about asking the staff about their wages and working conditions. If he was that curious, the Earl had said in a knowing fashion, he would be glad to go over the accounts with him himself.

But this, understandably, was a subject Anthony did not wish to go into with Elizabeth. Or, for that matter, with the Earl. So Anthony smiled complacently and went on quickly,

"And as you say, Morgan is not yet at the brink of the grave, and someone's bound to find out the truth sooner or later. So it would be better if you were the one to tell him, now."

Elizabeth could scarcely believe this reasonable creature was Anthony, and she stared at him in wonder.

"I don't know why you're eyeing me like that." Anthony yawned. "Uncle wouldn't mind a small change in plan. And I think Morgan would be loath to let his heir live in penury whilst he lorded it here in style. It would look bad and the gentry don't care for that. So it is better if you let the cat out of the bag, Coz."

Elizabeth stared at her cousin. It was late, she was extremely tired and should in fact have been fast asleep at this hour. But she had undressed, gotten into her night rail, and she had lain upon her bed in an agony of remorse. Until finally she had leaped up, thrown on a wrapper, and gone to hunt Anthony down.

Again, she had crept into his quarter of the house to have it out with him. She had envisioned telling the Earl of their true circumstances as a noble thing, and now Anthony had reduced it to sound mercenary practice. It was strange how in doing the right thing at last, he had made it seem as devious as the wrong thing had been.

She stood irresolute, her long gleaming hair tumbled about her shoulders, her hand at the neck of her long white wrapper.

"I think I'll leave you now, Anthony," she said primly. "I just wanted you to know how things stood."

"Things couldn't be better," he said blithely, seeing her to his door. "You worry too much, Elizabeth."

Elizabeth paused and gave Anthony a last long worried look, and then, clutching her wrapper about her, she slipped off down the hall.

"Well," said the Earl in a strange tone, as Anthony's door closed behind Elizabeth's retreating form, "I did not know our country cousins were in the habit of nightly conference. I wonder, does Miss Elizabeth think our Anthony in need of being tucked in each night?"

"Devil take it, Morgan," Lord Beverly answered in a

worried voice as he saw the expression of distaste upon his friend's face, "must you read impropriety into everything a female does? They're cousins, after all."

But the Earl, from the vantage point of the door to Lord Beverly's room, where he had been bidding his friend a good night, only stood and watched Elizabeth, in her nightclothes, her long hair flowing behind her, disappearing into the gloom as she traced her way back to her quarters.

"Cousins, yes," he said slowly, "but kissing cousins, my dear?"

"That's a monstrous thing to say," Lord Beverly gasped.

"Indeed it is," the Earl said wearily, passing his hand over his eyes. "Disregard it, old friend. I cannot help what I think. Or that I wonder at what transpires at such tender nightly devotions. But you are right, it is a monstrous thing . . . at least, to say."

— 8 —

There was no doubt, Elizabeth sighed to herself, that they made a striking pair. The Earl, in a russet riding coat, atop his high black horse, and Lady Isabel, all in cream and white to match the delicate mare she rode. When they saw Elizabeth making her aimless way back toward the house after her lonely hours spent in Simon's deserted Shakespearean garden, the Earl lifted his riding crop in salute, and then bent his head toward his companion to whisper something to the white plume that trembled above her ear. Lady Isabel laughed and smiled brightly toward Elizabeth, but since they were too far for words to carry, Elizabeth had to content herself with pantomiming a greeting and trying valiantly to exhibit a convincing smile as well. It hardly mattered, she thought a moment later, for they waved again and then turned and cantered off together toward the wide woods that surrounded Lyonshall. A lovely couple, Elizabeth sighed again, and she scolded herself: there was no reason that the sight of such a pretty pair should blot the sun from the sky and ruin the morning for her.

But, she thought, walking on and fidgeting with the green satin fringe of her shawl, she had spent the better part of her morning in the Shakespearean garden, starting at every sound, half-rising at every creak the wind caused in the trees, and beginning to feel her pulses rise with every rustle of a squirrel in the grass. Still, he had not come. Nor had he the morning before, nor the morning before that. Since the night she had told Anthony she was prepared to tell their host the whole truth of their circumstances, she had not seen the Earl alone. It was ironic that when she tried so manfully to keep up the pretense, she seemed to have met him everywhere and had spent so many hours in close converse with him in the garden. But once she was able and ready to speak in a truly free fashion, he had kept away from her.

She had seen him at mealtimes, she had seen him in the evenings, she had even played at cards with him. But the bond that seemed to have been built between them had vanished. He was polite to her, almost attentive in the way his eyes so often sought her out, he never for a moment made her feel ill-at-ease, but he had not been the easy natural companion she had grown to await with such pleasure. Even their card game had been an earnest, correct sort of pastime, and she had, sick to her soul at his proper distance, begged off early, pleading a headache. Only Lord Beverly had seemed to be disappointed at her departure.

There was an entirely new attitude about Lyonshall. A more businesslike workmanlike sort of atmosphere now prevailed as the Earl appeared to be getting down to the business at hand. He had called Richard Courtney into his study the day before, and the rest of the company had noted that the two had remained closeted for close on to three hours. While the other cousins had appeared to be reading, or chatting, or occupying themselves with careless diversions, still no one left the house for those hours. Every eye strayed toward the direction of the Earl's study with such frequency that Elizabeth was sorely tempted to suggest that they all throw off their pretense at indifference and rush to the door to put their ears to it together. Instead, she had idly perused a volume of poetry, and had watched with the rest of them as an awkwardly smiling Richard Courtney emerged looking intensely pleased and oddly relieved. He soon after returned to his rooms. Due to Cousin Richard's silent ways, no one was the wiser about the outcome of that little conference. But all secretly had feared the worst, since the Earl had summoned no one to his room since.

This morning he had gone riding with Lady Isabel, and the lady's glowing face showed that she was in high alt about it.

He should, Elizabeth thought stonily, have asked little Owen along, since it was, after all, Owen who might be the heir. But, she thought suddenly, perhaps it did make more sense for him to be interviewing Lady Isabel, for he might choose to make a package of it as Anthony had suggested and acquire a wife and an heir in one move. It would be a wise decision, but somehow the wisdom of it did nothing to alleviate the wretchedness she now experienced. To shake it off, she strode along toward the house with resolve. She would see that Anthony had a fair hearing, and then she would be gone from this place, she thought. She would have done her duty, and would only remember it all her days.

As she walked up the wide white stairs to Lyonshall, she noticed Owen standing in front of the great door, gazing out sadly into the distance in the direction that his mama and the Earl had ridden off to. The plump little figure, so oddly aged-looking, so apparently crestfallen, touched Elizabeth and freed her from her own morose thoughts.

"Good morning, Owen," she said brightly. "I see that your mama has gone off for a canter. Why haven't you gone as well? Are you feeling poorly today?"

He startled at the sound of her voice and gazed up at her from wide round blue eyes. "No, thank you," he said softly. "I don't feel badly at all. But I do not ride, you see, and I suppose that does make me feel badly."

"But I don't ride either," Elizabeth said. "Still, you are very young, and those horses seem to me to be very large. Perhaps if you asked for a pony?"

"I don't ride ponies either," Owen replied gravely, "and I doubt they are big enough to carry me. I'm rather stout, you know."

Since this was undeniable, Elizabeth could not think of an appropriately polite denial, and while she was pondering on how she could cheer him, he bowed and turned about to go. His grave polite manner, so different from the wild little boy Elizabeth had tended, put her off, but his apparent dejection challenged her to continue.

"Owen," she said suddenly, "I haven't a thing to do this morning. My cousin is off with Lord Beverly again and I doubt Cousin Richard is in need of my company. And as your mama and the Earl are off for a jaunt, why don't we two put our heads together and try to come up with something to do?"

Owen turned and looked at her steadily. "What do you suggest?" he asked.

"A walk," she said desperately. "How about a stroll through the gardens together? We can look at the flowers, and see if we can find any birds' nests. My Cousin Anthony used to be mad keen on birds' nests when he was a boy."

They had walked on down the garden path for a long while before Elizabeth received more than a simple syllable's reply to her chattering. For, "No," Owen had agreed, he had never seen such a profusion of blooms, and, "Yes," he nodded, lilacs were beautiful flowers, and, "Yes," that had been a pretty bird, but, "No," he had no idea of what it was either. But when she asked whether he would prefer to sit down on one of the many stone benches or whether he would rather walk on toward the woods where there doubtless were dozens of birds' nests to be seen, he had sighed and said quietly, "I should rather sit a while, Cousin Elizabeth, for I do tire easily."

They sat in not very companionable silence, till Elizabeth said with much false vivacity, "I imagine that as you are from London, you feel rather odd among all this country greenery."

"Not at all," Owen said, "for I have read much about it and it is just as I supposed it would be."

"Oh, do you read a great deal?" Elizabeth asked, pouncing on the one fact he had volunteered to her.

For the first time since she had laid eyes upon him, Owen looked just what he was, a small boy. He flushed and his usual stodgy face bore a distinct resemblance to Anthony's when he was a young lad and had nobbled half the cookies from a freshly baked rack.

"Yes," he said hurriedly, "but I pray you do not make much of it. It is simply a thing I do to pass the time."

"But that is delightful," Elizabeth said, with surprise at

his hasty demurral, "for I read a great deal too, and think it is a marvelous pursuit for any boy."

"Mama does not," Owen said, turning a pleading face toward her, "and I hope you do not tell her I mentioned it. For, you see, Mama thinks it is unmanly. And"—here he rushed on with uncharacteristic abandon, almost as if he were a bottle she had prized open and was now spilling forth—"she feels the Earl would agree. After all, the heir to Lyonshall should not be bookish. He should be," Owen went on, as if reciting a well-learned rhyme, "a man of action, a man of courage, and a sportsman, just as he is. Just as my father was."

Elizabeth bit back the word "Rubbish," which was forming on her tongue, for it would not do for her to condemn the boy's own mother. Instead she said lightly, "But when I have spoken with the Earl, I have found him to be a man of some erudition. And did you see his library? It is filled with interesting books, and I am sure he has read many of them. I don't think he would distain a lad who was interested in knowledge."

"Mama does," Owen said sadly and with finality.

"I don't agree," Elizabeth said, but seeing his reddened face, she added, "But I won't say a word to her. Promise," she added, making the sign of crossing her heart that she had learned from Anthony years ago. Her gesture, rather than her words, seemed to reassure him, and they sat quietly for a few moments, Elizabeth searching for something to say to him, Owen deep in his own unfathomable thoughts.

"Owen," she finally said, "what would you like to do, then?" Seeing his struggle for a reply and belatedly remembering that he had just owned to the vice of reading and was probably trying to think of something else to reply, she said quickly, "Or what would you like to have now? More than anything?" For she thought he would reply "A biscuit" or "A sweet," and then she could walk him back to the house and deliver him with a clear conscience to the kitchens, which seemed to be his favorite haunt. She had exhausted every effort in trying to companion him, and was weary of the effort.

"More than anything?" he answered, giving her question much consideration. "My spectacles, I suppose."

It was when they were back in her room, with the door securely closed behind them, that Owen finally dared put his spectacles on. Then he sighed a sigh of great relief and smiled up at her, his blue eyes finally focused and intelligent and his face now alight with enthusiasm. "For you see," he had confided as they walked back to the house, "it is very difficult to get on with people when you can't properly see them. I know the spectacles do not affect my hearing, but it does seem that I am rather farther away from people when I am not wearing them."

As Owen sat happily reading at her desk, chewing upon an apple, and swinging his feet, Elizabeth thought again, with a pang, of his simple explanation for secrecy.

"I look rather odd with them on," he said gravely, "and Mama says they ruin my looks."

"Well, I think not," Elizabeth said indignantly. "They make you look very intelligent, to be sure."

But seeing his disbelieving stare, Elizabeth said, "It shall be our secret, but surely your mama cannot mind if you wear them when no one is about? You might slip them on sometime and go for a stroll in the wood, and you may always put them in your pocket and wear them when you visit me."

Thus assured of her confidence, Owen chatted happily with Elizabeth until his nurse discovered his whereabouts and bore him away. He had seemed most interested, Elizabeth thought sadly, in her tales of Anthony's exploits as a youth and had hung on her stories of the dozens of birds' eggs her cousin used to collect. She guiltily envisioned the rotund Owen, bespectacled and furtive, creeping out in stealth to pursue that normal boy's pursuit. She only assuaged her conscience at her encouragement of his deception by the thought that such exercise would be better for him than his usual forays into the kitchens.

But he had raised her spirits when he had said as he left, with a secretly roguish look, "It was a lovely morning, Cousin Elizabeth. And I hope we can do it again sometime."

Secrets, Elizabeth thought when he had left. Secrets upon

secrets. Was there no guest at Lyonshall that did not harbor a secret from his host?

The day seemed sadly flat when Owen had left. Anthony was not due back for hours. So Elizabeth made her way down the stairs and quietly slipped out to the little garden where she had spent so many mornings. She did not expect to be disturbed there for she was sure no one but the Earl knew of its whereabouts, or indeed cared for its special air of quiet and peace. She knew that the Earl would not be there in the afternoon. Most probably, she thought angrily, he would be with Lady Isabel anyway. Only, she chided herself, she had no right to be angry at anyone save her own self. For who in her right mind would even consider that the Earl owed a thing to some impecunious female who was, at three-and-twenty, long in the tooth and untitled as well and, she thought fiercely, only visiting as a sort of mother substitute to one of his cousins at that? There was no way of knowing how many unkind epithets Elizabeth might have called down upon her own head had her thoughts not been so suddenly intruded upon. As it was, she was so sunk in self-recrimination that she did not note his presence until his long shadow fell over her.

"I did not," the Earl said in a hard voice, "introduce you to my brother's garden with the intention of having you mew yourself up here every waking hour. I know I mentioned that it was a special place, but really, my dear, it is not necessary to salute my taste by cloistering yourself here for the duration of your visit with us. Really," he went on with a harsh laugh, "it's as well that I didn't tell you I was fond of a turret or a tower, or I imagine we would have you pacing there all night like the unquiet spirit of Anne Boleyn."

The Earl, still wearing his russet riding coat, towered over her and looked down at Elizabeth with such a gaze of suppressed fury that she startled. She sprang to her feet, wondering if her presence in his brother's garden had somehow been a presumption. Perhaps, she thought hurriedly, it is some sort of sanctuary or sacred ground for him alone, and he is enraged that I have trespassed.

"I was only just leaving," she said. "It was only that it

was so pleasant here. But now you shall have the place to yourself again. For I must have lost track of time.''

"How time does flee when we are in the midst of such merriment, eh? No, stay, please, Elizabeth, I did not mean for you to bounce up like Miss Muffet,'' he said in a kinder voice, seeing how his words had caused the color to fly from her cheeks. She looked very young and very dismayed.

He had sought her out despite all his better judgment and he had come upon her. Just where he had known she would be. The sight of her, in her pale green sprigged frock, as innocent and tranquil-looking as some spring sprite, despite all that he had imagined her after that night's clandestine visit to her cousin's room, somehow obliquely angered him. Now he remembered Bev's words, and seeing her confusion, tried to make amends.

"Please do sit," he said. "I did not mean to chase you away. It is only that I am surprised to see how much time you have spent here.''

"Anthony and Lord Beverly are gone for the day, you know,'' she said seriously, sinking back again, "and there is little for me to do during the day. I did spend the morning with Owen, but now his mama has returned.''

"How did you and Owen pass the time?'' The Earl laughed. "In reminiscence of unforgettable desserts? Or a contemplation of the comparative merits of cookies and pies?''

"Oh, no," Elizabeth cried, wishing to rush to Owen's defense, but remembering at the last second that his erudition and myopic vision were a sworn secret, she continued lamely, looking away from the Earl, "He is really a very charming child.''

The Earl grimaced slightly at her averted gaze. So, she is withholding something about Owen now as well, he thought. Or is it just that she does not wish to overpraise her own Anthony's rival?

"But I am glad though that you came," Elizabeth said suddenly, still keeping her face from his direct gaze, "for I was about to seek you out for a private reason. There is something that I have to tell you. I must, and it is not a thing that I could say in company. If you have a few moments . . . ?''

The Earl stiffened and bared his teeth in an icy smile. "Of course. I am at your disposal," he said coldly.

"I have discussed it with Anthony," Elizabeth said straightforwardly, although continuing to look straight ahead of her, "and we have agreed that we must be honest with you. You see, we are not quite what we seem to be."

The Earl rose suddenly. He stood before Elizabeth with his hand gripped tightly upon a walking stick with an ornate gold fox chased upon its head. For one frightening, incredible moment, Elizabeth thought from the rigid set of his shoulders and the tension in his aspect that he was going to raise the stick against her.

"Certainly, then," the Earl said through clenched teeth, "if you are not what you purported to be, it is not a subject that should be discussed here where there is the possibility that we might be interrupted. Should you like to ride from here to some more secluded spot?"

He watched her carefully, but Elizabeth only looked about in confusion, for she could see no one, not even one of the usually omnipresent gardeners.

"Unless," he went on, "you would rather come with me to my study? But then, I fear, we should have a clutch of cousins waiting outside the door hanging on every second of silence and awaiting our return. If you are so anxious that the matter be a secret between us, I do think it best that you accompany me now . . . alone. Unless you have another suggestion?"

Elizabeth foundered for a moment; then, seeing no other alternative and fearing his tightly set face and impatient tone, she nodded. "Yes, of course," she breathed, rising.

"Very well," he answered, and turning, began to walk forward rapidly. He strode ahead of her, hardly seeming to use his walking stick at all. Elizabeth had to hurry to keep up with his broken but long-legged pace.

She was alarmed at the sudden change of events, but it seemed too late to question the propriety of his suggestion. Rather she temporized, and tried to bring up a change in his plan.

"But I do not ride," she said breathlessly as she struggled to keep up with him.

"I think," the Earl said, still moving swiftly along, "that you do, however, sit. We shall take a light phaeton. I do not promise to drive to an inch like some whipsters, but I can manage well enough."

Within moments they had arrived at the stables and the Earl had ordered up his open carriage. He swung himself up to the seat and Elizabeth had to content herself with a groom's hand up to the seat beside him. Seconds later they were tooling down the long front drive.

The Earl said not a word to her during the long ride, but only handled the reins and set the two horses to a furious pace. Elizabeth clung to her seat in horror, for if the Earl did not drive to an inch as he had said, he certainly drove to a quarter of one. They rushed on down the road with such velocity that Elizabeth had difficulty tracing their route. And when she dared chance a glance at his face, it was set in such hard lines she felt she was accompanying some sort of infernal furious driving mechanism.

It was a long while later that the horses slowed.

Elizabeth let out a long shaking breath to find herself still intact and at a standstill. The Earl jumped down in one long fluid movement, and then, tethering the horses to a tree, came round to offer Elizabeth his hand to descend. Seeing that he still held his walking stick, she attempted to descend without his help.

"You will break your leg if you distain my hand," he told her through gritted teeth.

She took his hand and found to her surprise that his strength was such that he hardly needed to bear his own weight upon the stick when he received hers.

Once on blessed firm ground again, Elizabeth took a hurried look around her. They were indeed, she thought, in a place where they could have private conversation.

A pond lay before them, in a natural hollow of the land. Great willows grew to one side of it and a long meadow stretched on beyond it. Wildflowers grew in profusion among the boulders to one side, and there was a beaten path that encircled the whole. Oddly, though it seemed an untouched bucolic landscape, there were two wrought metal benches along the path, one on either side of the pond.

"This," the Earl said as he walked toward the farther bench, "was a family conceit. Simon called it our 'last outpost.' For, you see, half the pond belongs to Lyonshall and the other to our near neighbor, Jason Thomas, Duke of Torquay. My brother was used to spend much time here as well, poor chap, since it was the nearest he could get to foreign travel, he often said. He and the Duke were great friends; they planned the place together. Although two more different sorts of fellows seldom inhabited the earth together," he mused. "Jason was quite the rake," the Earl said, continuing down the path, "but now he's married and the most conventional paterfamilias one could imagine. It is always the same with those reformed fellows. And as he is momentarily expecting his third or fourth dependent, I cannot remember which, it is unlikely he will intrude upon us. We shall have the place to ourselves and you can unburden yourself entirely without fear of interruption."

Having achieved the farther metal bench, the Earl sat, stretched out his long legs, and indicated that Elizabeth sit beside him.

"Now, then," the Earl said with a cold smile, "begin."

Elizabeth paused to marshal her thoughts and was about to speak when he went on, "What could it be? Is it that Anthony is not Anthony Courtney at all, but some impostor? Did the two of you do away with the infant Anthony Courtney years ago, like the little prince in the tower, in expectation of his future inheritance?"

She laughed at the absurdity, but before she could begin, he continued, "Or could it be that the true Anthony Courtney is even now the unhappy resident of Bedlam, or perhaps your Anthony himself is merely on parole from that august institution?"

Hearing her bubbling laughter ring out across the water, the Earl paused and then said carefully, "Or is it that you are not precisely his 'cousin' at all, but rather his wife or lover?"

The cold manner in which the last was said caused Elizabeth to gasp, cutting off her amused laughter in an instant.

"That is a monstrous thought!" she cried, half-rising in her agitation. "Even to say in jest!"

The Earl stayed her. "Sit down, Elizabeth, and grant me pardon," he said wearily. "It was indeed monstrous. I have been told that before. Go on, then. For you see, your hesitation gives rise to the most bizarre ruminations."

"Of course Anthony is who he says he is. And I am his cousin. I have raised him from infancy," she said angrily.

She paused for a moment and then turned to face the Earl and looked him full in the eye. She was now both angry and insulted, so her words tumbled out, clear and sharp in the mild afternoon air.

"It is only that we have presented ourselves under false colors. You see," she went on, drawing in a deep breath, "we are poor. Actually very poor. The clothes I stand in, the garments Anthony wears, all our finery was purchased from the proceeds of the sale of family bibelots. You might say that a Dresden shepherdess paid for this frock, Uncle's chiming watch accounts for Anthony's riding clothes, and a small horse painting by Stubbs for all my slippers and fans and buckles. Uncle lost his fortune years ago, and we, his two sisters, and Anthony and I, all live on what little remains. We are, in effect, that cliché, 'poor relations.' I did not have a season in London. Not because of my mother's fragile health, but because the cost was so prohibitive, I could not. In fact," Elizabeth said, pausing to note with a certain wrenching pride the startled look upon the Earl's face, "my mother enjoys the stoutest constitution. It was only another excuse for our poverty. Just as my refusal to ride was. For I do like horses. Very much, in fact. But we never could stable one, and it is difficult to learn to ride the kitchen cat. Which," she said in rising anger, "is the only livestock we can afford to keep. For he catches his own dinner each night."

"And," the Earl said with an oddly contorted expression, "that is more than I can say for my Scimitar. Quite right," he said, and then, to her complete amazement, he began to roar with laughter.

"Oh, pardon me, Elizabeth," he finally said, subsiding. "It is only that you looked so fierce. And that I had expected quite another sort of confession. But why in heaven's name did you strip the family coffers for this imposture as wealthy young springs of fashion?"

"Because," she said sorrowfully, "Uncle thought that you were an elderly gentleman of conservative leanings. He felt quite strongly that you would distain a poor relation, and choose a wealthy one as heir instead. He said that was the way of the world."

"Perhaps," the Earl mused, looking at Elizabeth with a softened expression, "that is true, after all. But not, as you must know, in my case. Then this is the whole of the secret matter you wished to confide to me?"

Elizabeth looked into his eyes and saw such a tender expression there that she had at once to lower her gaze.

"No," she whispered. "Not quite all."

As she was looking out toward the placid waters of the pond, she did not see his expression alter. Nor see the way he closed his eyes slowly, as if in pain. What now? he thought, for they always begin with the least and then pile up truth upon truth till the whole is indeed monstrous. As he waited for her to begin, he could hear very faintly the echoes of another soft voice saying, "No. It was not the first time. Yes, there were others. Many others." He seemed to hear Elizabeth's voice from just as far away. And then he sat up sharply, as the sense of her words finally registered upon his reverie.

"What?" he almost shouted.

"I work," Elizabeth repeated sadly.

"You work?" he asked in honest perplexity.

"Yes," she said. "I am a shopgirl. Only," she added with more spirit, for she was proud of her advancement in the world, even in the face of the fact that a man such as the Earl might be shocked by it, "I am rather more than that. I design bonnets as well," she said, lifting her chin and staring at him defiantly, "and I do that very well. Miss Scott says I have a natural talent for it. So though I do sell hats, I also have a hand in creating them. And they are very good ones. Although," she added with painstaking honesty, "I do not fashion the forms. We get those from London. But I do the trimmings. And I select the color schemes and nettings and. . . ."

The Earl stared at her as though she had said "I murder" rather than "I work," and Elizabeth, with sinking spirits, was about to rise and go back to the standing carriage, when he said incredulously, "That is the whole of it?"

"Yes," she said defiantly. "And I would have told you long before this, but I could not get Anthony alone to get his consent. So I sought him out the other night in his rooms and he agreed we make a clean breast of it. And if you now think us too far beneath you to consider as equals, we shall quite understand. We shall understand your attitude, at least. But we do not consider ourselves to be inferior in any fashion, except perhaps," she said with abandon, burning her bridges behind her, "socially."

"Elizabeth," the Earl said, placing one long-fingered hand aside her flushed cheek and gazing into her sunlit topaz eyes, "you are wrong. For it is I who am your inferior, I think. I entertained the most nonsensical notions about your state when you told me you had a 'thing' to be honest about. I wrenched you from Simon's garden because I thought what you were about to say was so . . . yes, monstrous, that it would profane that peaceful place for me forever. I apologize for that. But if you think I distain your condition or your courage, or your enterprise in working, then you are as wrong as I was in my estimation of you. Forgive me, Elizabeth. I have little faith in your sex, but I had no right to visit that deficiency upon you."

Elizabeth stared raptly into his eyes, and would have forgiven him anything, including murder most vile, but only said shyly, "I cannot forgive a sin that was not committed. For you only thought the worst of me. And if we were to condemn thoughts of others, we should never have a soul to talk with."

"To talk with," the Earl repeated softly, as though mesmerized by the changing sparkles of glinting light in her eyes. "Yes, that is the important thing, Elizabeth," he said, watching her closely, noting the arch of her neck, the provocative lift of her breasts, and the way the dancing refracted light struck shimmer from her clean light hair. "I am glad that you have unburdened yourself to me. Secrets are damnable things. If you have one in your keeping, it tends to grow alarmingly, as though it fed upon your silence. And they litter, you know, like barn cats in the dark."

She was gazing at him with a soft and quizzical expression and he wondered again at how many other secrets she had in her close keeping. She had said that she had told him all, and now here she sat, so relieved and so seemingly open and yielding to him. He could not ask her for another secret, but he distrusted her air of innocence. She had enchanted him, and had tempted him more than he wished to admit since he had grown to know her in the few short weeks of her stay at Lyonshall. He wanted to believe her, to toss all his hard-earned knowledge of the world away and believe her entirely. But he could not. He knew of only one other way to try to breach her innermost thoughts and discover her entirely.

The Earl tore his gaze from the smiling girl and stared out over the placid pond for a moment. Then he turned back to her with a peculiarly wrenched grin.

"Elizabeth," he said into the silence that had been broken only by birdsong till his words were spoken, "do you know why an affirmed rake like my neighbor, the Duke, agreed so readily to construct this little oasis of civilization in partnership with my scholarly brother?"

Though her thoughs said clearly "of course not," Elizabeth found she was only capable of nodding denial as she looked steadily at the lean countenance before her. The Earl had moved so close to her she could see the way his now green eyes studied each new tension upon her face and could feel his warm breath upon her cheek.

"The Duke had many house parties in his dissolute days," he began quietly, "and though he was admittedly as wild a nobleman as one could encounter, still he was, after all, a gentleman born."

The Earl's eyes danced with laughter as he went on, "And he knew that no gentleman could ever force his attentions upon a female in his own house who was harbored there as his guest. It just is not the thing, you know. So two benches were placed here at the boundary of Lyonshall and the Duke's lands. One sits upon our grounds and the other, the one we now adorn, lies on Torquay's lands. The center of the pond, you see, is the boundary line. Thus, the Duke could quite properly walk a lady around the water and court her there as ardently as he pleased. And no one could say that he was going beyond the bounds of propriety, for after all, she was not upon his own lands.

"Elizabeth," he said caressingly, "we are not, strictly speaking, at Lyonshall now. And you are not, just as strictly speaking, at my mercy as my guest. I never thought to use the Duke's own device, but I should like to now. May I?" he asked softly.

Again Elizabeth was without speech. Although not quite sure of his meaning, but as though mesmerized by his gentle voice and face, she gave him a small affirmative nod.

She felt his lips, warm and soft, lightly touch upon her own. And a moment later, found herself in his arms, and discovered herself overjoyed to be there. When he at last raised his head, and she at last could open her eyes to look at him, she found he was gazing at her with a searching expression. He looked into her wide and dazzled eyes, and with a low utterance, drew her to himself again. This time his mouth was as warm and searching as his gaze had been, and he deepened their embrace. She felt herself responding to him and answering his unspoken question fully and freely even though she had never experienced such a total encompassing of her senses before. His hands moved her as they searched intimately upon her, and still she stayed lost in his arms.

At last it was he who ended the embrace. He drew back and studied her again. She was too shaken by emotion, her eyes too blurred with unshed tears at her sudden thought, to see his expression clearly. For if she had, she would have seen that it was not loverlike in the least, but rather a look of chillingly cold appraisal. For he was waiting to hear her response to him. He had felt her body's response, but it was not enough. He awaited her spoken words. Would she say, he wondered, "Oh, no, we must not!" with shy confusion, as

Kitty had? Or, "How lovely," as all his light ladies did? She could not know that either answer, from either pole, would have damned her forever in his heart.

But she gave the one answer that no female ever had. As he watched, two huge tears gathered in her eyes. And to his growing consternation, they slowly overfilled and flowed down her cheeks, only to be followed by yet more until she was honestly weeping. Until she was weeping openly and tragically in the bright sunlight.

— 9 —

It was a scene that would have thrilled any pastoral painter. But it would have had to be done with a pastelist's palette in order to do it true justice. For the day was a soft one, dappled with sunlight and splashed with color. The pond lay still and blue, the willows were fragile hues of tender green and yellow, the flowers were the blue of columbine and iris and the varied tints of heartsease and primrose. The two human figures complemented their surroundings. The young woman was all in sprigged green muslin, her hair a shining light brown. The gentleman was an accent piece, in russet and brown, even to his thick hair. They sat as if posed upon an ornate wrought metal bench. But the scene would have appealed perhaps to only a select few artists, those that favored somewhat maudlin, dramatic postures. For the lovely young woman was covering her eyes and weeping as though her heart was broken and the tall elegant gentleman was bent toward her as if in supplication.

"No, Elizabeth, you must not," the Earl said as he withdrew a clean white square of linen from his pocket and pressed it upon the weeping girl, while saying in real confusion, "Have done. Really. I haven't compromised you, you know. It was only a kiss. I thought you wanted it as much as I. Truly, Elizabeth, you must not weep so."

Were they actually so provincial in Tuxford? the Earl wondered with alarm. They did not live in such gothic times that a kiss meant a lady's honor, or at least not in the circles he traveled in, and it was not as though he had forced her to

it. She was of age, and had come willingly to this deserted
spot with a gentleman, both alone and unchaperoned. Or was
it, a small thought intruded, a ploy to wring a declaration
from him? Was that what she was angling for with all this
sobbing? But taking another look at her as she sat frantically
dabbing at her eyes and taking deep breaths to control herself,
he doubted she was actress enough to give such a spontane-
ous performance.

"Come, Elizabeth," he said gently, taking another tack.
"Would you feel better if we had Anthony call me out when
we return?"

"Oh, it is not that," she wailed, a new freshet of tears
springing forth.

"No one has as yet written a sonnet to my lovemaking,"
he tried again, "but really, I have never reduced a female to a
puddle before. I am sorry," he went on a little desperately,
"that you disliked it so, but I promise, I vow, I will never do
it again."

"Oh, no"—Elizabeth turned a streaming face to his—"that
is not it at all. I have never had such a kiss before. It was
nothing you did to me," she snuffled, trying to restrain
herself. "It was rather what you must have felt. I am so
sorry, Morgan," she went on, in her extremity using his
Christian name.

"What I felt?" the Earl echoed in amazement.

"Yes," Elizabeth said disjointedly, "and knowing what I
do, it was cruel of me."

"What in fiend's name do you know?" The Earl raised his
voice in consternation.

"You know," Elizabeth whispered into the handkerchief.
Her companion watched in fascination as even the tips of her
ears blushed red.

"I'm a little thick today," he said slowly. "Pray refresh
my memory. Come, Elizabeth, it is not at all the thing to
carry on like Niobe, and then tell me that I know why, when
I haven't a clue."

"What Anthony told me," she said, now foundering in
embarrassment, "about your wound." Seeing his blank look,
she added, "Your other wound, why you called us all to

Lyonshall. Your reason for having to select an heir," she continued, noting the disbelieving look upon his face. "About . . ." She sniffed, hiding her eyes behind the handkerchief and saying with as much daring as she was capable of on such a sensitive topic, "About your . . . incapacity."

Peeking out and seeing a look of startled comprehension beginning on his face, she went on hurriedly, "And it was unfair of me to permit embraces, perhaps even to encourage them, knowing that it could bring you only pain. Or regret."

"Anthony told you about my . . . 'incapacity,' " the Earl said slowly. "And where did he get his information from?"

"From Lord Beverly, of course," Elizabeth said. "I am so sorry. I never meant . . ." But now she stopped as she saw his look of incredible glee.

"Of course. Bev. It would be from Bev," he said. "I begin to see it all now. And this 'other wound'—how exactly did the dear fellow phrase it? Now, it won't do for you to retreat and color up, Elizabeth, for the thing is in the open at last."

"He said," Elizabeth said, looking down at hands which seemed to wring his handkerchief of their own accord, "that you have more scars than any man can rightly be expected to bear."

The Earl's face grew still for a moment. "There's truth in that, at least. And I suppose you are too craven to tell me more?"

"No, there is no more I can directly quote," she said, her eyes still downcast. "But all was explained. So you see, I feel badly about that kiss."

"Yes," the Earl said. "Now, then, let us see if I have it right. Bev told Anthony that I could not . . . ah, produce my own heir due to my 'other wound'?"

Elizabeth nodded rapidly.

"And then, it follows that you weep because of sympathy for me?"

"No," Elizabeth said bravely, "for my own sake as well. I thought it might be pleasant, and a good way of affirming our friendship. I did not expect it to be so . . ." But here her courage failed her and she subsided. When she dared at last to look up at the Earl, she saw a wicked grin upon his face.

"Why, then, Elizabeth," he said silkily, "dry your tears. Because there is no other wound. Not one other. It was only my poor limb that Napoleon's supporters got a clear shot at. And I chose to select an heir for totally different reasons, not due to any 'incapacity,' but to end an impostor's masquerade. So," he said happily, reaching for her, "there is no need to pine. I can finish," he whispered, "anything that I choose to start."

But she broke free and shot from his arms. She stood and looked at him with alarm.

"But I don't want to finish anything," she protested. "Indeed, I only know how to start. I felt safe with you, Morgan," she cried as he rose and came toward her with a determined leer, "and now I do not. I don't want to. No, Morgan," she cried with panic, putting her hands up to deter him.

The Earl stood still, then drew back his head and laughed. Soon he was so doubled with mirth that he had to sit again. And finally, regaining control of his amusement, he patted the seat next to him and said as he saw her amazed expression, "No, come rest yourself, Elizabeth. A gentleman is free to pay court to a lady here, but not, I am sure, to ravish her. Even though he is not on his own ground. Come, come. I was only joking. A kiss is only a simple thing, rapine is not. And," he said shrewdly, "now a great many things begin to make sense to me. You believed me to be incapable of ruining you, else you would not have come here with me, nor raised your lips so trustingly. If you had not misunderstood what Bev had said, you would not have come with me today, would you?"

"No," she said with shame. "The thought never occurred to me, though."

"Then sit, my dear. And let the thought go out of your mind again. I have had a great deal of mirth at your expense. But I confess, it was delicious to see the look upon your face when you discovered your tame house cat had become a tiger. In all this time, then, you thought me . . . how did you

put it, 'incapacitated'? Bless Bev, he has given me a rare
day. No, don't look so horrified at yourself. It was an honest
mistake. Knowing Bev, and his way of speech, and the
arrogance of youth, it was only natural that Anthony would
leap to the conclusion he did. But, you know, Elizabeth,'' he
explained carefully, ''it was not at all the thing for a respectable young female to accompany a man off into the wilder-
ness as you did, and that is why I imagined you willing to
cooperate as you did. And I suppose that is indeed why you
did, thinking that I could go no further, burdened as I was by
my lack of . . . shall we say, 'capacity.' Deuce take it!'' the
Earl swore. ''It's difficult even to discuss the matter with
propriety.''

Elizabeth peered up at him, and then, both to her own and
to his surprise, began to giggle. In a moment, he joined her in
laughter and soon they both were laughing giddily together.

''My dear,'' the Earl said finally, when they were reduced
at last to only intermittent chuckles, ''let us begin anew. Let
there be no further secrets between us.''

Elizabeth squirmed for a moment, then stayed him with
one small hand.

''Then,'' she said slowly, anxious to be completely in train
with his desire for honesty, ''there is one other thing you
were not supposed to notice. And I haven't approved it with
Anthony as yet, but I feel I must clear house completely.
Anthony is, you see, a bit *radical* in his thinking. And Uncle
felt that as the Earl he knew was a Tory, we should hide all
mention of his political inclinations. There,'' she sighed,
shaking her head, ''that is, I swear it, all of it.''

''That is not quite the surprise you think it.'' The Earl
smiled, remembering his cook's agitation at Anthony's
interference. ''But as it happens, Father became a Whig at
Simon's instigation. And Anthony is young yet. The young
are entitled to all sorts of excess.''

Elizabeth was relieved to let the statement pass, although
privately she thought Anthony's excesses were far in excess of
anything her companion might imagine.

''Now, that the lot? You've opened the whole budget? No
secret lovers, no dire plots to impart?'' he gently chided her.

"All," she said with relief.

"Then the gentlemen of Tuxford must have execrable taste for you to be still heart-whole," he commented idly, catching up her hand in his.

"I have no dowry, nor any station. I am only a shopgirl, your lordship, remember, and at three-and-twenty, past all hope," she answered, allowing her hand to lie lightly in his clasp.

"Not only bad taste, then, but bad eyes as well, and hearts as small as pebbles," he said, raising her hand and placing a light kiss upon it.

"No, no, do not worry," he said as she regretfully snatched her hand away, "I will be good. But if it makes you feel better, and as a reminder to myself, let us stroll over to Lyonshall, where you will be completely safe."

He rose and offered her his hand, and with stately pace he led her to the seat at the opposite side of the pond. Though she laughingly protested, he told her with mock pomposity that now he knew she was such a proper sort of female, it wouldn't do for him to entertain her in a place where she had none of society's protection.

Once they had seated themselves again, he left off smiling. He took up her hand again, and said after a moment's hesitation, "Elizabeth, as you have told me all, it is only fair that I be as forthcoming with you. For I find that I want you to understand why I sent Anthony that invitation, and why I have doubted your every gesture. And again, much as I want to relate it, I find it is a tale that is difficult to tell with propriety."

"Then," Elizabeth said, watching his grave face carefully, "as it is a matter of propriety, let us go back to the other bench again. And then you need have no qualms. For I should very much like to hear it."

"Elizabeth," he sighed lovingly, "the gentlemen of Tuxford are very great fools."

And leaning back against the bench, he found himself telling her first about the impostor and then, quite naturally, the story of his marriage, as he had told no other human being in all the years since that evening in London when he had first seen his future wife. He became so lost in the tale, he did not notice how on occasion his companion's cheeks paled or reddened. For though he told the story with delicacy, certain facts were unavoidable and she was watching the remembered pain that came and went in his own face. And though he was never explicit in his relating each incident of the past, she could read him well enough to see the whole of it.

There were times in the telling when she felt that she was standing beside him, seeing his wife's betrayal with her own eyes. When he spoke hesitantly, seeking the right words, of his wife's confession of her past, she felt her own stomach knot up and knew the infinite despair at a wife's deceit, as if she were a hurt and confused young bridegroom. She saw Kitty through his eyes: young, beautiful, and mysterious in her allure. At the same time, she saw Kitty through her own eye's window: young, beautiful, but selfish beyond belief. In those moments, looking at the Earl's strong face and hearing his soft, deep, almost bewildered tones, she yearned to forget her own position and to lift one tightly clenched hand to try to smooth the lines of concentration from his solemn face. How, she thought again and again, almost as counterpoint to his story, how could any female leave such a man, deliberately lose such a man, heartlessly wound such a man?

The time slipped past and he scarcely was aware of her reactions, for her only comments were soft requests for further information, or gentle prodding to get at some forgotten details. When he had done at last, they sat in silence and watched the sun's late-afternoon path as it shone in the waters of the pond.

"Poor woman," Elizabeth finally said, "to be so afflicted. And how sad that you discovered her malady so late."

The Earl looked at her in amazement, and seeing his reaction, she went on, "For it was an affliction, Morgan. That is clear to see. We had a poor simple girl at home with much the same difficulty. But her family kept her close when they discovered it, and the physician in town said that it was not their fault, or even hers, but only an affliction of nature. In fact, he condemned the men that sought her out more than her, for he said they could help themselves where she could not."

"And you," the Earl said with something much like wonder in his voice, "said that it was Anthony that had the radical ideas. My dear, do you not know that you should be blushing, or holding up your hands in horror, or even being furious with me for broaching such a subject to a virtuous lady? No, don't protest. I should be called out for telling you that tale, if not for my behavior previously. My wits have gone begging." He shook his head in exasperation.

"Morgan," Elizabeth said firmly, "does that mean that if I were not virtuous you would tell me? That is ridiculous. Why do men think that a maiden lady has no idea of life? We may not 'do' things, precisely, but we do think about them, I assure you."

He laughed with delight. "My dear. Now I am even more penitent. I had no idea that I was entertaining a 'maiden lady.' "

"Are you hinting," Elizabeth said with a great show of icy aplomb, "that I am not a lady?"

When his laughter had subsided, he studied her intently. "Always the right word, always the right touch. My dear, you are a surgeon to the soul. Now, why do you poker up when I pay you a compliment? Had I said such a thing to Isabel, she would have laughed up and down the scale and then said a smug little 'thank you.' I may not," he said, "have gotten an heir as yet, but I begin to think I have a great deal to thank my fictitious heir, James Everett Courtney, for. I begin to think that I stand greatly in his debt."

But seeing her downcast eyes, he straightened and said in a bantering tone, "I go too far, too fast, in one day, and you are quite right to sit in disapproving silence. But what else can you do, poor lady? I shall have to buy you a fan, so that you can tap me smartly and cry, 'Oh, la, sir!' when I presume. That is how they do it in London, you know."

He rose, stretched his long body and picked up his stick, and then offered Elizabeth his other arm.

"It has grown very late. And though we are at Lyonshall, we ought to return to the main part of it. It is strange, but I feel much lighter in spirit now than when I came racing like a jehu to this spot. As if I have left off a large burden. I only hope it is not too heavy for your slight frame."

"But I have only heard it, I did not live it," Elizabeth reasoned, rising to stand with him and wishing to allay his fears, although she knew with a certainty that she would relive his story again and again and suffer for him anew each time in the late nights of her life. "And it is only right that friends should share their burdens."

"Are we friends, then?" he asked, looking at her lips. "Close friends?" he breathed.

"We are at Lyonshall," she answered nervously, stepping back a pace, half-wishing him to catch her up in his arms again, while the other half more sensibly knew they ought to be leaving.

"Do not worry." He sighed. "I remember that, at least. And if a gentleman accosted you this side of the pond, it would be tantamount to a declaration. Then Anthony would doubtless pop out from behind a tree and wish to start discussing a settlement, and Bev, at his side, would want to know the exact makeup of the bridal party."

Elizabeth laughed as they turned to stroll back to where the phaeton and horses were tethered. "Oh, never fear. You are quite safe in that respect. Anthony believes me to be ancient, far beyond the age where such things are even possible. And I, at least, well know that your thoughts do not turn in that direction. It would be," she added as he helped her up to her seat, "a wonder if they did, after your sad experience."

He stood for a moment, looking at her with an unreadable expression, and then said softly, "Once, when I was young, I stole into one of our farmers' orchards, climbed up into the boughs of a prized tree, and gorged myself with apples all the day. When I got home, I suffered not only the pangs of remorse at my father's lecture but also the pains of the most colossal stomachache I had ever had. But, you know," he said with a slight smile, "I still eat apples. In fact," he added as he turned to enter the phaeton, "I am very partial to them still."

Elizabeth colored slightly and sought light words to dispel

her embarrassment. She did not want to seem to be an ambitious female on the catch for a husband, although his words raised some impossible hopes in her breast. Sensibly, she shook them away, and said instead with a little grin, "Apple tarts, no doubt, are your favorites."

"Of course," he said, stifling a sudden laugh. "So much more exciting than humble pies."

"And so much cheaper," she added, delighted with the result of her daring as he threw back his head and roared with appreciation.

They joked and laughed all the way back to the long drive of Lyonshall. This time, he let the horses choose their own pace, so that by the time the long white drive was in sight, the sun slanted sharply and a faint glow of sunset lit the western sky. A lone figure paced the drive.

"Bev," the Earl called, "I cannot understand why you spend so much of your time in my drive. Isn't your room to your taste?"

"Much you care," the exquisite young man complained. "You're always off somewhere on some jaunt or other, leaving me to play deputy. Devil take it, Morgan, you've left me in the lurch again. Have someone stable your cattle, and then take over your duties as host. A fine thing to invite me here for a vacation, and then have me work my poor brain to the bone."

The Earl halted his equipage and gave the reins to a stableboy as he dismounted. His friend absently helped Elizabeth down, and then, without even greeting her, wheeled upon the Earl again.

"I come back from a pleasant trip to Town with young Anthony and find the place at sixes and sevens. And who's to order things? Aye, Lady Isabel would, if she could, but I wouldn't have that. So it's me that has to make the decisions. And with all the to-ing and fro-ing, I have half a mind to leave on the moment. London's quieter, I vow."

"Whatever has you in such a pother, Bev?" the Earl asked as he and Elizabeth made their way back to the house.

"Oh, nothing much," his friend said with a show of burlesque dismissal. "Only that one of your guests has decamped, and I don't wonder if he don't have half your silver in his satchel. And no sooner does his dust die down then another guest shows up at the door. I can't stop the one from going, and I can't tell the other not to stay. But pay it no mind, Morgan, pay it no mind.''

''No, why should I,''—the Earl smiled—''when you have so ably taken care of things?''

He turned and took Elizabeth's hand. ''I'll have to go and closet myself with this tiresome fellow and discover just what he's on about. But I shall see you at dinner.''

He bowed slightly over her hand and gave her a confidential smile that sent her wits wandering, then turned and motioned to Lord Beverly.

''Come along, old dear, and have it out with me.''

''About time,'' Lord Beverly grumbled, and began to follow him, and then stopped, hesitated, and turned.

''Oh, hello, Elizabeth. I didn't see you there,'' he said, before sketching a bow and turning to accompany his host.

— 10 —

Although it was but an ordinary Thursday evening, Elizabeth took an extraordinary amount of time dressing for dinner. She was in an unusually festive mood and felt unconscionably light and giddy as she went back and forth in her room, from the closet to the pier mirror, from the mirror to the wardrobe once again. She had not fussed so over her appearance, nor felt such an anticipatory tingling of her senses, since she had been twelve and her mother and aunt had agreed to have some of the neighborhood children in to celebrate her birthday.

A small warning voice reminded her that at that time her anticipation of the birthday festivities had far outstripped her enjoyment of what had turned out to be only a simple tea party. And a party, moreover, marked by embarrassment and disappointment. For the village girls, in their unaccustomed finery, had been struck dumb by what seemed to them to be a sudden elevation in their social state. They had concentrated so hard on which spoons to use and how to hold their teacups that they were mute with their efforts. And the squire's young daughter had seemed bored and uncomfortable among such an ill-bred crew and her every glance around her host's sparse parlor had eloquently showed how meager she thought their facilities to be.

But Elizabeth was not in any mood to heed small warning voices. For her head was full of a different, distant music, the echoes of hearty masculine laughter and the tones of a rich warm male voice.

She finally settled on a pale apricot silk with puffed sleeves and a discreetly daring neckline. As she checked once again in her mirror, she felt satisifed with her choice. For she saw that the color sparked the golden tones in her eyes and highlighted the sunny glints of her hair. She could not know that her eyes would have glistened and her color been just as high even if she had worn the mud-hued bombazine that she ordinarily wore in the shop. For it was not the dress but the voice she still heard that accounted for her high good looks this evening.

She did not know who the new guest was at Lyonshall, nor did she much care. So long as Anthony was still in residence, she little minded who else had decided to decamp. Although, she mused as she reached for a soft salmon-hued shawl to drape over her shoulders before she left her room, she would miss Lord Beverly if he were to go. But then she recalled that it had been Lord Beverly who had announced another guest's departure, and stifling an uncharacteristic giggle that had welled up at her own foolishness, she stepped lightly out of her room to go down to dinner.

She paused at the entrance to the dining room and looked about her with dismay. For she had been so long primping and posturing and mooning before her mirror that the other guests were all at table as she arrived. Her guilty gaze flew to the head of the table, but the long admiring look her host gave to her, along with a slow smile, chased all other thought of her tardiness from her mind.

"But here she is now," the Earl said gently. "Elizabeth, let me make you known to our new guest, Lord Kingston. Lord Kingston, our delightful non-cousin, Elizabeth DeLisle."

"Please," a deep voice insisted, "if we begin as 'Lord,' Lord knows where it will end. A simple 'Harry' will do, if you please. Your servant, Miss DeLisle."

Elizabeth made her curtsy and took her place at the table under cover of the company's laughter at Lord Kingston's adroit use of words.

As he was seated across the table from her, Elizabeth could not help noticing how well the new guest's way of speaking matched his mode of dress. For he was complete to a stand, the perfect gentleman of fashion. He was neither so much of a peacock as Lord Beverly, nor as discreetly dressed as the Earl. But everything about him bespoke the man of the mode. He was tall and well built, with a pair of wide shoulders. Every detail of him matched. The tone of his fair hair, which was swept from off a pale high forehead, was echoed in his cornsilk patterned waistcoat and biscuit pantaloons. The pale blue of his eyes was echoed in the blue of his tight-fitting jacket. Only the black silk sling that held his left arm found no counterpart in his dress that Elizabeth could see. But she guessed that his boots would be of the same color and glossy finish.

As the first course was served and removed, and Elizabeth listened to his deep amused tones dominate the dinner conversation, she understood that the glossy finish that no doubt enhanced his boots echoed his entire personality. There was nothing to dislike in him. And so it was odd, she thought, as she laughed politely at the end of some light anecdote he was telling about his travels to Lyonshall, that she did not care for him at all.

Anthony hung upon his every word, and Lord Beverly, who had been trying and failing to catch his young friend's attention, finally stopped and attacked his plate of fish with a disgust that simple plaice surely did not merit. Lady Isabel seemed as entranced as Anthony, but she sometimes stopped her fluttering laughter and did not resume it until she had seen her host join in. Owen simply sat and ate stolidly as was his wont, no more impressed with this glittering new guest than he was by his dish of snap beans, which he also studiously ignored.

When, somewhere between the service of the breast of capon and the fillet of beef, Elizabeth looked to see Cousin Richard's reactions to the new guest, she realized with some guilt that he was not at the table at all and she had never noticed. She ducked her head, but not before she felt the Earl's eyes upon her and saw the little smile he gave her when he saw her gaping at the empty chair.

"It is too bad," the Earl said then, "that you come upon us when our company is so diminished, Harry. My cousin Richard had sudden business in London, which called him away from us this morning. But he will return," he added with an amused nod in Elizabeth's direction.

"Most ungallant, Morgan," Lord Kingston commented, "to apologize for a missing guest when you have such lovely company still with you." And he turned his light blue eyes to gaze first at Elizabeth and then toward Lady Isabel before raising his glass to them in a silent toast.

Lord Beverly bridled and opened his mouth to sputter something in defensive indignation, but his host waved him down and drawled slowly, "But, Harry, that is my charm. I leave gallantry to such town beaus as yourself. It is my very boorishness which makes me unique."

"Then I might do well to change my tactics"—Lord Kingston smiled, lightening his tone to take rancor from the conversation—"if it would net me two such enchanting ladies at my own table."

Lady Isabel tittered happily, and Elizabeth permitted herself a weak smile, while all the while she longed, as she had not since she was twelve at that long-ago tea party, to stick out her tongue.

Lord Kingston was relating some dryly amusing tale of his deeds in the horse cavalry, which Elizabeth was listening to with a polite smile upon her lips, when he concluded by saying, amid the general laughter, "Lud, Morgan, you should have been there if you think the telling of it is humorous. For I have not done half justice to the expression on the lieutenant's face."

"But I thought," Lord Beverly said with puzzlement, after he had hastily maneuvered his mouthful of food to a place where he could speak coherently, "that you two served together. You did say," he went on, his eyes narrowing suspiciously, "that you were Morgan's 'comrade-in-arms,' when you arrived here. That's why I gave you leave to stay."

"Never fear," the Earl said on a laugh. "You haven't let in a bounder by mistake, Bev. Harry did not serve with me. Actually, we met in the field hospital. He was in with a wound in his arm, and I, as you know, with this confounded limb of mine. This incapacitating limb," he went on, ignoring Elizabeth as she scurried for her napkin to hide her sudden gasp behind. "We had several weeks with nothing to do but wait till we were robust enough for transport home. And I, at least, was glad of Harry's company. It was either that or the constant homesick ruminations of a captain from Yorkshire, as I recall."

"What a convenient memory, Morgan," Lord Kingston said sweetly, "for you to forget the kind attentions of Señora Vásquez, for wasn't it she who also took a great interest in your recovery? Actually, I never could be sure whether she wanted you to recover quite so rapidly as you did. And as I recall, she did not seem to think your medical problems incapacitating at all."

The Earl flashed a warning look at his guest before saying quickly, and with less than his usual aplomb, "Ah, yes. I had forgotten. She was a good woman who volunteered to ease our long hours of recuperation," he remarked casually to the company. "Her own husband had been lost at the front. She wished to fill her time, and she was very much like an angel of mercy, bringing delicacies for us, and books and papers and the like."

"Was that all she brought to you?" Lord Kingston went on, ignoring his host's admonitory glances. "I seem to recall," he continued, staring into his depleted wineglass, "a somewhat warmer relationship that filled more than her time."

Lady Isabel battered her host with a tiny beringed hand and tittered. But he ignored her and said, "It was merely that I had a command of the language and could communicate with the poor woman."

"Why, Harry," Lady Isabel simpered, "I do believe you are jealous of Morgan's ease with another language."

"The only language, save our own, that is worth speaking, my dear, is French, the language of love," Lord Kingston said dismissively.

"Oh, I wasn't thinking of any spoken words," Lady Isabel said sweetly, her blue eyes opened wide and innocently to belie the force of her speech. "There are other languages of love."

Lord Kingston glowered at the seemingly oblivious Lady Isabel, and their host spoke quickly as he put his napkin down and made as if to rise. "I think it is time for us to adjourn. As I recall, you were always a dab hand at cards, Harry. And musical enough to enjoy a performance by Isabel here, who is our resident songbird."

Several of the company spoke at once at the Earl's words.

Owen's husky little voice rang out for the first time that evening. "But I haven't finished my floating pudding," he complained.

Lord Beverly had already pushed away his chair and begun urging Anthony to join him in the salon so they could, as he put it urgently, "get the best seats, away from the curst fire."

Lady Isabel had begun to protest prettily that they must all be tired of her singing.

But their ears were commanded by Lord Kingston's cool voice, which rose above the general babble. "Are the gentlemen not to have port, Morgan? I confess to a small disappointment. I recall your constant yearning for your own cellars when we were away in Spain."

"As there are but two ladies in our party, Harry, we have been forgoing that masculine conceit here at Lyonshall. After all, it would be poor stuff for them to languish alone in the salon whilst the supposed gentlemen present guzzled for hours in close male camaraderie. Should they be condemned to tapping their toes or raveling their knitting for hours?"

"Of course," the fair gentleman said swiftly, "but as Owen here hasn't yet made a dent in his pudding, and the ladies are done, I'm sure they wouldn't object to us staying for a small space and enjoying some port."

"Not at all," Lady Isabel said huffily, gathering her skirts together. "Come, Elizabeth, we shall retire to the salon. But mind," Lady Isabel declared, looking very fetching in her anger, Elizabeth thought, like some disgruntled little cat that had its fur rubbed the wrong way, "if you linger too long, you will find us gone altogether."

The Earl's eyes narrowed for a moment and then he said in a calm, conciliatory voice, "We shall only remain for so long as it takes Owen to complete his dinner and have one glass of the vintage Harry so covets. After all, it is not only a potable wine, it is portable as well. And will taste just as well in the salon, if not better in your delightful company, Isabel,'' he concluded with a warm smile which seemed to mollify the lady.

There were too many currents here tonight, Elizabeth thought, too many stated and unstated undercurrents. Lord Kingston and the Earl seemed to be friends, but also to be vying with each other about something the other guests knew nothing about. She nodded to her host, and only thought once, as she left to follow Lady Isabel, that it was only a little disappointing that he had mentioned the wine would taste better in Isabel's company and had not mentioned herself at all.

But she had no sooner reached the door than she gave herself a silent cautionary shake. Whatever had transpired between them today, she must not let her desires lead her into thinking he owed her preference. He had not declared himself in any manner; in fact, he had joked over the matter of declarations. He was still the great Earl of Auden and she had changed in no way since the afternoon, except for the small matter of having inadvertently, somehow irrevocably, lost her heart. But she was still an impoverished spinster from Tuxford, and would do well, she chided herself, not to forget it, lest she make a fool of herself.

Elizabeth was relieved when Lady Isabel settled herself upon a divan and patted the seat next to her to signify that Elizabeth should sit down and be audience to her outraged running commentary on the contrariness of some gentlemen. For the first time since they had met, Elizabeth was glad of Isabel's company, for her endless prattle served to drive some of the lowering thoughts from her own head. So she nodded in all the right places and filled up the appropriate pauses and wished that the gentlemen would soon abandon their most superior port and join them.

When at length, the gentlemen did enter the room, Lord Beverly barely attempted to hide his bad temper. He swung down into a chair and looked broodingly at the fire. He seemed especially agitated as he watched a strangely elated Anthony, sitting by Lord Kingston, hanging on his every word, and encouraging him to speak more of his adventures in the world.

"For he's been everywhere," Anthony said enthusiastically in an aside to Elizabeth, "and had the most ripping times."

The evening did not rise to any great heights of enjoyment. It was as if Lord Kingston had brought the winds of discontent to swirl about the house, although it was a pleasant, mild evening. It was nothing he seemed to do overtly. For he divided his attention expertly throughout the evening. He chatted with Anthony, tried to bring Lord Beverly out of his sullens, passed reminiscences with his host, applauded Lady Isabel's singing, and played cards with Elizabeth with courtesy and a flattering amount of subdued flirtation. He ignored Owen. But then, since the boy sat, stuffed and half-asleep on a couch, as was his general wont to do in the evening, no one would blame him for overlooking the lad.

It was as they were all beginning to suppress yawns and Owen's steady little snores began to penetrate their consciousness that Lord Kingston made a suggestion.

"A delightful evening," he said coolly, "and I do wish I could share many such with you. But alas, I am only stopping off here for a short space. I am making my way back to Heron Hall to set up residence again at last. I have been remiss and it is time for me to set my estates in order. Soldiering is over, and loping off about the globe is delightful, but a man must eventually settle down."

He paused and let his eyes linger on Elizabeth for a small moment, and then went on blithely, "You did say I should stop whenever I was in the vicinity, Morgan, to stay awhile, and so I shall. And I do thank you for your hospitality. Still, I intend to make the most of this last respite before I take up my duties again. I was surprised, in fact, to find you in residence here with such charming company. Since it is my last fling, so to speak, I should like to make the most of it. And as we are all together, I hope you will all join me. What I am getting to, in my roundabout way, is to ask whether there are any subscription dances or fetes or theaters in the neighborhood? It would please me very much to have some jollity, and so far from London I am at a loss for what to do. Are there any such refinements hereabouts, Morgan?"

The Earl stood near to the fire and watched his guest with a measuring look. But then his face cleared and he said smoothly, "Oh, yes, Harry. But we had our sheep-shearing contests a month or so past, and I fear you have missed it entirely. We do have a tinkers' fair in a fortnight, and they have a Punch and Judy show, and if I am not mistaken, the ladies' social for the benefit of foreign orphans is to be held on the twentieth of the month in the rectory. But," he went on, ignoring Elizabeth's suppressed giggle, "all is not lost. We have to make much of our own festivities in these parts, and I would be a poor host not to attempt some pleasures on our own. I am glad you have brought it up, for I have been remiss too. I am out of practice. Indeed, I fear it is too late in the day to throw up a ball or any other such glittering fete. But I can and will engineer a dinner party for us. No," he went on, deaf to Lord Beverly's murmured "Dashed impertinence," "I should have thought of it myself. Nothing too elaborate, I fear, no orchestras or waltzes, neither can I scare up jugglers and party tents. But sixteen or twenty of my neighbors, and perhaps some country dances after, why, yes, that I can and shall do. I had thought," he went on over Lord Kingston's polite denials about not wishing to be rude or encroaching, "I had thought this house party to be a purely business affair, but have found it to be quite different. It's an excellent idea," he said decisively, "and I shall put it in train tomorrow. In a week's time, I think, for then Cousin Richard will be back with us."

After peeking to be sure of her host's mood, Lady Isabel allowed herself to be delighted with the idea, and volunteered to be of all the help she could. Elizabeth murmured that she would be glad to help, as well. But Lord Beverly only sat and muttered darkly about mixing business with pleasure, and "curst man-milliners," and making such a skeleton at the feast of himself that all were generally glad when the Earl announced that it was time for them to retire for the night and take their cue from Owen and join him in easeful slumber.

"Tomorrow morning, then Tony," Lord Kingston said lightly as he went up the stairs. "Be early, for if we're to make a day of it, we'll have to have an early start."

Anthony nodded happily, made a perfunctory good night to the others, and followed Lord Kingston up the staircase. Lady Isabel summoned a footman to carry Owen and then quietly and thoughtfully made her way up to her own bed.

"Actually," the Earl said, delaying Elizabeth with a slight touch upon her arm after the others had gone, "I could give a ball, but I shan't. Are you thinking it is mean-spirited of me? Or because since I seem to waltz when I am only trying to navigate a straight line, I am not overeager to spend an evening watching my guests in each other's arms?"

"Oh, no," Elizabeth breathed, "but does the thought pain you that you cannot dance?"

"No." He laughed. "Not at all. I did not care for it one way or the other before the wars. But I thought from your frown that is what you were thinking."

"No," she said, "only that I was surprised at your agreeing to a dinner party at all. For we came here, Anthony and I, with the expectation that there would be only an interview, and then we would be off home again. I was surprised to find that we were staying even for such an extended visit. And," she went on, thinking aloud, "Bev is right, you know. We were all assembled here for purely business reasons, to settle the matter of the succession. You need not feel that you must entertain us lavishly as well."

They seemed to be alone in the great hall, the sounds of the other, departing guests receded far abovestairs. She saw his face only partially in the light of the candles, and it seemed to her to be secretive, composed only of planes and shadows.

"I do not feel I must indulge you," he said slowly, taking a step closer to her, "but Bev was right in one way at least. A mere interview is a poor, cold way to discover another being's heart. Only by learning to know my cousins well can I hope to make the right decision." He paused and then went on in a lower, gentler voice, "The getting of an heir, you know, should not be a dispassionate business. No matter how one decides to go about it. Do you agree?"

Elizabeth was glad that the darkness hid her face and the flush his words caused upon her cheek. She only nodded as he went on, "So it was not my pleasure-loving friend Harry, not entirely, that caused my decision. It will be a pleasant affair.''

"I am sure," she said. He was so close, she took a tiny step back, and had a second to wonder at her longing to have stepped forward instead. She was torn between wanting to stay and hear whatever else he had to say, and wanting to be left quite alone to sift through his words and ponder their import when she could think coldly and rationally. And that would have to be somewhere far away from his disturbing presence.

He seemed to understand, for he looked down at her in the semidarkness and said at last, with a smile that shifted the pattern of shadows upon his lean jaw, "Don't worry, Elizabeth. We are here at Lyonshall now. Not only at Lyonshall, but actually within it. I shall not forget, lady guest. So no harm shall come to you here."

"That's what you say," a sudden intrusive voice complained, cutting into their strangely intimate moment. "I wouldn't trust that caper merchant for a second, Elizabeth. He's too smooth by half."

"Bev," the Earl groaned, turning to see his friend saunter toward them, "I thought you were already abed."

"Too aggravated," Bev said angrily. "Invite a chap in, and he tries to take your house over. If I had my wits about me, I would have sent him off the moment he came in."

"He is my friend, and it is my home," the Earl said carefully.

"No friend of yours, Morgan. You've too soft a heart. He hasn't been inside your doors for a day and he's got you setting up fetes and soirees and Lord knows what."

"But you like parties, Bev." The Earl laughed. "You're forever whining about my going to London with you to make the round of gaiety."

"That's different," Lord Beverly said sulkily. "And you be careful, Elizabeth. The fellow's been around and knows how to get round people. Why, he's even talked Morgan here into giving him an adjoining room for his valet. Now my man's fit to be tied. No, don't grin, Morgan, just because you choose to be an eccentric and rusticate without a valet, there's no cause to give mine heart spasms whenever he sees Harry's toplofty fellow prance by. Mind, Elizabeth, he can talk anyone round.''

''I shall keep my head,'' Elizabeth said demurely, knowing from her experiences with Anthony that the Earl's friend was in no mood to listen to reason.

''Just watch yourself,'' Lord Beverly warned, ''for it might be a family failing. He's got young Anthony wrapped about his little toe already. 'Tony' indeed,'' he muttered.

''Good night; Elizabeth,'' the Earl said firmly, ''and good dreams. We shall have a lovely party. And I shall get to know my cousins much better.''

As she went up the stairs she could hear Lord Beverly's grumbling continue unabated. But as she reached the head of the stair she heard the Earl's rich voice say thoughtfully, ''I shall watch them all carefully, Bev. Both my cousins and my guests. Don't forget that.''

— 11 —

Lyonshall was transformed. Elizabeth could only stand and gape in wonder as the great house began to put on its best company manners. Anthony was overwhelmed as well, but dared not show it in the face of the flattering attentions he had received from such worldly fellows as Lord Beverly and especially his newfound comrade, Lord Kingston. So he went his way with an air of insouciance. But Elizabeth could often catch a glimpse of the awe in his eyes in unguarded moments. Lady Isabel announced herself well pleased with the results of her work, which had consisted of mainly drawing up plans and chivying servants to her will. But Lady Isabel and the others were used to Town ways, Elizabeth thought. She herself had never seen anything so splendid go forth.

For if the parquet and marble floors were gleaming before, they now were mirror-polished. And if the great hall was impressive in its ordinary way, now it was magnificent, with vases of flowers and ferns and even entire boughs of blossoms artfully arranged in every previously quiet corner. Branches of candles were brought in and placed everywhere belowstairs in preparation for the dinner party, as if it were felt that the night's natural darkness were some sort of lower-class shame not to be tolerated in such an establishment as Lyonshall. A platform had been constructed and set up in the disused ballroom, the whole of it entwined with leaves and flowers, so that the musicians engaged for the country dances could appear to be playing from out of some sylvan glade rather than in the heart of the great house itself.

Preparations had begun the very morning after the Earl had announced his intention of giving a dinner party, before his invitations had even gone forth, as though it were understood implicitly that only fire or flood would prevent any guest from obeying such a summons. Now, only a scant week later, Lyonshall stood proud and ready for its company, and never had Elizabeth felt such a rustic.

For it was not only the house that had been transformed. It seemed that everything had been changed since the night Lord Kingston had arrived, and all the easy relationships that had existed had been subtly altered. Elizabeth had tried to resume her normal pursuits, but even that effort did not recapture the previous tone of her days. The addition of one house guest to their number seemed to have shifted the delicate balance of their lives and caused new alliances to form.

As was her habit, she had gone down to the Shakespearean garden the very next morning after Lord Kingston's arrival. Happily enough, it hadn't been long before the Earl had joined her. They had scarcely begun to speak when Lady Isabel had come trilling toward them down the crushed-shell walks. That she had followed the Earl's progress was apparent, and that she sundered all the special peace Elizabeth had found in the garden became clear soon enough. For she prated on about the loveliness of the place, and then began to suggest red roses here, and a fountain there, and opine that a swing might not go amiss to the left and a gazebo be the sweetest addition to the right, till the Earl's face had grown still. Then he suggested that they all go for a stroll to some more suitable spot.

It was Lady Isabel who took the Earl's arm as they walked, and she who monopolized all the conversation for the remainder of the morning. She filled every moment with light and, to Elizabeth's untutored ears, sophisticated and clever converse about London Society and all sorts of amusing personages known only to herself and the Earl. As Elizabeth knew nothing of the people spoken of, or of their foibles and fancies that so amused Lady Isabel and her host, she soon found herself sitting silent. Although it could not be said that they ignored her, for from time to time the Earl would turn to her and make some explanatory comments, still there was nothing Elizabeth could add to any of the conversation. Thus she was only too eager to go in for a light luncheon when the Earl suggested it. And then she sat mute as a stone all through the meal, as the previous conversation continued. Even Lord Beverly had begun to enjoy all the gossip as Lady Isabel charmed him from his brooding with it as deftly as an expert fishmonger could prize a winkle from its shell.

The Earl had business to attend to during the afternoon, while Lady Isabel napped and Lord Beverly moused about the house and grounds, keeping an eye out for Lord Kingston's and Anthony's return. Elizabeth read aloud with Owen all the day. Yet again, at nightfall, Lady Isabel, encouraged into veritable torrents of chatter by her morning's successes, kept by the Earl's side, and Lord Kingston and his new acolyte, Anthony, kept each other close company. Elizabeth and a bad-tempered Lord Beverly sought to keep each other tolerably amused, but it was soon apparent that each had an ear stretched to a different conversation in a different part of the salon.

So it went for a week before the night of the party. Elizabeth could not determine if it was due to a lack of interest in herself or to the press of duty, but her host appeared to have little time for her now. It was true that the Earl did seek her out at odd times to chat pleasantly to what seemed to be both their satisfactions, but she could not be sure that it was any more than a kind host's kind consideration. For no discussion went on between them for very long before either Lord Kingston or Lady Isabel, or even Lord Beverly, spied the Earl and drew him away from her. Anthony was so besotted with his newfound friend that he had only a few words in passing for Elizabeth. And even though Cousin Richard returned after a few days, he was now so drawn and distracted that his previous manner could almost be described as gay by comparison.

Still, no one's thoughts were far from the business at hand. Lord Kingston had been apprised of the Earl's search for an heir, and as Anthony hurriedly confided to Elizabeth, his new friend Harry believed Anthony had "the inside track." Elizabeth was not so sure. All were aware that Cousin Richard had received yet another private audience with the Earl when he returned from London. And their host surprised everyone by having a private coze with little Owen for upwards of two hours one misty morning. Though his mother had drawn him aside for the rest of the afternoon, she seemed no wiser about what had transpired than Elizabeth. For she questioned Elizabeth closely after she had seen Owen chat with her. But Owen had said only that he and the Earl had played jackstraws and had some gingersnaps together. Now only Anthony awaited his private interview.

As Elizabeth fastened on a pair of golden ear-bobs the evening of the party, she wondered whether Anthony's approaching interview would be soon, for it would surely signal the end of their visit. Once all the cousins had been questioned and judged, there would seem to be no further reason for their presence here at Lyonshall. She had learned the Earl customarily spent only the summer here, and then could be expected to take himself off to his estate in Sussex, or his home in the North, or even on one of his jaunts upon the Continent. If Anthony were not named heir, she doubted she would ever set eyes upon the Earl again. And even if he were, she thought, with sudden clarity, the shock so great that her hand trembled of itself and one ear-bob slipped to the floor, why should she ever be in the position to see him again? The sudden realization that her pleasure in this visit, in his company, was as ephemeral as any of the pleasant days spent here, caused her to sit for a moment and draw in a deep breath.

But, she thought, tossing her carefully arranged curls back and forth, she had been misguided if she imagined there could be one thing more. If her host had flirted with her, it was only the fashion to do so in his circle. If he had stolen a kiss, it was known that kisses were very common coin in his set. If he had confided in her, it was, after all, easier to confide in a stranger. Perhaps it had even been necessary for him to tell her his strange history. For his pride may have been bruised when he discovered she thought him less than a totally virile man.

To even wish for so small a thing as a lasting friendship might be foolish fancy. For he had not touched her again, and though he sent her warm glances, and cheered her with small courtesies, he had not said or done anything further to encourage greater intimacy. Soon she would be back in Tuxford, in the shop and amongst the hats and customers. There, and perhaps only there, would she be able to fully appreciate how very unrealistic each one of her secret hopes had been. A cat may look at a Queen, she thought, even as a shopgirl may be smitten by an Earl. But both must understand that they might only look.

Elizabeth stood and replaced her ear-bob. The most that she could expect was that in his kindness, even if he did not choose Anthony, he might be able to give Uncle some financial aid to ease the family's difficulties. And if that were all she hoped for, all she truly hoped for, then she could escape Lyonshall with her dignity, if not her heart, intact. She would enjoy tonight, she vowed, and not be intimidated by the worldliness of the company, and keep the evening as a bright memory. And that, she thought with determination as she kicked her deep-coffee-colored shot-silk skirt behind her as she rose to go, was all she would or could ask for.

At first, as Elizabeth stood with the other house guests and greeted the arriving guests, all she could see was an assortment of well-dressed people who bowed and curtsied and seemed genuinely pleased to meet her. She could not then, even if a knife had been placed to her neck, couple one name with one person. More than a dozen and a half new faces swam before her.

But by the time the company had been ushered into the large dining hall and been shown to their seats, Elizabeth realized that she had been utterly wrong in her estimate of the composition of an Earl's country dinner party. The only invited guest that had been mentioned at all was a near neighbor, the Duke of Torquay. And then, his name had been spoken only in passing, when the Earl had laughed and told Lady Isabel that her old favorite, Jason, had sent his regrets and would not be there, as his wife had just presented him with a third son. Elizabeth had swallowed hard, assuming that all the guests would be of similar rank.

But once her eyes had been cleared of their social panic, she saw that most of the ladies' frocks were neither so ornate nor so up to the second of fashion as Lady Isabel's, or, indeed, even her own. Few of the gentlemen present even aspired to Lord Beverly's sartorial excesses, and none to the quietly correct dignity of their host's apparel. As the introductions began to register at last upon her, her spirits rose. She realized that they all were simply country folk, as provincial as herself.

As she relaxed and raised a toast with the others to King and Country, she saw seated at the table: a vicar and his wife, a local squire and his lady, a few landowners and their mates, an elderly scholar, and various others from the locality. They all seemed merry and blessedly unaffected. The conversation swelled around her, and when a footman refilled her glass for a toast to her host, she raised her glass with alacrity. Then she settled in her chair for what now promised to be a delightful evening to remember.

Elizabeth was seated in her usual place, as befitted one of the two female house guests, on her host's right. Lady Isabel had her accustomed chair opposite. But the newly arrived gentleman next to Elizabeth was a grizzled, brusquely spoken old fellow who informed her immediately that he was his lordship's "country sawbones." Before much time had passed he informed Elizabeth with a worried frown that he had not examined his patient for a time, but it was a constant irritation to him as to why that deuced leg did not heal properly after all his attentions to it. He seemed to feel that the Earl's limp was a personal affront, and after brooding for a few moments, declared with decision that as he had seen his lordship into the world, he was in no hurry to see him out of it, so that he'd better arrange to have another look at that bothersome limb again before he left this night.

Elizabeth bit back a smile at the doctor's grim insistence and envisioned the Earl forced to strip off his tight-fitting trousers at table to accommodate his determined physician.

But the doctor's merry, round-faced wife put in quickly, before Elizabeth could entertain herself with any more such improper thoughts, "Aye, Dennie, and wouldn't his lordship look fine, displaying his wounds betwixt the prawns and the porridge. Pay no mind to him, Miss DeLisle. It was hard enough dragging him away from business to get him here, so he's trying to drum up some more to keep him busy during dinner. Don't let him go on about medicine, my dear, or you'll be bored to flinders by dessert, and then he'll try to force a restorative on you."

Once chastised by his wife, who then turned her attention solely upon an elderly gentleman at her side, the doctor minded her admonition so well that Elizabeth found him vastly entertaining. He told her anecdotes about the Earl's childhood with such wit that she was soon warming his heart by her delighted response to his stories. He did not know that he could have hit upon no more enthralling subject for his captive audience of one. Lady Isabel was occupied in desultory conversation with the local squire. So the Earl, being drawn into conversation about rotated wheat on one side and the time he had pretended measles to get out of churchgoing on the other, made poor work of consuming his dinner.

As the meal went on, through its amazing variety of courses and varied wines, Elizabeth became aware of some stir at the other end of the table. Anthony and Lord Kingston sat there, separated by only one shy young female. But they seemed to be largely ignoring her admittedly meager charms and having their own rollicking good time drinking and joshing with each other. It was the inordinate amount of laughter and noise they were creating that drew Elizabeth's attention to them. She narrowed her eyes as she saw how rapidly Anthony was tossing down the wine before him, and drew in her breath when she saw how quickly the Earl's well-trained footmen replenished it. She was surprised, as Anthony did not usually drink so heavily, and shocked since she had not seen or imagined the cool Lord Kingston acting so recklessly unbent before.

Through the course of dinner, Elizabeth's gaze went toward Anthony again and again. At one point Lord Kingston seemed to be recommending a canary wine, at another, she saw her cousin and Lord Kingston gaily toasting the blushing girl between them. And then, before her incredulous stare, they raised a nonsensical toast, with equal enthusiasm, to Lord Kingston's favorite horse. Hers were not the only eyes scrutinizing the uproarious pair, for she often saw the Earl look up to watch them, as well as Lord Beverly frowningly taking note of the increasing levity. Even Dr. Woods eventually turned his attention to them. "A little wine for thy stomach's sake," he muttered, "but more than that, and a man's a fool."

A crystalline spun-sugar cake that made Owen's eyes widen to resemble his dinner plate was brought out, and the talk began to become more general. Those at the table were leaning over to address others that they had scarcely seen all night, and the conversations widened in concentric circles from two original speakers to four and then at last to encompass the entire table. This, Elizabeth was sure, seldom happened at formal City dinners, but somehow here in such congenial neighborly company, it seemed quite proper. The forthcoming charity fete was discussed thoroughly, as it was a topic dear to the hearts of many of the women present. And then somehow, some way, somewhere among the company, the subject of foreign travel was brought up.

A lady in pink declared that now the hostilities were over she hoped her dear husband would see his way clear to taking her to Paris—at last, she added on a sly note. Amid the laughter, and the service of a spectacular rainbow ice mold, Lord Kingston asked, from way down the table, if his host was soon to be off to Paris as well, now Napoleon was safely cooped at last. As the Earl began an answer, Elizabeth saw to her dismay that Anthony's face was unbecomingly flushed, his eyes glittered, and he brushed away at a lock of hair that had fallen across his forehead. He seemed to be muttering something angrily to Lord Kingston, leaning ungracefully almost athwart his female companion's dessert plate.

"I think not," the Earl said, taking no notice of the rising mumbles coming from Antony, "for I understand France is still in sad disarray after so many years of war. Rather I think

I should prefer to remember it as it was, a graceful and fruitful land. I may go back in a few more years, when it is prosperous once again.''

This time Elizabeth, as well as everyone else at the table, could catch some of Anthony's remarks. ''Once graceful and fruitful for a few,'' was one fragment she heard, and ''Never be prosperous until Napoleon's safely back,'' was another. Elizabeth grew white as the glazed angel-food cake the footman now bore in, so leached of color that Dr. Wood gave her a glance of purely professional interest. She hoped that Anthony's slurring had obscured the words to those unfamiliar with his speech or his tendencies. She spoke up quickly, in a brittle, falsely gay voice, ''But Italy—now, Italy is a land I hear is lovely, warm, and delightful.''

''Still, Paris . . . ah, Paris,'' Lord Kingston persisted, riding over the Earl's answer to her comment. ''Now that was a city of splendor. The nights alive with gaiety, the days with excitement. How I shall miss the Paris of old, and it is gone now, irretrievably gone.'' He sighed.

This time no one heard what Anthony mumbled, but it was clear to all present that he was extremely agitated about something.

''What's that you say, Tony?'' Lord Kingston asked in puzzlement. ''Didn't quite catch it. Perhaps you ought to pass up that Moselle, my boy,'' he said indulgently, with an understanding smile.

''Aye,'' Dr. Woods agreed, leveling a meaningful look at a hapless fellow across the table, ''for nothing courts gout faster, eh, Fowler?''

But now Anthony struggled upright and blurted clearly, ''You heard me, Harry. I said, you've the right of it, Paris is gone. Gone to the dogs. And never will be right again until Napoleon's back in his rightful place.''

''I agree, young man,'' the vicar called out, misunderstanding Anthony completely, ''and I fear his proper place is not in this world at all. But rather somewhere below it,'' he concluded, his own face flushed with his attempt at what he considered to be a slightly scandalous comment worthy of the exalted company.

"His rightful place?" Anthony shouted, rising up on one elbow to thrust an empurpled face toward the offending vicar. "His rightful place is Emperor of all Europe! That's his rightful place. And I tell you, nothing will go right until brave men everywhere"—and here Anthony swept out his arm with such force that the timorous young female next to him cringed backward as he overset a water glass—"brave men everywhere bear arms in his defense. They've sent him to an island, an island," he entreated Lord Kingston, as though there were no other sensible creatures present he could convince, "a tiny island, when his proper domain would be this island, his proper kingdom, all kingdoms on earth!"

"I say!" cried the squire.

"For shame!" sputtered the vicar.

And, "What sort of joke is this!" challenged another gentleman.

But one landowner, a previously quiet fellow, leaped to his feet to declare ringingly, "Our brave Billy went off to fight the Corsican monster, and I can tell you, he still wakes screaming in the night at the remembered battles."

In the general uproar, Elizabeth scarcely saw the Earl rise effortlessly and signal two footmen. Then he made his way, amazingly swiftly for a man with halt gait, toward Anthony.

But Anthony seemed oblivious of all that was happening about him.

"That's 'cause he fought on the wrong side, you see," he said confidentially to the angry landowner as he gripped the tabletop with two hands. "Had he fought for Napoleon, you see, instead of against, why, then, you see, what a different story it would be. For Napoleon—" he began to go on, but stopped when he felt the Earl's hand upon his shoulder.

The Earl looked down at him with a pleasant smile. "Anthony, old chap," he said softly, "I think you need some fresh air. That Rhine is deceptive stuff. It goes down like lemonade, and doesn't announce its true nature till too late. A bit of air will clear your head."

"Don't need air," Anthony denied, trying to wrench his shoulder from the Earl's seemingly light grip and failing.

"Need Napoleon back. It's what we all need, don't you know?"

The two footmen positioned themselves behind Anthony and at the Earl's nod lifted him effortlessly to his feet. Then the Earl wrapped one long arm about Anthony's shoulders and propelled him, still protesting, from the room. As Anthony left, no longer unwilling but rather dazed, his words floated back to the stunned company. "Don't you see," he said piteously, "that we've been all wrong? Oh, I know you must be angry about your leg, and all, but surely you must see the right of it?"

When the last of Anthony's mumbled plaints had faded, Elizabeth found herself sitting at a dinner table with her host absent, her cousin disgraced, and every other person present absolutely still. Then all at once, each person realized the situation, and all attempted to leap into the breach at once. A general babble arose.

"Wine," said the doctor sagely, patting Elizabeth's hand. "Wine's the culprit. Probably a very sane young fellow when he isn't in his cups. Don't worry, my dear. He won't harm you. Auden's got him under control."

"He is a very nice young man," Elizabeth managed to choke. "He is my cousin."

"Wine," repeated the doctor, looking darkly at the glass in front of him, as though it contained some murky poison. "Think I'll just nip out for a moment to my carriage. Got just the thing in my bag for the lad. That is, if the housekeeper don't think of hot soapsuds first," he added mysteriously, and bowing, left the table as well.

The dinner was in disarray about her, but instead of joining in the fevered attempts at normal conversation as Lady Isabel so correctly did, Elizabeth sat still. It was not until one large tear began to course its way down her cheek that she heard the Earl's voice, low and level, whisper into her ear, "Hold up for just a little longer, Elizabeth. All will be well."

She mopped away the offending teardrop as the Earl, now standing at the head of the table, said brightly to the assembled guests, "The young man attempted to solve the age-old question of whether white, red, and pink wine can coexist in the same vessel. Alas, it is still true that they cannot.''

A little wellspring of laughter greeted his comment.

"He offers his apologies, but unfortunately, you will have to take my word for it, as he is undergoing Dr. Woods's famous cure for such experiments right now," he went on.

A small groan went up and at least one gentleman laughed sympathetically. "If he survives that"—the gentleman chuckled—"he'll live to a ripe old age."

"I'm sure he will join us, older and much, much wiser, later this evening," the Earl agreed. "But for now, I think it would be a capital idea if we adjourned to the ballroom. Our desserts, obedient as they are to our every command, will follow. As will music, and if you promise not to tell the good doctor, more spirits."

Appeased, his company rose, and some of the charm of the evening seemed recaptured. The ladies went out on their gentlemen's arms, and Elizabeth, scarcely believing her ears, heard no further comment about Anthony's treasonous statements beyond a few whispers about how wine took some fellows.

Elizabeth rose blindly and almost stumbled into the Earl, who stood behind her.

"I must go to him," she whispered.

"You must not," he said, placing his hands firmly on her shoulders. "Bev is with him, and the doctor as well, and all that went down is about to arise again. I hardly think Anthony needs you now, or, for that matter, would welcome your company. You will go and mingle with my guests and put it all out of your mind. And I shall accompany you and be sure that the others forget it as well. Come, Elizabeth, a little spirit, if you please."

Looking up, she saw a stern look flash in his eyes. She did not wish to anger him further than Anthony already had, so she placed her hand upon his arm and went quietly with him.

Once they were inside the vast ballroom, almost the first sight to meet her eyes was that of Lord Kingston, once again urbane and cool, quite soberly holding forth to a group of gentlemen.

"He is not with Anthony, no. I expect he had no wish to dirty his hands further. Or his clothes, for that matter," the Earl said obliquely. "I cannot, alas, open the dancing," he sighed, "but then, I have repair work to do. I shall ask you, Elizabeth, to do that honor with Cousin Richard. Now, come with me, and remember that it is not quite the end of the world. Or else our vicar would be much busier than he now is."

Somehow Elizabeth managed to begin the dance with Cousin Richard. He was, as usual, closemouthed. But two things that he did surprised Elizabeth even in her well of wretchedness. He told her immediately, with a rare smile, that as Anthony was only a young cub, no one would give the matter a second thought. And then he danced with her exquisitely. Soon the set was joined by others, and before long the four musicians were playing merry country tunes for several reeling couples.

As soon as she could, Elizabeth left the dance floor, leaving a startled Lady Isabel to discover Cousin Richard's unexpected grace. Elizabeth did as best she could to obey her host's instructions. She commiserated with Mrs. Woods about the folly of marrying a doctor and thus spending every social evening alone whilst he found some occupation for himself. She agreed with a Mrs. Stanley that the cost of both butter and lace was prohibitive these days. As she felt it was the least she could do to make amends for Anthony, she listened to the initially offended gentleman tell her in lurid detail every one of his son Billy's war-struck nightmares. After a while, she could not tell if it was that everyone was being exquisitely correct socially or if they had indeed forgotten the extent of Anthony's comments and marked it all down to his intoxication.

At length, when the evening was half gone, a pale but blotchy-faced Anthony crept into the room. Lord Beverly stood at his one side, Dr. Woods at the other. In the hush that had fallen upon his entrance, Anthony said wretchedly in a weak voice, "Terribly sorry. I had no intention of disrupting dinner. Beg forgiveness."

"Lad looks like he's been dragged through a hedge backwards." The doctor's wife sighed.

"Of course you're forgiven, lad. Just remember in future, wine and politics don't mix." The squire laughed.

"Wine and rich food don't mix neither, as he's doubtless discovered," one of the other gentlemen commented. Before long, almost every one of the assembled guests had walked over to Anthony to condole with him. The elder ladies clucked in motherly fashion and their daughters smiled in sympathy. The gentlemen made hearty jests about the power of spirits and recounted some of their own youthful indiscretions. After what Lord Beverly deemed a decent interval, he nudged Anthony rather forcibly in the ribs. Anthony grimaced, then made a wobbly bow and excused himself from the company.

The musicians played on, the guests seemed to have forgotten the whole, but Elizabeth stood at the sidelines and despaired. Her self-imposed exile did not last. For Owen, who for once was not sleeping his dinner off, perhaps because the music was too loud, appeared before her with a plate of tipsy trifle. "This is awfully good, Elizabeth," he said shyly. "Do have some. It is exceptionally good," he urged.

"Owen's right," the Earl said, looming up from the shadows. "It is awfully good. Thank you, Owen. I'm sure Elizabeth will like it. She had no dessert, you know."

"I know," Owen said sagely, as though he well knew the lack of dessert accounted for most of the world's sorrows. Then he made a stiff little bow and left to peruse the dessert table for anything he might have missed.

The Earl put the plate down carefully, then faced Elizabeth. "Come. It's all righted now. No need to castigate yourself. For he was far too far down the table for you to stop once he was in full spate. But it really doesn't matter."

"The things he said—" Elizabeth began.

"Were things that everyone believes to have been brought on by an excess of wine," the Earl said quickly.

She looked the Earl full in the face and blurted, "But they weren't. It's what he truly believes."

"He is very young," he answered patiently, "and the ideas of our youth tend to be extreme. Were you never young, Elizabeth?" he asked quizzically. "Bev was used to dress all in scarlet and pink," he mused. "The most shocking shade of pink. I used to think his poor father would have apoplexy when he saw his only begotten son decked out like a fortune-teller at a fair. And even Simon, the most level-headed fellow once he got his growth, was enraptured of the idea of running off to sea in his salad days. And I . . . You well know how I covered myself with glory in my youth. So you need not blame Anthony, nor yourself. I think half the problem is how very seriously you have taken him. It is not wise to take young men too seriously. Or older ones, for that matter." He laughed.

"And, no," he said, looking at her steadily, "he has not ruined all his chances. And," he added with a small smile, "even that matters less each day."

Elizabeth could not quite understand his comment, and dared not try to understand further. She only smiled and felt her anxiety slip away. She stood wreathed in smiles, glowing dumbstruck, like a morning glory in the sunlight of his shadow. And then he turned away to chat with another guest, leaving Elizabeth alone to damn herself for six sorts of a fool.

— 12 —

The guests crept about the great house with unaccustomed stealth. Except for Lord Beverly, who, bereft of his boon companion, occupied his time with strolling in the gardens, occasionally moved by some inner thought to slashing the heads off intrusive flowers which called themselves to his wavering attention. Elizabeth, watching Lord Beverly from a window, was tempted to go outside and warn him of the danger of incipient murder that she had seen gleaming in the head gardener's eyes as he observed Lord Beverly's unorthodox method of working off his impatience. But she could not bring herself to stir from the house. For it was Anthony who was being interviewed by the Earl this morning, and fiends with hot pincers could not have budged her until the interview was over.

The Earl had not seemed angry with his rash young cousin the day after the party, nor the day after that. Both Elizabeth and Anthony had breathed sighs of relief as things went on in much the same manner that they had before. But this morning the Earl had put down his coffee cup and gently interrupted Anthony in mid-sentence as he was outlining his plans to accompany Lord Kingston to Town to see to the acquisition of some new neckcloths.

"Oh, pity," the Earl had drawled. "I did hope that you might be free this morning, Anthony. For there were some things that I wished to converse with you about . . . alone."

Anthony had put down his buttered toast and given Elizabeth one stricken glance. Between the space of two heartbeats,

Lord Kingston had said lightly, "Go ahead, Tony. The trip can wait, for it never was of prime import. And needs must when the devil drives, eh, lad?"

Elizabeth could see Anthony struggling with his reply. He had come to think himself very much the man-about-town in his days at Lyonshall, and she knew he would have dearly loved to say something equally flippant and outrageous. She knew Anthony detested the idea of being thought as a suppli-cant for the Earl's favors, especially in front of Lord Kingston. But, she saw with blessed relief, Anthony was not blind to reality. He choked for a second and then said casually, "Harry's quite right, Cousin Morgan. I've got a drawer full of neckcloths anyway. I'm at your service this morning. We can ride out tomorrow, Harry—that is, if it's all right with you?" he added with a very youthful look of entreaty toward his new friend.

"Certainly, certainly," Lord Kingston said smoothly. "I shall not wear the willow, not with two lovely ladies present, at any rate."

Anthony had gone off like a sheep to the slaughter, Eliza-beth thought, and the rest of the company trailed off in their own pursuits. But again, none went far from the study where the Earl and Anthony were met. Lord Kingston had initially tried to capture Elizabeth's attention with light flirtation, quizzing her about life in Tuxford and her plans for the future. But even though a few scant weeks ago she would have been thrilled to receive the attentions of a gentleman such as he, now she had no thought of him.

It was not only because she was nervously thinking about what was going forth in the Earl's study. Somehow, Lord Kingston, with all his graces, made her feel uncomfortable. He was so pleasant, so charming, so very flattering, that he set her teeth on edge. For all his unpredictable behavior and for all his occasional thorniness, Elizabeth always welcomed the Earl's company. Of course, she admitted to herself, that might well be only because of her personal feelings toward him. But, she thought further, perhaps it was also because the Earl treated all who came across his path, male, female, servant, or child, in the same manner. Whereas Lord Kingston treated only the ladies with unflagging courtesy and condescension.

She would, she realized in her contrary way, be far more pleased with Lord Kingston if he made one of his snide or cutting remarks toward her on occasion, as he did to any of the gentlemen. Surely, she reasoned, she could not always please him, just because she was a female. But so he treated her. And so she did not seek to make his acquaintance any further than she already had. Perhaps for that reason he seemed determined to coax a smile, win a laugh, achieve a coy and pleased response from her. He seemed to have intensified his efforts in that behalf of late.

Elizabeth borrowed a line from Cousin Richard and pleaded letters she must write, and in that manner escaped from Lord Kingston's attentions.

It was odd, Elizabeth thought, after she had escaped Lord Kingston's presence once again, that he did not seem to pursue Lady Isabel. For the two seemed a perfect pair. Both seemed staples of the ton, both cared for finery and gossip, and both affected the same air of elegance. But neither seemed too impressed by the other. Lady Isabel's uninterest was understandable. If she had set her cap for the Earl, that was certainly comprehensible enough to Elizabeth. But she could not fathom why Lord Kingston seemed so bored with the lady, even though he claimed a passing acquaintance with her. Perhaps, Elizabeth opined idly, it was an acquaintance that had ended badly.

Now Elizabeth sat in the library with a clean sheet of paper before her and pondered nothing other than Anthony's progress. She could no more have written to her Uncle at this moment than she could have burst into the Earl's study, as she longed to do, to discover what was being said. She did essay a line or two to her uncle, but looking down at the insipid stuff she had written, she realized he would have thought her run mad to waste postage on such inconsequential drivel. She was engaged in tearing the paper into squares when Cousin Richard came hesitantly through the door.

"Terribly sorry," he said, seeing her mutilating the letter.

"I did not know anyone was in here," and he began to leave the room.

He looked so distraught, so pale-faced and shaken, that Elizabeth sprang to her feet. "Oh, no, Richard," she cried, "I was only just leaving. You needn't leave on account of me."

He hesitated and then came back into the room. She had never seen him looking so wretched. His long thin face was set in dour lines, his hair was disarrayed, and his hands clenched and reclenched on the morning paper he held.

"It's only that I was looking for Morgan, you see," he said anxiously.

Elizabeth realized that Richard had come late to table this morning, and that Richard seldom seemed aware of what went forth in the house, so she said quickly, "Anthony is with Morgan having his interview. In his study," she went on, seeing the look of consternation upon Richard's grim countenance.

"But I must speak with him. Now," Richard said with agitation.

"You could send word in, if it's an emergency," Elizabeth said doubtfully, unable to imagine an emergency dire enough to interrupt such a confidential matter.

"No, no. I can't do that," Richard muttered, pacing the room rapidly. "Elizabeth," he finally said, stopping to look at her, "I shall give you the message for Morgan. Tell him that I am called away. Tell him I had to leave for London again."

"Again?" Elizabeth blurted in surprise. Then, to make a recover, she said with genuine concern, "Is it bad news?"

"Very bad," Richard replied.

"Oh, dear," Elizabeth said, coming forward to lay a hand upon Richard's hand in sympathy. His hand, she discovered, was cold and trembling. "I am so sorry," she said, looking at the miserable young man. For coming up close, she could see that which one often forgot, that Richard was only a young man after all.

"I don't deserve your sympathy," he said with some force. "Ah, well," he went on, looking down at her, "of all the fools assembled here for this judging of suitable heirs, you alone seem to be the most honest and the sanest of the bunch.''

''Richard!'' Elizabeth said in shock. Not only were his words bitter and insulting, but he had never said so much in such a short time before.

''I would not have wished to come here,'' Richard said, as though compelled to speak by the searching look in Elizabeth's eyes. ''I would not have come here,'' he said forcefully, ''if I had any choice. Understand, Elizabeth, I am a proud man. Or was,'' he said bitterly, ''a proud man. I have little enough to be proud of. A small estate, halfway to ruin, and little more than the lining in my pockets to repair my fortunes with. But I went to London to see if I could raise some blunt to put my estate back in order again. I wished to raise horses. I am good with horses,'' he added, staring at Elizabeth as if to dare her to deny this.

''I don't know why I tell you this, except that I must leave the message for Morgan, and you are a good sensible female. I see that. Oh, yes''—he laughed sourly—''I do see everything that transpires here at Lyonshall, though I say little. For I think I am overwhelmed with shame at myself, coming here to do the pretty in hopes that Morgan would be my fairy godmother. A great hulking Cinderella I'd make, too, wouldn't I, Elizabeth?

''No matter,'' he went on. ''It is almost over and I can at last be myself. I found no eager patrons in London and was almost about to go to the moneylenders, though I knew the danger in that course, when I received an invitation to a rout at an old school friend's house. I met Caroline there.''

Elizabeth noted how he paused when he said the name. How his face and voice softened at the uttering of the name.

''She is the loveliest creature, Elizabeth. Wellborn, graceful, and beautiful. But also well endowed with a modest fortune. But that, I swear, is of no moment to me. In fact, I would far prefer her to be in rags, for then I would have had a chance with her. As it was, I paid her court. And she told me that despite her father's urging her to take someone with more money, she preferred me. I stayed on in London, my ambition outstripping my funds, just so that I could be near her. But when Morgan's letter came, I saw that I might at last have a way to clear her father's objections. As heir to Auden, surely, he could not turn down my suit again."

A look of hope lit his eyes. Unconsciously he held Elizabeth's hand too tightly, as he went on. "And her father agreed. Agreed, at least, that being named heir would make me more suitable. But he promised nothing. So I came to Lyonshall. And found that I hated myself for it. I do not like to be a beggar. I did not like to parade myself before others, as if in some sort of contest. I would earn my way in life. Perhaps that is why I was so withdrawn and surly. For so much as I needed and wanted Morgan to choose me, so much I also despised myself for vying to be picked as heir. It was not Lyonshall I wanted, it was only Caroline."

"Ah, Richard," Elizabeth sighed, touched by the confession that seemed to have been wrung out of him by circumstance.

"I wrote to Caroline constantly while here. And then one day I received a letter from her, in which she said that it seemed her father was looking upon another man's offer with great interest. That's why I hastened back to London the other week. She seemed overjoyed to see me. Genuinely glad to see me. As soon as I could I returned here, for she urged me not to let the others steal a match on me. Elizabeth, do you know what a misery it is to pretend to be someone you are not?" he asked with passion.

Elizabeth winced at his words. And she took his trembling hands in hers, and held them still. "Poor Richard," she said, looking at him with great sorrow-darkened eyes. "Oh, I know. I do know. Have you told Morgan, my dear?"

"That depends," the Earl's cold voice said harshly, "upon what he has told me."

Elizabeth dropped Richard's hands as a guilty child will drop a stolen treat. She looked over Richard's shoulder to see the Earl, leaning heavily upon his stick, staring back at her with a twisted smile upon his lips. Anthony, puzzled, stood beside him.

"Morgan. I must go. I was just telling Elizabeth, so that

she could relay the message to you. Look at yesterday morning's *Times*, Morgan. Look at it!'' he cried, thrusting the paper toward the Earl.

The Earl held his hand out stiffly to receive the paper. He seemed abstracted as he took it, and his eyes never left Elizabeth. Finally he gazed down at it and looked to where Richard pointed with a shaking finger.

''Oh,'' the Earl said softly, once he had read the words. Then his expression softened as well. He placed a hand on Richard's shoulder. ''What can you accomplish by returning now?'' he said quietly. ''It is done. You must accept it.''

''I must see for myself,'' Richard answered, forcing himself under control again. ''I must have it from her own lips. At least that,'' he said.

Richard took the paper back and gave it to Elizabeth. ''There is the end of my tale,'' he said to her. ''Perhaps it is the end, but I must go and see.''

But Elizabeth did not read the paper, she only started and asked in confusion, ''But Morgan knows?''

''Yes,'' Richard answered as he made to leave, ''he knows everything. Good-bye for now,'' he said to the Earl. ''I will return only when I know all the truth.'' And he left the room.

The Earl looked after him and then said in a musing tone, ''Not quite everything. But I do know the lad is only letting himself in for more misery by returning to London. But I think him lucky, though he does not know it as yet. For she was only playing with him. It is the other fellow who is the really unlucky one.''

While Anthony looked at the Earl in confusion, Elizabeth scanned the lines on the much-crumpled paper. It was the social pages she held. After a moment, Elizabeth cried, ''She's engaged herself to a Baron!''

''Yes,'' the Earl answered in a now bored tone, ''as she most likely always intended to do. And it is the poor Baron who will regret this day, long after Richard has put her down to experience. But it is not quite fair to discuss this further in front of Anthony, as he has not been made privy to Richard's dilemma. And I am not sure he ought to be, without Richard's express permission.''

"Of course," Elizabeth replied. "I shan't say a word. Anthony, I'm sure Richard will tell you the whole when he returns.''

Anthony shrugged, and the Earl put in swiftly, ''Now that Anthony and I have done with our little talk, we decided it was time to come and release you from your lonely waiting. But this morning seems destined for secrets. For Anthony and I have also agreed to keep our discussion to ourselves for a while. Can you bear it, Elizabeth?'' he asked quizzically.

"If I must," Elizabeth said in disappointment.

"Oh, don't worry, Liz," Anthony said cheerfully, ''for Morgan's not come to any decision. That much I can tell you.''

But as the three began to speak of more general things, the Earl wondered at the truth in that statement. For when he had entered the room and seen, for that one moment, Elizabeth's rapt face gazing up at Richard, he had for that one moment felt himself propelled back in time. For it was not the first time he had seen a trusted female's face from a vantage point beyond another man's shoulder. Now, looking at her clear, smiling, animated visage, the Earl sighed and wondered if he had not indeed come to a decision after all.

Elizabeth sat upon her bed and finished brushing out her hair. This really, she thought as she rose to put her brush back upon her night table, cannot go on much longer. The summer was slipping away, and the Earl seemed no closer to a decision than he was when they had arrived. Almost, she hated him in her thoughts, as she prepared for bed, for he should not, she thought censoriously, take so long about it. But even as she thought it, she reconsidered. For the moment that he did make up his mind, she knew she would be gone from this place, probably never to return. She sighed heavily and was prepared to blow out the candles when she heard a slight noise at the door, something between a scratching and a rustle.

Elizabeth felt a shiver of alarm. The first thought to come

to her was that of rodents. And if—she shuddered, drawing the covers up around her—the Earl housed rodents in his ancestral home, she would be out of Lyonshall before sunup.

But the noise abated and she heard then only the usual sounds of a summer's night filtering in through her half-open window: crickets, frogs, and the rustling of the leaves on the great trees that surrounded the house. Taking up all her courage (and her night rail's skirt as well), Elizabeth eased herself up and out of bed. She raised her candle high and saw a slip of paper lying on the floor near to her door.

She scanned the few words upon the paper. "Come at once to the blue salon. We must discuss Anthony," was all it said.

Elizabeth took only a second to try to puzzle out the hand. She had never seen any of the other guests' writing, and as the writing on the original letter that had come to Tuxford could have been done by the Earl's secretary, she could not know if it was the Earl that had sent her this curious note. And she did not know who else would wish to speak about Anthony at this late hour, when all in the house were abed.

A second later, she thought that perhaps Anthony had come to some harm, and the writer of the note wished her to know about it before any other inmate at Lyonshall. He had, after all, lately been in the habit of going out at night with Lord Kingston, "to bend an elbow" (they had laughed) at the local inn at the outskirts of Lyonshall.

It only took a few more moments for fear to encompass her entirely. A greater fear than she had had at the thought of rodent invaders. For Anthony was in her charge and Anthony was her own, and her fear for him riveted her to the spot. The note, however, said "at once," and rereading those words broke her from her immobility.

She hastily threw on a night robe, tossed her hair back, and barefooted, left her room and flew down the stairs toward the salon, with no thought of propriety, but only of Anthony. She raced to the door to the salon and flung it open. There, she saw at once, stood Lord Beverly, in the loudest, most colorful red-and-gold-patterned robe she had ever seen. Although to be truthful she could not help thinking, she had seen no gentlemen but Uncle and Anthony in their nightwear before.

Lord Beverly's golden curls were tousled and his face looked curiously vulnerable, as though he had just been awakened.

"Where is Anthony?" she gasped as she saw him.

"Deuce take it. How should I know?" Lord Beverly answered angrily. "You're the one I was going to ask that of."

"What has happened?" she demanded, thinking him only stupid with sleep.

"How should I know?" Lord Beverly asked. "I checked his room before coming down, and he's not there. What was it you wanted to tell me?" he demanded, coming toward her with an odd gait, and she saw that he did not have his slippers on the right feet.

Mutely Elizabeth held out her note.

Lord Beverly took it, and rubbing his eyes, he gazed at it for a long moment, and then fumbled in the pocket of his incredible dressing gown and withdrew a paper. He gave it to Elizabeth and said, "Someone's a joker. Got the same note myself. Thought the young cawker had gotten himself into a scrape, and that Morgan wanted my assistance with him. I've pumped him out once before. Thought Morgan didn't want the ladies to see him in a state again. And I knew," he said triumphantly as Elizabeth still stood gaping at the identical notes in her hand, "that Harry would be no help in that case. Need a fellow who's got his wits about him for that sort of job."

"But perhaps he is in trouble," Elizabeth quavered, "and we are both needed."

Lord Beverly put his head to one side and pondered. "Might be something in that," he said slowly. "Then we ought to stay awhile. No end of trouble a green lad can get himself into. Harry might have taken him to a cockfight, or he might have gotten into a brawl with some of the local fellows. If he's battered and bloody, they'd need some strong stomachs to see him right. They might be at Dr. Woods's now and need some help with him when they get home."

Elizabeth felt her legs grow weak, and she felt a rush of wind in her ears.

"Steady, now," she heard Lord Beverly's voice say in

alarm. She felt his hands about her shoulders, and found herself propelled into a chair.

"Head between your legs. Ah, umm . . . limbs," Lord Beverly said nervously. "Have you any salts with you? Should I burn a feather? Have you any feathers?" he went on desperately, withdrawing his hands from her shoulders as if they were boiling hot. "Put your head down," he shouted, and then said, as if to himself, "Brandy! That's the thing. Hold on, Elizabeth. Don't swoon, whatever you do."

But Elizabeth had gotten sufficient control to shake her head in denial when he was back with a brimming glass of brandy that he tried to force upon her.

"Excellent restorative," he urged, slopping some of it on his amazing robe in his agitation. "Down it all at once and you'll feel more the thing. Go on," he insisted.

"Bev," she said in a reedy voice, "if I drink that lot, I'll emulate Anthony at the dinner party. Both ways," she said in a more normal tone, eyeing the glass in distaste. "For brandy makes me most vilely ill. I'm better now, thank you. It was just the thought of Anthony covered with gore that overset me."

"I'm sorry," Lord Beverly said as he perched nervously on a chair and watched her. "Didn't mean to excite you. As it happens, might all be a hum. Might be nothing to it. For here we are, and there's no one else about. I came down immediately I heard the noise at my door and saw the note. Didn't even bother to draw my trousers on," he complained, and then, horrified, said quickly, "That is, didn't get my slippers on right. Forget my trousers, will you, Elizabeth?"

"I've forgotten them." Elizabeth giggled in spite of herself and her worry.

"My slippers," he said again with emphasis as he bent to change them to the right feet. "Would you mind," he asked imperatively, as Elizabeth watched him, "turning your head? Got no hose on," he explained as he completed his task.

Elizabeth was smiling as he said, "There. Right as rain. You can look now."

"Do you think we ought to wait here?" she asked nervously.

"Think we ought, don't know if we should," Lord Beverly said slowly. "For we're all alone, together in our nightclothes, you see."

He eyed her. There was no doubt, he thought, she was a ravishing-looking female even in her disarray. Especially, he amended, in her disarray. Although the night robe covered her, its thin material clearly hinted at the curves on her body beneath. Her honey hair lay soft upon her shoulders and her eyes were bright with emotion. There was nothing seductive in her attitude, he knew, but everything deliciously promising in her aspect.

But she looked upon him as a brother and trusted him as one, he knew. And she was an innocent. Further, he had his own ideas as to his dear friend Morgan's emotions toward the chit. He sighed softly. It was a good thing, he thought, tearing his gaze from her, that he wasn't in the petticoat line after all. When he glanced back at her, she was looking at him expectantly.

"Very nice peignoir, by the by," he said as Elizabeth's hand flew to her neck to button the last button she had left undone. "You might go up, and I'll wait," he thoughtfully concluded. "Nothing amiss with a chap as near to naked as nothing, if he's sitting alone in a house at night."

"How can I go up, even to dress properly, when Anthony may come in, needing my attention?" she demanded. "And you are dressed, Bev. I've forgotten your trousers, remember?"

They sat in silence, listening to the mantle clock ticking for a few minutes. And then Elizabeth said, "How long do you think we ought to wait?"

"Depends," Lord Beverly said, cudgeling his brain. "I checked Anthony's room, but I didn't check Morgan's. Still, I'd hate to wake the poor fellow over nothing if he is in there. It was a damp day and I know he has the devil of a time getting to sleep with that curst leg of his when the weather's lowering. Hate to roust him for nothing. I'd say we ought to wait an hour, and then forget it as a prank if no one comes by then. Still, I'll keep my door open, don't you worry, till Anthony toddles in."

"Who would play such a trick?" Elizabeth asked wearily, pulling back her heavy hair with her hands.

"Owen might, the lad's too stuffy by far. Perhaps he's been aching for a bit of mischief."

They sat quietly, each thinking of who would send such a summons for a jest, till Lord Beverly stretched and said in an offhand manner, "Long as we have to wait, Elizabeth, would you care for a game of cards to pass the time?"

"Yes, yes, fine," she answered, still troubled by thoughts of the possible dangers Anthony might have fallen heir to.

Lord Beverly rummaged in a drawer and came back with a deck of cards, but he scarcely looked at his first hand when he said thoughtfully, "I could do with a spot of something, couldn't you, Elizabeth?"

"No," she said distractedly, thinking of Anthony and trying to concentrate on the cards in her hand. "I told you, I don't care for any brandy."

"Not spirits," Lord Beverly replied, his shocked blue eyes widened, "but something to eat. When we were boys, Morgan and I often crept downstairs at night for a little feast in the kitchens when all the others were asleep," he said nostalgically. "There might be a leg of fowl, or a bit of that excellent pudding, or even a slice of cheese left over for us. What say I just nip out to the kitchens and bring us back something?"

"I'm sure Morgan would be thrilled with us gorging in his salon at two in the morning," Elizabeth said depressively. "Really, Bev."

"Well, then," he said, "why don't we both go to the kitchens and have a quick bite? We can leave a note here, saying where we are. It beats sitting here and fretting ourselves to pieces, don't it?"

Her fair-haired companion wrote a note in letters so wide a blind man could see them, and propped it up on the mantel.

"There!" he said in satisfaction. "That'll do it. Come along, Elizabeth."

He paused at the door.

"You haven't any slippers. Would you like to borrow mine?" he asked gallantly.

It might have been the lateness of the hour or the vision of herself pounding along in his slippers, but Elizabeth gave out a clear, ringing laugh.

"You could just say no," he admonished her, "without bringing the house down upon us."

Lord Beverly remembered the back way to the kitchens very well and they made their way there with exaggerated stealth. Once they had achieved their destination, with not a stubbed toe nor an alerted footman to interrupt their progress, Lord Beverly lit some candles and waved Elizabeth to a seat at a long wooden kitchen table. She waited there while he bent to start a fire ablaze in the huge fireplace, and then sat patiently as he hummed while he foraged. Soon the table was littered with bits and pieces of a magnificent late-night repast.

Elizabeth busied herself with ladyfingers and the remains of a bowl of syllabub, while Lord Beverly happily concocted a dish of ham, fowl, and cheeses on bread for his sustenance.

"Do you know how to make cocoa?" Lord Beverly interrupted his praise of their capital idea of a feast to ask hopefully.

"Shame," said a deep voice, and both Elizabeth and Lord Beverly startled with guilt at the sound.

The Earl, in a dark blue dressing gown sashed with gold, stood watching them, his eyes hooded, gripping his walking stick.

"Shame on you, Bev. Putting a lady to work for you. Do I not sustain you well enough during the day, that you need to make inroads upon the kitchens in the night? And with an accomplice to make cocoa with you as well?"

"Where is Anthony? What has happened to him?" Elizabeth cried, rising from the table as Lord Beverly started toward the Earl.

"Why, here he is," the Earl said casually, and Anthony, shamefaced, came out of the darkness behind him.

"We went to the Rose and the Bear for some fun," he said with boyish embarrassment, "and the time flew by. Sorry to give you a start. I'll be off to bed now," he said lamely.

"And I as well," said Lord Kingston, who appeared at his side. He sounded curiously aggrieved. He looked toward Elizabeth. "It seems that as I have had little luck during the day, I must remember to call on you some night when I am in need of nourishment, at least," he said silkily, eyeing her robe and bare feet.

And then he bowed and left with Anthony.

"But why did you send us that note?" Lord Beverly asked the Earl as soon as the other two had left.

"What note?" the Earl asked, standing quite still and watching them.

"Why," Lord Beverly said, fumbling in his pocket, "dash it, I must have left it in the salon. Show him yours, Elizabeth."

"Do," the Earl said softly, investing that one syllable with such innuendo that Elizabeth colored up.

"I left it in the salon as well," she said.

"All I saw was a hastily scribbled note, in letters a yard high, that said cryptically that you might be found in the kitchens."

"Well, both Elizabeth and I received the same note after we went to bed. We went to bed separately, that is," Lord Beverly said in desperation, as he looked into his friend's stern visage, "but we met in the salon in our nightclothes, even though I was half-dressed. . . ."

"We received identical unsigned notes summoning us at once to discuss Anthony in the salon. I feared some accident, so I came flying as I was. As did Bev," Elizabeth said, putting up her chin. "And we waited for him. Or for you, for we thought it was you that had sent the note."

"I see," the Earl said, his lips twitching. "And you thought nothing of the impropriety of the situation?"

"We did not care, we were so worried," Elizabeth said defensively.

"I cared," Lord Beverly yelped.

"What a seductress you are, Elizabeth," the Earl said on a laugh, limping forward to inspect the table. "Within a day, I find you holding hands with Cousin Richard in the morning and cozening up to Bev by beguiling him with cocoa at night. No wonder Harry was scandalized by you."

"Harry doesn't know a thing about Elizabeth and me," Lord Beverly said angrily.

"No, he doesn't, unfortunately for him," the Earl answered absently, as though lost in thought.

"It was likely that sneaking little Owen making a may-game of us all," his friend grumbled.

"Doubtless," the Earl said. "But then, he keeps shocking hours, since I, only a few moments past, received the same sort of note as well. I met Lord Kingston and Anthony quite by what appeared to be accident as I was entering the salon. It's a good thing you two weren't there then, in your dishabille. That might have been hard to explain away, but as few ardent lovers carry on midst the mutton and savories at this hour of the night, there was more of gluttony than passion apparent in your meeting. I congratulate you, Bev, on your interesting choice of trysting spots. Few Romeos have hit upon the idea of kitchens for their secret amours. But so long as I am already here, why are you being such a selfish lout?" the Earl continued more lightly. "Can't you pass some of that beef over here?"

Elizabeth, suddenly conscious of her flimsy attire, rose to leave. But the Earl caught her by the hand.

"Do stay, Elizabeth," he said sweetly, "and finish your syllabub. Although," he said consideringly, "I believe there's more left about your lips now than in the bowl."

As Elizabeth sat and scrubbed at the sticky residue on her upper lip, Lord Beverly carved some meat for his host. "Just like old times, eh, Morgan?" he chortled.

"Not quite," the Earl replied with a gentle smile, watching Elizabeth. "Some things improve with age."

— 13 —

Elizabeth arose oddly refreshed after far too few hours of sleep. Her first waking thought was of the previous night. It had been a strange affair. She had spent hours in the kitchens with the Earl and Lord Beverly, and had delighted in the close camaraderie that seemed to have sprung up among the three of them. The lateness of the hour had made it seem as if they were the only people left awake in the universe, cast away on their kitchen island, making their conversation light and almost childish in tone. They had laughed immoderately through the small hours of the night.

Yet it had been a curious time. For while she had been quite comfortable in her unorthodox attire before Lord Beverly, the mere presence of the Earl caused her to feel almost as a wanton. She had become acutely aware not only of her night rail and the thin robe covering it but also of her body beneath. Where Lord Beverly's garish robe had been amusing and the thought of his trouserless state only endearing, she had been unsettled by the Earl sitting next to her in his long dark blue dressing gown. When, between jests, she had found herself wondering just what lay beneath his garb, and startled even herself by her sudden blush, her eyes had caught the Earl's and the wicked glint in them hinted that he knew the reason for her confusion. Even after she had gone to her bed, intrusive thoughts of him had kept her awake longer than they ought to have, and had quite banished the mystery of the notes themselves from her mind.

But the Earl and Lord Beverly had not forgotten. And

when they broached the matter to Owen at breakfast, his eyes had grown alarmed and then shuttered. He denied knowing a thing about any missives. Still, he had seemed troubled and guilt-stricken, at least to Elizabeth's practiced eye. But before she could frame a question for him, his mother had pooh-poohed the whole matter and only said coquettishly to the Earl that she might never forgive him for not inviting her to their night's revels as well. Then she had told Elizabeth not to tarry over breakfast, for the ladies were arriving at noon. Only then did Elizabeth remember the tea party at all and she made a hasty retreat to her room to change her dress.

Lady Isabel had persuaded the Earl to agree to her having a small tea for the local ladies. Isabel had pouted quite prettily that as she was becoming a hermit here at Lyonshall, did the Earl not think it would be a good idea for his two mon-strously outnumbered female guests to be permitted to have some of their own sex for company? It seemed quite natural then for her host to smilingly agree. But Elizabeth now realized, her spirits sinking, his acquiescence did put Lady Isabel in the nominal position of hostess at Lyonshall, as it was she who had arranged the party and invited the guests. And perhaps that was the purpose of it all, Elizabeth decided glumly, as she checked her appearance in a small gilt mirror in the hall.

She sighed as she encountered her own weary reflection. She had dressed in a demure high-necked rose-sprigged muslin. She had wound back her hair, and wore only a single simple gold ornament. It was well enough, she concluded, if one discounted the slight smudges beneath her eyes. She sighed again; as this was her first highly social tea party, she had so wanted to look correct. But she had little time for further ruminations, as the butler approached her and politely in-formed her that the ladies had already arrived and were awaiting her in the small salon. Elizabeth thanked him, took a deep breath, and went forth to greet Lady Isabel's guests.

Lady Isabel sat at a tea table, the sunlight making a halo of her fair hair. She was dressed in a morning gown of creamy lace. Her position at the table and her casual but firm air of command made it appear that she was, in fact, hostess of the great house. A fitting and quite natural hostess for an Earl, Elizabeth thought with sad justice, though the thought caught at her heart.

Four other women were present. Mrs. Woods, the physician's wife, the vicar's wife, and the plump mate of the neighboring landowner were recognizable to Elizabeth at once. But the fourth female was a stranger to her. And a spectacular stranger. She was of middle years but slim as a girl. Her gown was of the finest Brussels lace and her hair was almost the same shade as that of her hostess, though Elizabeth noted that she took care to sit out of the sunlight, for when a few stray mischievous sunbeams struck her tresses they struck more brass than gold. Her eyes were small and sharp, as were all her other features. She might have been an attractive female, Elizabeth thought as Lady Isabel waved her to a seat and murmured introductions, if she did not seem so finely honed and almost whittled to a point.

"And Lady Serena Rector you do not know, Elizabeth," Lady Isabel said, "for she is only lately arrived in the vicinity. She is staying on with family in the next county. But she is a dear friend of mine from London. And when I heard she was passing through the district on her way to her dear friends, the Fitz-Harolds, I hit upon the scheme of asking her here with us."

"I should not have missed it for the world," Lady Rector replied in a bored, thin little voice which belied her words.

Elizabeth took a seat next to Mrs. Woods, as that lady's sharpness was only of the mind and somehow her solid presence was comforting.

Lady Isabel led the conversation, and it was hard work for a time. For they were a disparate group. Three were local females who seldom strayed far from their district, and two were ornaments of the highest ton. Elizabeth contributed little, as she was too unaccustomed to social teas, and feared putting a foot wrong. Their initial conversation was labored. Mrs. Henrick, the local landowner's wife, had social pretensions and so only hung upon the two London ladies' words as though committing them to heart. The vicar's wife turned out to be sadly downtrodden, and only agreed with whatever was put to her. Mrs. Woods said just what she thought, and Elizabeth was nerving herself to do the same.

But as the teacups were refilled and the cress sandwiches were nibbled away, they discovered under their hostess' expert lead that there were commonalities that quite transcended class and station. Lady Isabel led them into talk about matters common to all their sex and they began to chat busily and happily about children, and then fashion and frocks, and then the talk turned inevitably to bonnets.

Lady Rector, with an animation that seemed quite out of proportion to her general state, was rhapsodizing about the most dear and cunning hat she had set her mind on purchasing in London, and had lost through her indecision to a chit who had waltzed into the shop and purchased it in a trice from beneath her very nose, when Lady Isabel cut in and said helpfully, "Why, Serena, you are in luck! For if Madame Dupont refuses to make up another, Elizabeth here could most likely fashion it for you in no time."

The others all stopped in mid-sentence and stared at Elizabeth, who sat feeling cornered and confused at the turn of the conversation.

"Are you clever with your hands, my dear?" Mrs. Woods asked. "That is a lovely talent. It's all I can do to mend a shirt. Anything more than that, and I'm off to the seamstress."

"Oh, much handier than that," Lady Isabel caroled. "Elizabeth is no amateur at such things. No, indeed."

They all looked to Elizabeth for further comment, but she only stared back, dumb with panic.

"She's far too shy about her expertise," Lady Isabel said merrily, "and hasn't said a word about it, even to me. But I have it on the highest authority that she is an expert at the manufacture of millinery. In fact, though she is far too modest to brag about it, Elizabeth actually works with a milliner in her hometown of Tuxford. Just think, she spends each of her days working in a shop, making up the sweetest little hats in her corner of the kingdom, and she is too self-effacing to admit to it."

Lady Rector stared at Elizabeth with the greatest of interest, through narrowed eyes, and then asked her friend, as though

Elizabeth were incapable of speech, "Works as a milliner? In a shop?"

"True," Lady Isabel trilled. "Aren't you in luck, Serena? Elizabeth only came here as companion to her cousin Anthony, who is cousin to Morgan. Elizabeth is not related to him at all. However, she's a goodhearted girl who gave up a month's wages just to see that her young relative arrived safely to Lyonshall. I am sure that she finds time hanging heavy without her usual occupation to fill her hands. And her purse," she said in a low but clearly audible whisper to Lady Rector. "And I am positive that with your way with words, you can describe that bonnet to perfection, and Elizabeth can have it ready for you before you are off on your travels again."

"Is it true, girl?" Lady Rector asked immediately, dropping all affect of boredom, as well as her previous term of address of "Miss DeLisle" as she questioned Elizabeth. "Can you do it? There's a pound note in it for you if you can. It is luck indeed, Isabel, if I can have that hat. For I did long for it so. It is a chip straw," she said to Elizabeth, "with a few blue feathers and a nosegay at the side. And a wide blue ribbon to support the whole. I'll pay for the materials as well, and if you are half so good as Isabel claims, I'll be well satisfied. And if she is not," the lady went on to the general company, "it is only money. And if it does not come out right, my maid will be glad of a new bonnet to impress the staff with. As she is a dream with a pressing iron," she confided to Mrs. Henrick, "it will be well worth the price, however it turns out."

Mrs. Woods was stunned, and sat with her mouth open as Elizabeth rose and stood to face the others. Her face was white save for two high spots of color upon her cheeks. Her topaz eyes flashed brighter than the sunlight on the tea left unfinished in her cup.

"I am afraid not, Lady Rector," she said clearly. "For there wouldn't be time to do the creation justice. I shall be leaving Lyonshall shortly and I would not want to get your hopes up by taking the commission. A pound note is very generous, I'm sure," she added, curtsying as low as she would to a Queen, which Lady Rector noted and stiffened in affront at, "but I shall have to write it off as a loss. If, however, you are ever in Tuxford, we should be glad of your custom. If you will excuse me, ladies," she said while she still had the control to keep her voice steady, "it has been delightful, but I do have letters to write. So sorry to disappoint you, Lady Rector. Good afternoon."

As Elizabeth left, so blind with grief and rage that she achieved the door only by instinct, she could hear Lady Rector announce, "Well! I must say, Isabel, I knew the countryside was primitive in many ways, and one must make do, but to have me to tea with a milliner! And when I tried, really tried to make the best of it and offer the chit a few shillings, to be so cruelly distained! Even Madame Dupont, on her highest ropes, is not so high in the instep, and would never think of taking tea with me."

"I should think she would kill for the privilege," Lady Isabel's soothing voice went on as she tried to smooth her friend's feathers, and Elizabeth closed the door behind her.

Elizabeth stood in the hallway and drew in deep breaths. It will not do, it will not do, she told herself severely, to rush through the house in tears. As she sought to contain herself, the butler appeared at her side.

"Is anything the matter, miss?" he inquired with concern.

"No, nothing. It will pass," she said, turning her face from him so that he could not see her glittering, swimmming, tear-filled eyes.

"Might I suggest the library, miss?" the butler said after a moment, watching her closely. "For there is never anyone there at this time of day. It is a pleasant spot to relax in, miss," he urged, beginning to walk toward the library, as Elizabeth followed, "and I shall see that you are not disturbed, Miss DeLisle," he said softly.

When he had closed the door behind her, Elizabeth finally let the tears fall. But only for a moment. After a few minutes of ragged weeping, she sat up and dashed her handkerchief across her eyes.

One more tear, you silly chit, she threatened herself, and I am done with you. If they have embarrassed you, she thought angrily, it was no more than deserved. For they had not, after all, lied about her condition. Nor had they invented tales about her behavior. They had only spoken the truth. And if, she cautioned herself, you yourself had forgotten that truth here among the idle and the wealthy, then you are the only one to embarrass yourself, the only one to have illusions shattered. So she sat up rigidly and gazed out of the long lettered French doors, unseeing, as she dared herself to drop one more tear over the matter, and refused to think, here and now, about its implications.

"Now what sort of trouble have you gotten yourself into?" the Earl asked, echoing her own thoughts as he entered the library.

"No trouble," Elizabeth replied stiffly. "It is just that I am unaccustomed to tea parties." All she could see as she kept her eyes downcast was the silver head of his walking stick as he stood beside her chair.

"And unaccustomed to incivility, insult, and cruelty as well," he said.

She turned her face toward him and was glad that she had not seen him as he came in, for his lips were pressed into a tight line, and his face was hard.

"I know the whole," he said, settling lightly on the arm of the chair she had flung herself into. "What Mrs. Woods did not tell me, Weathering did."

"I am sorry if Mrs. Woods found being forced into company with a mere shopgirl, a milliner, to be degrading," Elizabeth said defiantly.

"It was the 'two-faced witch' and 'that stick of an old tart' that she complained of, actually," the Earl said, his voice lightening. "I did not hear any mention of shopgirls. The only reference to you was couched in terms of 'that poor dear child' and 'the dear young lady.' She parted from Isabel shortly after you did, with an astonished vicar's wife and Mrs. Henrick in tow. And not silently, either, from what I hear. She did say that she had a few choice words for her hostess as she exited. Then she turned the house upside down searching for you, but Weathering was vigilant. He was also quick to guide her to me," the Earl said ruefully, "and she let me know in no uncertain terms what she thought of my 'two fine London ladies.' I shall have to swallow a great many of her husband's evil possets till I am in that woman's good graces again. And if it troubles you, whatever the vicar's wife thought, she is certain to unthink, being wise enough to know to whom her husband owes his living. And Mrs. Henrick knows well what society she will be left to after the dear 'ladies' depart this vicinity. Mrs. Woods made it clear that 'Emma will come round, and Mary too, if she knows what's good for her.' So come, Elizabeth, the only harm that's been done is to the name of good manners, and Isabel's spite should not sink you so low.''

"She only spoke the truth. It was not a secret,'' Elizabeth said staunchly, wondering for the first time who it was that had told Isabel the truth of her occupation.

"No, no secret,'' he agreed, "but neither is it common gossip. And do not look at me like that, Elizabeth. Your eyes speak volumes. It was not I. More likely it was Anthony that told Harry, Bev, and everyone else. Not that it matters. For it doesn't. Yes, yes,'' he said, now rising, "you think it shameful. And think that everyone in society would as well. Some would, but the majority would know that it is far wiser to work at a trade and survive than die in a socially correct manner as a perfect, idle, starving lady.

"Lady Rector is a rare old piece of goods. I wonder where Isabel got her direction. She is a practiced harpy, and there's not a man or woman of sense in the ton who will credit half a word she utters. Had I known she was coming, I would have canceled the whole,'' he mused.

"It has gone on quite long enough,'' he said suddenly. "I would stay and convince you of the foolishness of this morning's matter, but I am about to end all the nonsense. My man of business has come. I wrote to him some days ago. Yes,'' he said, as she stared up at him, "it is almost over. I have made a decision. I shall closet myself with him this very afternoon, and then I think we can all breathe easier.

"Bear up, it will only be for a little while longer,'' he said, looking fully at her. Before she could ask a question, he spoke briskly. "Now, I suggest you leave here, for if you

crouch in the library all afternoon, Isabel will have achieved
all she set out to do. I did not think you so tame a creature,
my dear.''

He held out his arm and Elizabeth rose and placed her hand
upon it.

''Quite so,'' she said, holding her head high as she went
from the library with him.

''Very good,'' he bent to breathe into her ear. ''Now, do
smile, or Weathering will have my head.''

Elizabeth did not have to face Lady Isabel that afternoon.
She did not know if the Earl had spoken with her, but Lady
Isabel decided to have a light luncheon with Owen in her
rooms. Anthony was out riding alone, and the Earl, his
man-at-law, and Lord Beverly had gone together to the Earl's
study. Finding herself alone, Elizabeth selected a promising
book from the library and settled herself at a bright window
seat in the same small salon where she had been so roundly
insulted in the morning. She felt that by revisiting it she
would show the world that the whole incident was of no
import to her. And in truth she did not ponder it. But she read
little of the book before her, she was so busily thinking, not
of the morning's events, but of her future. Most especially of
what her future would be when the Earl at last had set his
decision down upon paper.

Anthony, Richard, or Owen? she wondered. Which would
make the better heir? And then, omnipresent, the thought
came to her that, to herself alone, it mattered little now which
he chose, despite all of Uncle's hopes. She only wondered
whether she would ever set eyes upon him again once she left
his home. Perhaps, she thought, growing drowsy in the sunlight,
he would stop off in Tuxford one day to see how his cousin
did. Perhaps if Anthony was named heir, he would have him
to Lyonshall again to go over accounts, and Elizabeth could
come along for the journey. Perhaps, she thought at last,
half-conscious from her lack of sleep, he would want to kiss
her again. Just once again, she thought, laying her book
down and her forehead against the cool windowpane.

''How lovely,'' Lord Kingston said.

Elizabeth started up with such force that the book slid to the floor. She reached for it, but Lord Kingston retrieved it first, and she found herself looking up into his intent blue gaze. He held the book, and did not offer it to her outstretched hand.

"Your pardon for awakening you," he said quietly, "but you looked so very lovely, like some sleeping dryad surprised in the wood."

"Dryads don't read much, I think," Elizabeth said crossly, "and there's not a tree in sight."

"Why do you always attempt to take the wind from my sails?" he asked seriously.

Elizabeth saw the frown which only slightly marred his smooth even features and watched the late light play upon his fair hair. He was a tall, straight, well-looking man, and now that he had left off wearing his black sling, claiming that only the damp troubled his wound these days, he looked a picture-perfect man of fashion. She wondered again why she remained so impervious to his gallantries.

"I suppose," she answered just as seriously, being still too dazed with waking to take care with her words, "because everything you say to me seems so rehearsed. And quite the same as the things you say to Lady Isabel. And whenever I do say a thing you don't expect, you seem displeased."

"How am I to communicate with you, Elizabeth?" he asked plaintively, sitting down on the seat beside her. "My usual manner you distrust. I have asked Tony about you time out of mind, but he doesn't understand your attitude either."

Elizabeth stood up abruptly. "It doesn't matter, really," she said, "for soon we shall both be on our separate ways."

He reached out and grasped her by the wrist and said earnestly, "But it does matter to me, Elizabeth. Very much."

Elizabeth did not wish to be rude enough to pull free from him, so she only said simply, "Lady Isabel is far more conversant with the art of light flirtation. I wonder that you do not concentrate on her, for you two are of the same world. I am only a shopgirl from the provinces, Lord Kingston, and you shouldn't wonder at my gaucheries."

"But I do," he said, rising, and still holding her fast by

the wrist. "And I know Lady Isabel of old. She is like all the others of her ilk. It is your freshness, your naturalness, which enchants me."

Elizabeth grew alarmed at his insistence and reached out for the book he held, so that she might make a retreat. But he only dropped the book and then grasped her by both hands.

He gazed down at her, and then, curiously, looked quickly at the clock upon the mantel. Seeing her puzzled expression, he said hurriedly, "There is time for us. Someone always comes to interrupt our conferences, but I see that this once I have time to speak my heart. Elizabeth, you delight me. I think you have been so dazzled by Morgan that you have not given me a chance. But Morgan, you see, can feel nothing toward you. His late wife destroyed all faith in women for him. I can see that a female might find him intriguing, but, Elizabeth, there is no hope for you from that quarter. But I am heart-whole, or was, until I met you. It is high time you considered me. But," he said, cocking his head to the side, "it is my words which have always displeased you, isn't it? I think"—he smiled, pulling her toward him—"it is time you judged my actions."

He wrenched her to him and held her close. And lowered his head and kissed her gently before she knew what he was about. His lips were cool and undemanding, but still she fought free of his embrace.

"Lord Kingston," she gasped, trying to pull her arms away, "you go too far. I am not interested in lovemaking. You can only anger me this way. Please let me free."

He stood for a moment, considering her. Then his eyes turned to the clock once more.

"On the contrary," he said, smiling. "I think it is only that I have not gone far enough."

This time she was prepared for his onslaught and dragged her hands together so that when she was pulled close they at least acted as a buffer between their bodies. This time, however, he was adamant, his mouth was open and hot upon her lips. This time he kissed her savagely. While she struggled he quickly transferred both her fists to one large hand, so that he could grasp at her breast with his other.

Elizabeth felt no responsive delight in his kiss, and his gripping hand at her breast caused no thrill to her senses such as the Earl's gentle touch had aroused. She felt only suffocating panic and disgust.

He had forced his tongue against her gritted teeth, when she suddenly remembered the advice Anthony had given her in jest long ago. She relaxed a moment and he took heart from her surrender. As he groaned against her mouth and gripped her closer, she eased one slippered foot behind his highly polished boot. Feeling her slight movement, he chuckled low in his throat and thrust one leg between hers as he strove to lower her to the chaise. Then she gave him a sudden strong shove which sent him backward, stumbling over her impeding foot. He went reeling back, releasing her as he attempted to regain his balance.

She stood appalled, backing away from him. He recovered himself and stood upright, only looking at her. He did not appear to be a man driven by passion. Though his cravat was askew, he did not breathe hard, nor did his cool light blue eyes register anything but calculation.

Elizabeth neither slapped him nor burst into tears. Rather she wiped her mouth savagely with the back of her hand and cried in ringing tones, "That was revolting! If that is how you thought to win me over, I think London females must be wanting wits! I find you quite revolting! A popinjay, a fool! Pray leave me and never, never speak to me again!"

But he made no answer. He only looked beyond her to the doorway of the room; then he shrugged. "What could I do?" he said simply. "I misread the situation and went a bit too far."

Elizabeth wheeled around to see that the Earl and Anthony stood within the room, goggling at her.

"A bit too far?" Elizabeth cried in disbelief.

Anthony was the first to step forward. His fists were clenched and he looked from Elizabeth to his friend in troubled confusion.

"Come, Tony," Lord Kingston said, straightening his cuffs. "You are a man now. Your lovely cousin went to my head. It was only a bit of light lovemaking that got out of hand. I don't often lose control, and for that I do apologize, but she does not know the strength of her own charms. I understand your anger, to be sure. But I am a gentleman. If it will satisfy you, I will offer for her. Although," he went on calmly, "in London a mere kiss would not be considered such a shocking disaster. Still, I am your friend. And Elizabeth is your cousin, and lovely. I could do a great deal worse. And so could she. For with all her protestations, which I do understand, my dear," he said placatingly to Elizabeth, as though they shared a great secret, "it seemed to me that she was enjoying it well enough till I forgot her youth and inexperience," he went on with a lifted brow that robbed his words of meaning.

"But then," he sighed, "I was ever self-congratulatory, eh, Morgan?"

The Earl remained quiet, though his face was shuttered and grim, while Anthony stood taut and flushed with anger.

Lord Kingston went on smoothly, "Still, if you won't accept my apology, or my offer, you may wish to call me out. Come, Tony, cry friends, or it will be pistols at dawn, old fellow. Shouldn't you rather have me as a brother than an opponent?"

Anthony glanced to Elizabeth's horrified face and made up his mind.

"Pistols, then," he said tightly, "for I know Elizabeth too well to stomach these lies."

"No," the Earl said coldly, limping into the room. "Not in this house, or upon these grounds. Go to London if you wish to do battle. I shall not countenance it. Harry, we will talk about this later. And, Anthony, Harry is correct only in that such things are not considered so rigidly in the sets he travels with in Town. But he has apologized. And we are none of us tattlemongers. It need go no further. Elizabeth, come tell us, do you think it a bloodletting matter?"

"No," Elizabeth said quickly, thinking that Anthony had never held a pistol in his young life, while Lord Kingston often bragged about his marksmanship, even with one "bad wing," as he called it, at Manton's in London. "But," she said quickly, "I did not . . ." Her words trailed off into silence when she saw the chilled and chilling expression of distaste upon the Earl's face.

"So, then, it is forgotten," he said quickly. "Harry, if you are to pursue a courtship, it will not be in this house. At any rate, there will be no further opportunity here again. Elizabeth," he said, looking hard at her, unmoved by her stricken face and rapid breathing, "I think that there is no further reason for you and Anthony to remain here at Lyonshall. The business at hand is done. No," he added, noting her indrawn breath, "have no fear, this afternoon did not weigh at all. The decision has been made—decided and signed. It would have been past time to do so, no matter what else transpired. All the parties involved will be informed by letter of the outcome. It would be callous to do otherwise. But you two should leave. Tonight, I think."

Elizabeth's thoughts were in turmoil. If she defended herself now, she would only cause Anthony to rush to her defense again. But she wanted desperately for the Earl to know her innocence in the matter.

As though he knew what she was about to say, a slow, sad expression crossed his previously grim features. He looked down at her and almost whispered, "For now, it is best that you go. Believe me."

But Elizabeth could only search his face, and in a last effort to communicate the whole of her feelings, she murmured only one incoherent question: "Is there nothing else?"

At length, quietly and with finality, he spoke. "What else could there be, Elizabeth?"

— 14 —

"It is wrong. And wicked," Lord Beverly stormed as he paced the front hall. He gestured toward Anthony's and Elizabeth's luggage.

"Morgan's been my friend since we were in short coats, but when a chap is wrong, he's wrong. That blasted Kitty," he raged. "It is not right to speak ill of the dead, but she's behind it. Not that she could be, of course, as she's dead. But her memory, you know. Now he wouldn't trust his own mother—if she were alive, that is."

"It doesn't matter, really, Bev," Elizabeth said softly, putting a hand tentatively on his sleeve, "for his lordship did say his business was concluded, and so we must leave at any rate."

"Then why has he left the others to stay on? It's devilish bad business," Lord Beverly brooded. He had run his long fingers through his tousled blond hair so often that he looked quite deranged, and not at all the figure of impeccable splendor he so often was.

Anthony said nothing. Indeed, Elizabeth thought, it was unlike him to remain silent for so long. She would have thought him ready to flow into a full spate of condemnation of the aristocratic classes, and at least have a thing or two to say about the downtrodden. But now that he was, in fact, for the first time in his young life actually downtrodden, he said nothing. He only stood white-faced and hot-eyed as he waited for the coach to come round to the front entrance to pick up their belongings and themselves.

Elizabeth herself had scarcely had time to think about the turn of events. Her night of missed sleep, her encounter with Lady Isabel's spite in the morning, capped by Lord Kingston's assault not a few hours past—all had combined to leave her feeling only bruised in spirit and sadly lost. The thought that the Earl thought her capable of playing up to his friend was the cruelest blow of all. As she had watched the maid pack her belongings, her mind had been blank of all but that single terrible thought.

Now as she watched Lord Beverly pace and cry out at the injustice of it all, she began, for the first time, to think of the reception that awaited her at home. Uncle would never be so unkind as to blame her, and Mother and Aunt would doubtless condole with her about the wickedness of the wide world. But their hopes would be dashed. There was no way that she could envision that Anthony had been designated heir. One did not, after all, expel one's heir presumptive from one's house in the dark of night. Owen, then, or Richard, she thought. But it no longer mattered which of them the Earl had decided upon. Their own cause was lost.

When the footman informed them somberly that the coach had come, and had begun to carry their luggage out, Elizabeth at last awoke from her reverie. "Is he . . . his lordship not seeing us off?" she asked Lord Beverly in a whisper.

The fair young nobleman flushed to his eyebrows. Then he bent his head and kicked at a trunk. "No," he said, as though in shame, "he has appointed me to the task. He is busy with his man of business."

Elizabeth had not expected the others. Lord Kingston had been nowhere in evidence since their afternoon encounter. Perhaps, she thought bitterly, he had feared she would reconsider his offer. She was not surprised at Lady Isabel, nor at Owen's absence, and Cousin Richard was gone from the area. But she was staggered to hear that their host was not there to see them gone.

Not even a good-bye, Elizabeth thought in shock. Then they were truly in disgrace. To leave in the night, to leave upon orders, was insulting enough, but that he had not even bade them farewell was the last crushing blow. But curiously, that knowledge did not sink her further. Instead, a great and white-hot, healthy fury rose in her breast, burning away all the wretched self-condemnation and pity she had been engaging herself with. It was, she thought, bringing up her head, unjust. It was, moreover, uncharitable, unfair, and needless to heap that last glowing coal upon their heads.

"Well," Elizabeth said, so fired with anger that she scarcely knew what she spoke, "so be it. You need not bother, Bev, to make any lengthy farewells to us, nor to stay any longer. We are obviously lepers, and we shall leave the way we came, alone and unattended. Good-bye, Lord Beverly. I don't know if we shall ever meet again, but it has been a pleasure knowing you. Come along, Anthony, it is past time that we left."

"Dash it all, Elizabeth," Lord Beverly cried, seizing her traveling case from her gloved hand. "Do you think me a flat? I swear I deserve better. Much I care what Morgan thinks. You two are my friends, and I shall at least ride as far as the village with you. And if I had my way, it would be the others I was waving farewell to, and well you know it, too. So don't come saucy with me, or I shall . . . I shall ride on the roof of your carriage if you don't let me in."

Even in the midst of all her turbulent emotions, Lord Beverly was able to wring a giggle from Elizabeth.

"Come, then, if you wish," she said at last. "But as I think it only foolish to prolong our good-byes, I cannot see the point to it."

"Much I care," that gentleman muttered darkly, as he escorted his silent friend and his cousin to the waiting carriage, "if you see the point or no. It is what I shall do."

But no sooner had they settled in the carriage, and the footman had closed and latched the door, than Lord Beverly took on a new aspect. He sat up straight and waited for the coachman to crack the whip and start the horses moving. Then he leaned forward with an excitement and enthusiasm that they could see in the flickering carriage-lamp flame was written large upon his face.

"The point is, my friends," he chortled, "that we are not going to Tuxford. Not this night."

Even Anthony came out of his trance at this statement. "What the devil are you saying, Bev? Of course we are going home." Then with some of his more characteristic fervor, he said, "We haven't the funds to go sporting to London. We are not quite of your class, Bev, we are, after all, only a poor milliner and her layabout cousin."

Elizabeth was startled to hear Anthony's new assessment of himself, but before she could refine too much on it, Lord Beverly leaned so far forward his nose was almost touching the belligerent Anthony's.

"Oh, do be quiet, Anthony! Or shall I call you 'Tony,' as your so dear old chum Harry does? At any rate, be quiet. I waited until we were alone. Lyonshall's bristling with ears. I have a plan."

Elizabeth groaned. "Bev, Bev . . ." She half-laughed. "Do let it be. It is over. His lordship himself has said so. Let it be."

"Oh, 'his lordship,' is it?" Bev said mockingly. "When only a few days past you two were smelling all of April and May, and it was all 'Morgan' this and 'Elizabeth' that, and I vow that if it had gone on one more hour it would have been 'Morg' this and 'Liz' that, and the devil knows what else an hour from then."

Elizabeth flushed and sat back abruptly. Anthony turned to look at her with curiosity. She was sure that he had never even noticed the closeness that seemed to have sprung up between his host and his cousin.

"Are you two," Bev said in ringing tones, "going to take this meekly, like the little sheep that graze in Tuxford hills, or are you going to fight back?"

This coherent, almost poetic phrase was so unlike their old friend Bev that both Anthony and Elizabeth sat speechless.

Lord Beverly looked very pleased with himself and let the moment's silent applause for his statement lapse. Then he went on eagerly, "No, I tell you no, and no again. That would be spineless and cowardly. You have to fight back, I say."

"Yes," Anthony said sourly. "What do you propose, Bev? Shall I set fire to Lyonshall, or shall I have Elizabeth creep back to steal a few family treasures? Really, she is right, it is quite clear that Morgan is quit of us. Somehow we have given him a disgust of us, and he wants to see our backs as soon as can be."

Elizabeth, stunned to find Anthony unusually mature and reasonable and Bev almost sensible in his speech, sat back and let the two previously incoherent males of her acquaintance carry the conversation forward.

"Yes, but why?" Bev asked slyly. "Because there have been all sorts of smoky doings to cast you in the shade. Secret notes, and gossip, and such. And that rogue Kingston making up to Elizabeth like she was a cyprian, when I suspect he's got no more interest in her that way than he would in his horse, begging your pardon, Elizabeth," he said belatedly.

"Certainly," Elizabeth said, feeling both vindicated and vexed by his appraisal of Lord Kingston's interest in her.

"Not," Bev said hurriedly, "that you're not a smasher, not that I have any designs in that way either, of course, but not because you're unattractive, you understand."

"I do understand," Elizabeth said kindly, wishing to rescue him from the net he was weaving about himself.

"Then," he went on, "I think it would be fainthearted, and craven, yes, craven," he cried as Anthony tensed, "to just go creeping back to Tuxford without attempting to at least clear your names."

"And how," Anthony asked wearily, "are we to do that? For I shall not come crawling like some sort of serf, to beg his high lordship to pardon me for my sins."

"Nor I," Elizabeth said softly, thinking of the terrible look in the Earl's eye when they had last met, and knowing that not for all the profit in the world, nor for Uncle, nor for Anthony, nor especially for herself, would she face such a look again.

"No, no," Bev said impatiently, "that's not what I had in mind at all. Can't do a thing without proof. And I shall try to get at that proof, indeed I shall. But what to do with it if you two are back home and miles from the spot? I want you both to stay on.

"I will not have allies, and who am I to trust at Lyonshall? I don't like that Cousin Richard above half, he's so cat-footed and sneaking, there's no telling what he's up to. And Owen? He'd sell his soul for a pudding. And Isabel? The lady has got no warm feeling for you, Elizabeth. And as for Kingston, I know he's a bad sort, only I can't puzzle out what he's got to gain. He ain't even a relative of yours, for which you should thank your lucky stars, for you've got a right bad lot as it is to call kin. No, I need you," he concluded. "You must stay on."

"Where are we to stay?" Anthony asked, his interest growing, but his newfound reasonableness taking the upper hand. "Hidden in the stables?"

"Really, Anthony," Lord Beverly answered, at last leaning back, "there is a perfectly good hostelry in town. It is rather old, of course, and had fallen on hard times. But new owners came last year and spruced it up a bit. You'll be tolerably comfortable there. Why, you know it already, it's the Rose and the Bear. The landlord's a good sort of chap and a few coins will buy his silence. You two register as Mr. and Miss Smythe or Jones, or whatever, and none will be the wiser. In that way, as soon as I get wind of something, you can come running. Your family don't expect you back at any time in particular, do they?"

While Anthony admitted that was true, Elizabeth did rapid calculations in her head. "Bev," she said sadly, "even if we were to agree to this scheme, we could not stay above a few days."

As Lord Beverly began to protest that the matter would not take above a few days, she went on, "And we would not stay upon your charity."

"No, indeed," Anthony echoed.

"And," Elizabeth said, oddly unwilling to defeat their friend's scheme, but impelled by her own straight thinking to attempt to do so, "really, Bev, if we do have enemies who have sullied our names, what can you hope to discover, after all? The heir has been named, that is done. And I doubt any evidence of malice would deter his lordship from his course. He has evicted us. He believes the worst of us, and there is little to dissuade him. And even if you do, what will it profit us?''

Lord Beverly stood up in indignation. Only to sit down again promptly, as he had struck his head upon the ceiling of the carriage.

"Gain?" he gasped when he was able. "Why, what is more to a man than his good name?"

As the carriage slowed to a stop in front of the Rose and the Bear, all the occupants were silently pondering the irrefutable truth Lord Beverly had spoken.

The inn was a comfortable one, Elizabeth noted as the posting boy rushed to gather up her luggage. It was a long, low building, half-timbered and worn with age. But new carpets and curtains gave it a friendly appearance, and the sparkling cleanliness of the place was pleasing. A great fire roared in the grate in the common room and Elizabeth sank gratefully into an inviting overly padded chair. The events of the past day were beginning to tell upon her, and as Anthony and Lord Beverly held conference with the innkeeper, she could no longer know if they were doing the correct thing. She only yearned for a wide, soft bed and hours of uninterrupted oblivion.

She had only just closed her weary eyes when the innkeeper's wife came bustling up to her. Elizabeth sat up to see a very good-looking, softly pretty blond female of middle years peering down at her anxiously.

"Oh, you're that tired, then?" the woman said. "Then it's only like the gentlemen to leave you sitting here alone, cold and lonely. Come along, Miss Smythe, and I'll have you tucked up into the sweetest bed, as soon as you can stare. Now, now, the shot's been paid, and all's set. I'll just take you along to your room, it's the finest one we have, and get you to bed. Don't bother to seek them out," she said as she led the dazed Elizabeth up the dark and winding stair. "I'll tell the gentlemen where you've gone."

Elizabeth walked obediently, tugged along by the woman, to the highest regions of the house. She soon found herself within a charming room done up in shades of rose and white.

But the first thing to catch her eye was the huge canopied bed that dominated the room.

"Yes, it is lovely, isn't it?" the woman said comfortably. "It cost the world, and Ferdie wondered at the expense of it, but I say, and have always said, that a bed's the most important part of a house, and so it is. For you take care of the spirits and the horses, I said," the woman went on, deftly stripping Elizabeth's pelisse from her and assisting her to undress, "and leave the beds to me. Well, I won't tell a young miss what he said to that, but if you come back in a few years, I will, it was that clever. Now, then, dear," she said, helping Elizabeth into her night shift, "off to bed with not a care. For I know all, and all is safe with me. If you need aught before morning, give out a call for 'Rose'—that is me. 'Ferdie' is the 'Bear,' you see," she sang from the door, after she had led Elizabeth to the bed and blown out all but one candle. "And we both welcome you. Now to sleep."

Elizabeth, smiling gently in the dark, felt, just before Rose's expensive bed called her far from the room and her troubles, that all might not be so dark after all. But that she would have to wait for morning to see clearly.

Lord Beverly arrived at Lyonshall as the clock was striking the hour of a new day. He gave his cloak to a sleepy-eyed footman and made his way, with exaggerated stealth, to the Earl's study. The room was dark, save for a few candles burning and the glow of the fire in the grate. Lord Beverly stole into the room and closed the door quietly behind him. But even that small sound alerted the occupant in the room. He did not rise from his chair, nor turn around, but the Earl's weary voice only said quietly, 'It is done, then?"

"Yes," Lord Beverly said, walking to the desk and finding a decanter and pouring himself an unusually large libation. "Done. And a deucedly bad business it was. But I did just as I ought. Where's Tompkins?"

"In his room. Sleeping the sleep of the just. He's been hard at it all night. Papers, Bev, papers stacked high." The Earl sighed, accepting the glass his friend poured for him.

"Richard's come back, poor lad," the Earl said into the

stillness of the room, as Lord Beverly posed brooding into the fireplace, with one booted foot upon the fender.

"That's cheery news," Lord Beverly said sourly.

"You're too hard on him, Bev, he's only young."

"We'll have two more visitors from London tomorrow evening," the Earl said after a time. "Sooner, if they catch the early stage. Then we may be done with the whole of it."

His friend only grunted and drained his glass.

They stayed in silence, listening to the logs tick and sing in the fire, till the Earl said at last, dropping the words into the quiet like stones, "Did she weep, Bev?"

"Not her," Lord Beverly said proudly. "Not a tear. Just held her head high and marched out. Just like a man."

"Not quite," the Earl said softly. " I thank you, Bev. It cannot have been pleasant for you."

"No?" Lord Beverly said in anger, whirling about to point his glass at his friend. "How can you say that? I dearly love to throw a young defenseless female and a green lad out into the streets in the middle of the darkest night. Do call upon me again when you have need, your lordship."

"Come, come," the Earl said wearily, groping for his walking stick. "In another moment you will have filled the skies with sleet and invented a whirling north wind to give the tale more substance. It was a damnable thing, as it was, but I had no choice, Bev. Even you saw that."

"Oh, aye," his friend said quietly, "that's true enough, but it don't mean I had to enjoy it."

"We had to do it, I saw no other course," the Earl said, standing. His friend saw the stark sorrow in his face, such as he had not seen in years. He made a bleak gesture of denial.

"No, Morgan, you've the right of it. Don't blame yourself further. We had to do it, for it couldn't go on, you and Tompkins were right. It's only that I didn't like it above half."

"Only pray we were right, Bev, and that there were no wrongs done that we cannot right in time."

They walked to the stairs together, and Lord Beverly waited as his friend made his laborious way up them.

As they reached the door to the Earl's rooms, he paused

and turned to Lord Beverly. "She did not weep, you say?" he asked distractedly, passing a hand over his eyes. "I do not know that I would not have felt better if she had."

His friend laid a gentle hand upon the Earl's shoulder. "M'father used to say, 'Sometimes you've got to do the worst in order to get the best.' But then," he mused, laying his head to one side, "I recall he always used to say that before I got a thrashing."

The Earl stood tall and straight, and clasped his stick hard in his hand. He looked at his friend and essayed a grim smile. "A great deal I have done in my life, I would give much to have undone. Tonight's work must stand large amongst those doings. But yet, there are some things I must have done right. You are my friend, after all."

Lord Beverly only shook his head and said softly, "Blast it, Morgan, that makes me feel worse than ever."

They bade each other good night, and Lord Beverly walked brooding to his room. As his door closed, another door did the same, but more slowly and with stealth.

The watcher sighed and turned back from the door. Then a glass of ruby claret was raised in salute.

"Done!" The watcher spoke softly on a note that could not contain its relief and joy.

"And well done!" another voice whispered with satisfaction.

— 15 —

The morning brought Elizabeth bright sunshine, a mild breeze, and hot chocolate in bed, but no wise counsel. In fact, as she dressed, she could no longer see the point to their remaining in this charming inn near Lyonshall without either her family's or the Earl's knowledge. Lord knows, she thought, catching a last glance at herself in the mirror before running lightly down the stairs, how I was mad enough to see reason in the plan last night. Bev must have bewitched me with his words. It is certain, she decided as she went to join Anthony in their private parlor, that we must soon be gone.

Anthony was in high good spirits as he finished off the last of his breakfast of beefsteak and ale. The night had brought him even greater enthusiasm for his friend's proposal. As Elizabeth seated herself, he told her of his eagerness to get started. When he began to go on about how it might not be a bad idea for him to aid Bev by doing a bit of lurking in the woods to see what he could spy out, Elizabeth laid her toast down firmly upon her plate.

"Anthony," she said severely, "I agreed to the scheme, which seems more cork-brained by the moment, only because Bev said he only wanted us to wait here, upon his summons. I will not have you going off on your own. Only think," she said, imploring him, "how dreadfully it will look if the Earl finds us still upon his premises after he directly ordered us home. We shall look like pensioners, like poor groveling creatures. There is nothing worse than a beggar upon one's doorstep, and how else is he to think of us if we are discovered?

No," she said, watching his face fall as her words registered, "it may be tedious, but we shall wait upon Bev. And if, as I suspect, he makes no progress soon, I suggest we part friends, but that we do part from him, and this place. I cannot bear any further insult, Anthony, I cannot!" she concluded, surprising even herself at the force of her words.

Anthony was instantly remorseful. He patted her hand awkwardly and cursed himself for a lout. If nothing more transpired from their visit than had already, Elizabeth thought as she heard him trying to comfort her, it would be enough, this newfound maturity. Doubtless it came from his close association with the various adult males at Lyonshall, and it yet clung to her cousin. For in the past he would have sulked if his project was balked, and blamed her for his incarceration in the Rose and the Bear. Now he sighed and then said stoutly, "You are quite right, Elizabeth. For you were the one to bear the brunt of it all, even though I was the candidate for heir. We shall wait for Bev, then, I promise."

The afternoon came and then wore on without word from their friend. Elizabeth occupied herself with an attempt at reading, and Anthony with popping back and forth from his chair to the window in expectation of seeing his friend arrive with news. Every farmer, every townsperson, every servant that arrived at the door to the inn was watched closely by Anthony from behind a curtain. It was a sweet August day, and Elizabeth would have dearly loved to throw off her affect of calm, resigned patience and go walking forth along the country lanes. But if she were to go, so would Anthony. And if she were to show restlessness, she would only agitate him further.

It was only after Anthony had delivered himself of an even dozen "Where the devil can he be's" that the anticipated arrival came. Lord Beverly, looking most dashing, Anthony cried out, upon a slapping gray, rode up to the courtyard. A few moments later, he was in the parlor with them, his face all smiles and gladness.

"Things are all in train," he shouted, clapping Anthony upon the back. "Even better than we had hoped. Young Anthony," he chortled, beaming like the late-afternoon sun

above them, "get yourself dressed to a shade. For we are
going to have a talk with Morgan."

Elizabeth and Anthony stayed frozen in their places. Of all
the expectations they had harbored, this one was not amongst
them.

"I shall not go to beg my case," Anthony said straightly.

"No need, no need," Lord Beverly replied joyously. "It
has all come out. We only need, that is to say, *I* only need
you to be there at the moment of truth. Then it will not be
you who asks the pardon, I assure you."

Elizabeth stood slowly and said with wonder, "We never
expected such a turnabout. How did you achieve this, Bev?"

"No time for that now," Lord Beverly said quickly. "Only
needs must go. There'll be time later to talk it all out, I
promise you."

"Very well," Elizabeth said, running her hands over her
hair to make sure it was still neat, though how she could have
disordered it by merely sitting and waiting all afternoon, she
did not know. "Anthony looks well as he is, and I think I
need only my shawl and we can go."

Lord Beverly paused, and his face reddened slightly. He
spoke, but did not lift his eyes to Elizabeth. "Ah, no, my
dear," he said awkwardly. "Morgan wants to see Anthony,
not you."

Elizabeth felt the color drain from her face. Of all the
indignity she had yet been exposed to, she thought, this
surely was the worst.

"I shan't go without Elizabeth," Anthony said immediately.

"Look here," Lord Beverly said. "It isn't the end of the
world. Morgan wants you at Lyonshall, Anthony, right now,
and he don't want Elizabeth there. I'll wager he has a good
and tight reason, too. No need for you to poker up. All will
be made clear in time," he said, his voice fading at the
obstinacy he saw on Anthony's face.

"Anthony," Elizabeth said softly, coming up to him and
laying a hand upon his sleeve, "Bev is right. I'm not needed.
Perhaps it is to protect me from insult that Morgan does not
wish to see me. I fear he is sadly disappointed in me. No,"
she went on, staying his rebuttal, "I know you feel I have

been wronged, but at least I can receive no further wrong here. If there is to be an heir to Lyonshall, and if you are he, my presence will make little difference. There was a time," she said carefully, "when I thought Morgan liked me very well, and, I confess, I was glad of it. But that in itself may be why he does not wish to see me, so as not to give me any false expectations. Although, to be truthful, I never did think of anything to our friendship beyond friendship. Oh, dear, I fear I am beginning to sound like Bev now, in one of his flights. Go, Anthony. Even if you are not named heir, clear up the matter. Little though you may like it, the Earl is a powerful man. You are kin, and Uncle could do with all the help he can get. Do not cast away this chance out of gallantry, especially when I assure you there is no need for it."

Anthony listened and then nodded to Lord Beverly. "Then I shall come, but I do not like it."

"No more do I," Lord Beverly muttered, his usually pale face ruddy with suppressed emotion. "Listen, Elizabeth, he only said he did not want you today. It may all change tomorrow. Wait here, then, till we return or send a summons. All will be right, I promise."

Then he led her cousin outside. He tossed the innkeeper a few coins, and a mount was led out for Anthony. Elizabeth watched through the window as they both rode away.

When they had gone, and even the echo of their horses' hoofbeats had faded, Elizabeth at last sank down into her chair again. She had the maddest impulse to simply pack and leave for home, and send them all to the devil. But after a few moments she began to think more clearly. The Earl detested her; that was one fact. Anthony might yet again be in his good graces; that was another. But whatever transpired, she now swore, she would never, never enter Lyonshall again. It was a matter of pride and of honor. She would remain here at the inn, and whatever the outcome, the only destination that would lead her from this pleasant parlor would be the road homeward.

She was very glad of her decision, and did not know why such clear thinking should make her feel so very much like weeping. Then she stood up with determination. She badly needed a good long walk to clear her head, she decided, and so went to the door, flung it open with unnecessary force, and from there marched to the door of the inn.

"And where are you off to, Miss Smythe?" Rose cried, bustling in from the taproom.

"I am in need of a stroll, some exercise to blow the cobwebs from my mind," Elizabeth explained as she placed her hand upon the door.

"Oh, no, never that," Rose said with determination, placing her hands upon her hips. "I do not wish to disagree with a guest, and a lady, but I have my express orders from your brother and from that lovely young lord. Last night they told me that you must not leave, nor must anyone discover your presence here. And as I took good coin of the realm from them upon that head, I cannot allow you to go out."

Elizabeth tried over and again to explain the change in circumstance to the obdurate landlady, but she was adamant. She steered Elizabeth back to her parlor, and listened to all her explanations, and sighing, said, "This all may be well and true. But I cannot budge. I have given my word, you see. Please, Miss Smythe, I've a business to tend to, but if you insist, I shall have to sit with you like a nanny. For I gave my pledge. But if you give me yours that you will not stir from here, I can go back to my custom and help poor dear Ferdie with earning our livelihood."

Defeated and embarrassed, Elizabeth reluctantly agreed. When her gentle and misguided jailer had left, Elizabeth sat again and prepared to wait for what she was sure would be creeping, interminable hours. So it was that she was startled when Rose came back only few moments later, bearing a note in her hands.

"You are called 'Elizabeth,' Miss Smythe?" Rose asked slowly, scrutinizing the note she held.

"Oh, yes," Elizabeth cried gladly.

"A boy brought this for you, then, for we haven't another Elizabeth hereabouts."

Elizabeth took the note eagerly and quickly read the few lines scrawled upon it in a heavy, dark, masculine hand.

"Elizabeth," it read, "Please come to Lyonshall at once,

alone. But come round the back way. I shall meet you in the Shakespearean garden and explain all.''

It bore no signature, but it needed none. Such an imperious summons to the lost Simon's refuge could have come from only one person. The urgency of the message drove all of Elizabeth's vows never again to set foot at Lyonshall from her mind. He needed her, that was clear. And, she thought as she absently handed the note to Rose, he had said "please."

"I must go, you see," she explained rapidly. "There is proof enough."

"I dunno," Rose said thoughtfully. "It isn't signed, you see."

"Perhaps there wasn't time. Oh, I must go at once," Elizabeth cried as she went toward the door.

"Aye," Rose said slowly, "but still you cannot walk there. Not in your thin slippers. It would take until dark. And I don't fancy sending you off alone. I'll have Ferdie get out the gig, and we'll have you driven there. I do suspect," she said, seeing her guest's great hurry to go, "that you don't even know the back way to Lyonshall. It's for servants and deliveries, and not for the Quality."

It seemed an eternity till the gig was brought round, and Elizabeth could only thank her benefactor briefly, she was in such a flurry of impatience. As they drove off she said not a word to the stableboy who held the reins, she was so occupied with mentally urging the horse along to a faster pace.

Rose had been right, she did not recognize the narrow road that led round the back of Lyonshall. There was little traffic here; only one farm cart was seen trundling by, and one large closed coach by the roadside, which must have lost its way, for the horses were feeding idly and the occupants could not be seen. It was a quiet country lane else, protected from the setting sun by the interlaced boughs of the towering trees that stood on each side of it.

The boy slowed the gig. "We're almost there, miss," he said respectfully.

All Elizabeth could see was a wood filled by enormous trees, and a narrow path that led between them. As the boy began to turn the horse to enter the path, Elizabeth said quickly, "No. Stop here, I will walk the rest of the way."

Clearly torn between what he perceived to be the duty owed to a young woman of Quality, and that same female's orders, the boy halted the gig. As a sop to his conscience, however, after he helped Elizabeth down and turned his horse to go, he pointed toward the path with one mud-streaked finger. "If you foller that there," he volunteered, "a long ways, never stepping off, although it curves like a snake, you'll be at the end of the wood. Then there's the grassy part, and then the house itself. Do be careful, miss," he called back over his shoulder, "for you can turn an ankle quick as a snap on them stones, if you ain't careful."

Then, feeling that his advice was as good an amulet as any against Rose's possible wrath, he tipped his battered straw hat and departed.

The path was difficult to travel in her thin slippers, Elizabeth realized, but nevertheless she stepped lightly and quickly in her impatience to arrive at her destination. There were times during that long walk up the back drive when her eyes would dart to the cool woods at the side of her path, and she would long to make her way through the soft bracken rather than the stony path. But she remembered the stableboy's warning, and kept to the path no matter how her feet stung. Due to the twisting nature of the path, when she turned to see how far she had traveled, she could no longer see where she had entered the grounds, and when she looked ahead, she could not see the outline of Lyonshall. But she went on as rapidly as she could, for she could see the sun growing redder as it began to sink beyond the tops of the ancient trees.

A sudden turn in the path gave her the view of Lyonshall at last. She could see where the trees ended abruptly and the long sloping lawns commenced. Narrowing her eyes against the setting sun, she could pick out in the distance the great willow that stood at the foot of Simon's garden. Then she realized that it did not lie directly in back of the house, as she had thought, but rather off to the right side of it.

As her present path would lead her only directly to the back entrance of Lyonshall, she noted with relief that she could at last take a transverse route over the softer ground of the wood and in that manner achieve her goal even more quickly.

Elizabeth entered the blessed shade of the wood and stepped over the cool mossy earth with alacrity. She was fretting about her ruined slippers to prevent herself from worrying about her approaching interview with the Earl, when she noted a tall figure, backlighted by the brilliant sunset, coming toward her rapidly. For one moment she thought that it was he, but a breath later she remembered that he was incapable of such a fluid stride. And though the sunlight created a blazing halo about the figure's head, she realized that no light could transform deep auburn hair to such a glittering light yellow shade.

She stood still then, watching the figure approach. The moment's pause helped her to get both her fluttering breath and heart back to their normal states. As she waited, she realized that this cool copse was the last clearing in the wood. Only a few steps farther and the forest ended, and then only a fair easy walk up the manicured lawn would bring her to the garden.

When the figure was still too far for her to see the face properly, but close enough to speak to, she called out, "Bev! What has happened? Why was such a hasty summons sent? For I came running, as you see, as fast as I could."

"And I am sorry that you did, for it is a wretched business for me, Elizabeth," Lord Kingston said as his long strides brought him to her.

For that moment, Elizabeth's speech failed her, and she could only gaze up at Lord Kingston. Then she blurted, "It was you? You sent me the note?"

"No," he explained carefully in such a strange tone that she stepped back a pace, "I did not. Morgan did, to be sure. But as you may have noted, he often fails in his resolve. And when he decided that he could not, after all, face you again, he deputized me to his purpose. Blast!" Lord Kingston said savagely. "It is not an easy thing to be Morgan's house guest. First he has Bev send you away, then he calls upon me to depress you further. If the bonds of friendship between us

were not so strong, I would have denied him. But as it is
. . ." He shrugged.

"Bev failed?" Elizabeth asked in confusion.

"How could he else?" Lord Kingston sighed. "For once
Morgan gets hold of an idea, he is intractable. When he
discovered you were still in the vicinity, he was furious. He
took his rage out upon Bev first, then poor Tony. He sent
for you, I suspect, to do similarly. But at the last, he decided
he could not even look upon you again. 'Do the business for
me, Harry,' he said, and stalked away. I wanted to spare you
the pain of actually coming to the garden to get your congé,
so I set out to intercept you. I did not know that you would
arrive so soon. I planned to meet you at the gates."

"Oh," Elizabeth said, for she could think of no other
reply. She had not known him as well as she had thought, but
as she stood and tried to absorb all she had been told, still she
could not envision the Earl so cruel, nor so lacking in spirit as
to send another man to do his battles. But then, she
remembered, he had told Lord Beverly to see them from
Lyonshall.

"Then," Elizabeth said suddenly, avoiding Lord Kingston's
eye, "I shall leave. There is no need to explain further, I
understand."

She turned to go, but he stepped in front of her and
blocked her way. "The least I can do," he said softly, "is to
accompany you back to the inn. I have a carriage waiting at
the gate, for it was there that I expected to meet you. Come, I
will walk with you."

He offered her his arm, but Elizabeth shook her head.
"No," she said resolutely, "I need no further assistance. In
fact, I should rather walk, for in that way I can clear my
thoughts. It is kind of you, my lord, but I assure you I am not
such a fine lady that I have not walked miles farther at home.
Thank you anyway, and tell his lordship I shall not fret him
again, for I shall never return."

"I think," Lord Kingston said slowly, now taking her arm,
despite her attempt to pull away, "that I must insist."

Now that he was in front of her, Elizabeth could see his
expression clearly without the radiance of the sun to obscure

it. And the expression she read alarmed her. She tried to drag herself away and grew more anxious as he held her fast. Although now the sun was at her back so that he could not read her countenance, he seemed to understand her well enough.

"Useless," he said implacably. "You shall come with me, Elizabeth."

The last bursts of the sun's fading light sent radiance to touch upon the scene, making Lord Kingston's neckcloth dazzling white and Elizabeth's hair shot silk. It touched upon the leaves, upon the stones, and struck a glint upon the pair of spectacles that peered out from behind a tree. But neither of the pair struggling in the clearing noticed it. The eyes behind the spectacles grew wide with fear and foreboding. He had come after birds' nests and found a hornet's nest instead.

After only a second's pause, the glint disappeared as the owner of the spectacles decided rapidly that discretion was, in his case, both sadly and easily the better path to valor. The small figure wasted not a moment, but crept bent double, a difficult feat for such a bulky little parcel of a boy, silently from the scene. And then, once he had achieved the wide lawn, he straightened and began to run flat out.

He had kept his own counsel unhappily but conscientiously for all these past weeks, remaining silent through intimidation and the inescapable awareness of his own helplessness. But he knew full well from his own bitter experience that his new true friend, Elizabeth, was now in certain though unspecified danger. The decision was sudden and irrevocable; no true hero from any of his treasured secreted books would ever have let a maiden fair suffer due to his own cowardice. So he ran as though possessed. And he was, both by fear for her and by fear of his own wild recklessness.

But it was difficult for such a rotund figure to make much headway, though he was impelled as though pursued by demons. Thus it was that when he finally reached the Earl's study, he was panting so that it took several long gasping moments for him to state his case so that it could be half-understood.

"Elizabeth, Elizabeth," Lord Kingston said, shaking his head sadly as he imprisoned her hands in his and held her fast, "what am I to do with you? Here I try to be a gentleman, and all you can do is run from me like a frightened deer. Now, come, be a good child and come with me as a lady should. For all I want to do is the right thing."

"The right thing," Elizabeth said through clenched jaws, "would be to let me go my way unmolested."

"Oh, is that what you fear?" He smiled. "I'll admit I am tempted. Have been tempted since I first saw you. But I fear your reaction yesterday quite put me out of sorts. I am an expert in such matters, I assure you, and I could see that your thoughts did not match mine in that direction. Still," he said, smiling down at her, "it is never too late. Now that Morgan has spurned you, you have no future except that dreary little shop. No fortune, no prospects. You could still do better with me, Elizabeth. You are a devilish tempting little creature. There is nothing for you here, or at home either. Why not cast in your lot with me? I am not hard to take, I'm considered quite expert in the ways of love, in fact. Come with me to London. We'll live at the top of the mark, and I will see that you don't regret it."

"I would not marry you for any reason," Elizabeth cried once again, trying to tug free of him.

"I did not mention marriage," he said coolly.

Elizabeth started and then said, in an effort to match his coldness, "You are not a gentleman, and I may not be a lady, but that does not make us a pair. Release me instantly."

"Or what?" he said angrily. "No, it was a bad idea to start with. It's as well you turned me down. For it was the work of impulse, and Isabel would skin me if she found out. No, I shall stay with my original thought. You shall come with me, Elizabeth. And if you continue this struggle, I can, I assure you, guarantee your compliance. But I do not think you'll relish a bruised jaw, nor I the effort of carrying you down to the carriage. Now," he said calmly as she ceased her resistance and only gaped at him, "you will walk with me, my dear, and you will enter the coach with me. Then I will bid you a tender farewell. And you will leave Lyonshall, just as you wished, forever. No, don't look at me like that. I'm no murderer. I have too much wit for that. But you will be sent on a journey across the seas. And by the time you get back to England, if you do indeed decide to return after your weary travels, all will be changed. Morgan will be gone from here, as it is not his custom to remain for long. Even if he is in residence, I do not think you will have any reputation or word to be honored, not after your odd disappearance and your long sojourn abroad.''

Elizabeth felt cold to the bone and only whispered, ''Why? What have I done to you?''

He looked at her oddly, and then cupped her chin with one hand. ''You do not know, do you? Little innocence, it is not what you have precisely done, it is what you were about to do. It does not suit me for Morgan to be wed again, it does not suit me for him to decide not to name an heir. You were about to upset my plans, that is all, my love. Although,'' he breathed, looking into her startled clear topaz eyes, ''I do understand his change of plans, I do sympathize indeed.''

He drew closer to Elizabeth and pressed a kiss upon her lips. She recoiled instantly and began to fight, trying futilely to free herself. He raised his head and gave her a look of such anger that she flinched.

''No? Then I shall desist. I do not have to take what is not freely given. But I wonder if the fellows I have hired to see to your safe transport will have such reservations. Nor do I much care. But,'' he went on savagely, dragging his hand slowly down her breast and along her body with insulting languor, ''I think you shall. Come, Elizabeth,'' he said abruptly, dropping his hand so as to more safely secure his grip upon her. But he hardly had need to, for Elizabeth only stood still and stared at him in horror. She whispered with sudden dread comprehension, ''Morgan never wrote that note, did he?''

''So slow for so swift a lass. No, sweet, he did not. I had only to follow Bev this morning to get your direction. You can imagine our consternation when we discovered you were not, after all, on your merry way back to your hat shop. But now you shall undertake another journey. Not so merry perhaps, but surely swifter and farther. Do not look so stricken. After all''—he laughed—''what is a reputation to a shopgirl? It is time for us to go. You have your choice: either walk with me or begin your journey with an aching head. It is all the same to me.''

Elizabeth only dug her feet in and shut her eyes. She did not welcome pain, but she knew that she could never meekly accompany him, no matter what the penalty. She stood in the glade listening to the late bird calls and the sound of the wind in the canopies of the trees. She heard her captor heave a great sigh and mutter about what a fool she was. She braced herself for a blow that never came. For her eyes snapped open as she suddenly heard a new sound, that of distant voices hurrying close. Lord Kingston dropped his fist and wheeled about as he heard them as well.

But when Elizabeth turned to see the first of a collection of people entering the clearing and felt herself grow dizzy with exultant relief, she also became aware of the fact that Lord Kingston still gripped her close. He had, in fact, thrust her in front of himself. She felt him fumble one hand into his jacket and then hold her so tightly about the waist as to almost cut off her breath.

Her first thought when she saw the Earl, moving with rapidity although leaning upon his walking stick, was as to how she would ever explain this compromising situation to him. For she was in Lord Kingston's embrace again. Now she despaired. Even though she knew her entire future had just been threatened, her only present concern was as to how he would ever trust her again.

But he only glanced at her once, and then gave his full attention to Lord Kingston. Bev was beside him, and had started forward to her with a glad smile, but the Earl pushed him back. Through the confusion and fear that surrounded her, Elizabeth could still recognize some familiar faces before her. There was Owen, half-crouched beside Bev, and the Earl's man of business, and a tall footman she had often seen. But the two other men crowded close were strangers to her.

The Earl stepped forward and signaled them to quiet and then smiled at his friend. ''Harry,'' he said softly, ''don't be an idiot. The race is run. There's nothing more to profit from it. It is over. Let her go and we will talk.''

"Talk?'' Lord Kingston snarled. "Talk, is it? About what, my dear? Whether I shall go to Newgate or Australia? Keep such talk to yourself.''

"Harry,'' the Earl said reasonably, limping closer, "you are not a fool. Where can you go from here? Do you think you can just turn and walk away with her now? It's too late, my friend. You had a lively dance, but the music has stopped. I'll swear you are a more reasonable fellow than this.''

"Oh, I am reasonable,'' Lord Kingston said with a smile in his voice. "Reasonable enough to know that you will take care when you see this.''

Elizabeth felt her arm jerked back, and saw from the corner of her eye the pistol Lord Kingston produced from behind her back.

"I am a reasonable shot, you recall,'' he added tightly.

The Earl only stepped closer and said dryly, "More than reasonable, if you can get us all with one ball, Harry. Come, there are ways we can work this out, still. But not if you harm Elizabeth. Then there will be no recourse. There yet may be an honorable way out for you, but not if you add murder to your list.''

"Isabel, was it?'' Lord Kingston spat. "That jade. Did she think to take all and throw me to the dogs? Well, I know enough to settle her. Or was it that fat toad Owen? He never liked the idea of my becoming his papa, though for all I know I might already have had that honor.''

"Neither,'' the Earl said, coming so close that Elizabeth could see the glint in his eyes. "It was I. I knew the moment you came to Lyonshall, my friend. 'Tall, fair, well-set-up young gentleman' was the description I heard in London. That and the fact that James Everett Courtney, my designated heir, knew all about me and my home. Who else, Harry? When you stepped through the door, I knew. I remembered all those long and lonely hours in the hospital when I told you of my life. And then when you said you were on your way to rusticate at Heron Hall, I was sure, for I had heard that Heron Hall was on the auctioneer's block, it was so encumbered by mortgage and debt. And then, Harry,'' he went on, standing still and so close that Elizabeth could hear his every indrawn breath, ''it was foolish of you to pretend to no interest in Isabel, and no strong attachment to her at all. That made no sense. I know you of old. Neither did your schemes. I wonder at their crudity. Did you think I would pay heed to a drunken youth's maunderings, or fail to note who filled him with spirits? Did you think I would believe Elizabeth attracted to you, even for an instant? I am not such a fool to think all females akin to my dear late wife, and no actress could simulate Elizabeth's very real disgust of you.''

But seeing Lord Kingston's lips pull back and his grip on Elizabeth become cruelly tight, the Earl changed his tone and sighed deeply. ''But that must have all been Isabel. How could you have listened to her or credited a thing she said? I only waited till I could get documented proofs, whilst you were under my roof. Do you see that fellow there, Harry? Mr. Jensen, the fabulous bootmaker. He knew you on the instant.''

''I never forget a foot,'' one of the strange gentlemen spoke up fervently, before his companion elbowed him in the ribs.

''And the other fellow is employed by Bow Street. I thought to have the matter settled between us, Harry,'' the Earl said sadly, ''but then I saw that you and Isabel had further plans. She summoned you, of course, to discredit Anthony and Elizabeth. And would have done the same for Richard, if he were not so busy doing it for himself. But it was foolish of you to come, Harry. Did she actually convince you that if all obstacles were removed I would fall into a romance with her? Or did you think I would settle all upon Owen, and then you two could find a way to dispense with his inheritance . . . and eventually myself as well?''

Lord Kingston's face flushed, and Elizabeth felt his body grow suddenly taut.

''No matter,'' the Earl continued. ''It hardly matters now. Though I confess that when Isabel was told all the truth, she went into strong hysterics. She did not know you as James Everett Courtney. Was there no honor among thieves? Don't take umbrage, you were wise not to trust her. Come, Harry, this is sad stuff. Come back with me, we shall see what we can yet retrieve from our lost friendship, in the name of gentlemen. Loose Elizabeth, Harry. You have tried your damnedest to do her injury. That must end now. Indeed, I only sent her away so that she could be safe from your plans until I had the evidence in my hands.

"She has no part in this, Harry. Free her now. She did not even know of my suspicions or plans. How could I have told her, when her emotions lie so close to the surface of her eyes, and her face is so transparent? You and Isabel would have had the truth from one look at her, moments after she herself did," the Earl went on, at last letting his gaze rest sadly upon Elizabeth. "I had to send her away when I realized how far you were prepared to go, but only so far as the Inn. For I knew the whole wretched business was drawing to an end. Loose her, Harry, and be done with it at last."

"I shall be done with it," Lord Kingston shouted, "for I hold her now. And if that is the only way I can get at you now, through her, I shall. Damn your eyes, I shall!"

The Earl shook his head. "Harry, Harry, do be sensible. I longed to destroy you that day in the salon, but my hands were then tied. For I could neither challenge you nor order you from my house until the net was closed about you. What do you think I will do to you if you harm her now? But more to the point, what will it profit you? You are many things, but not a murderer of defenseless females. And I did not think you a man to hide behind a female's skirts," he added with a sneer.

"Nor am I," cried Lord Kingston, pushing Elizabeth away from himself with such violence that she stumbled and Lord Beverly had to rush to catch her and hold her upright.

"But you, my dear friend," Lord Kingston said, pointing his pistol straight at the Earl, so close that the barrel touched his chest, "are a man. And what is to stop me from finishing you here and now?"

The Earl simply stood and looked at his erstwhile friend with a weary expression. He shrugged. "Nothing, I imagine. But, Harry, what will it profit you?"

Lord Kingston hesitated and then, a look of wild despair upon his face, began to lower his pistol slowly toward the ground.

"You are wrong!" cried a young high voice almost cracking in its excitement. "For I shall stop him!"

Anthony burst into the clearing, disheveled and breathless. He carried a long chased-silver dueling pistol in his hand, and he stood facing Lord Kingston and the Earl, and pointed the pistol toward them.

"Drop it, I say!" he shouted, the pistol wavering wildly as his hands trembled in agitation. "For I have taken it from Morgan's study, and I know how to use it, Harry. I have been your dupe, but no more. I demand you drop your pistol. At once!"

Lord Kingston wheeled to face Anthony and said with a trace of his old insolent drawl, "And have you even cocked it, young half-cocked fool?"

"I have," Anthony shouted. "Now, drop yours or I shall fire!"

The Earl raised his hand in a motion of denial to Anthony, and Lord Kingston turned to note his gesture with amusement.

Then Anthony, wild with anger, raised his pistol, and holding it with two hands, closed his eyes and fired.

The explosion cast him back a step, and it was moments before the smoke cleared. Lord Kingston dropped his pistol and clutched at his heart in mock distress. "Behold me terrorized, young Tony. I doubt you could hit an elephant at two paces."

"Do not denigrate the boy," the Earl said softly, in amazement, "for he has at least hit something. But I fear," he said on a thread of voice, before he sank to the ground, "that it was me."

— 16 —

"Incredible!" Dr. Woods said in amazement as he entered the room where Elizabeth had paced and waited. "Quite incredible. I shall have a paper out of this, see if I don't," he went on, drying his hands on a towel and muttering as if to himself. "Present it in London, see if I don't. Won't it be grand to see old Wilfred's face when he finds out what his old classmate from the provinces has come up with? He'll turn green as turtles from envy. A paper and a treatise, see if I don't have both."

"Will he live?" Elizabeth cried in agitation. She had waited all this hour, after Lord Beverly had gently but firmly turned her from the Earl's bedchamber. They had borne him back to his rooms, bloody and insensible, and she had wanted to stay with him but had been sent away. So she had waited alone. Anthony, white-faced and stricken, had stayed with Bev and the Earl until Dr. Woods arrived. Lord Kingston had been sequestered with Mr. Tompkins and the man from Bow Street. And Owen had gone to his mama, who was said to be prostrated with grief at the turn of events.

Now at last Dr. Woods had come to her, but all he did was speak to himself. "Live? Of course he will live, girl," Dr. Woods said angrily, as if annoyed that she had interrupted his train of thought. "Fellow's got the constitution of an ox. He's lost a great deal of blood, but he'll do, he'll do. But what a coup!" he began again, as though thrilled by some inner discourse. "The look on those London experts' faces when they hear my paper. Aye, that will be worth the price of

211

admission. I'll get to it at once, tonight, if Mrs. Crawford
don't decide to birth that infant at last. Then, the look on their
faces," he caroled to himself.

Elizabeth ran to the doctor and beseeched him, "What are
you talking about? How is the Earl?"

"He'll do, I said," the doctor said emphatically. "Weren't
you listening? But what a happy circumstance. Here he goes
off to Sir Wilfred, and Sir Corbett, and a slew of other fine
fellows in London. Top-of-the-trees fellows, with teaching
positions and fine addresses and heavy fees, and they all
shake their heads sagely and tell him there's naught to be
done. And then his old family sawbones, a simple country
fellow"—the doctor chortled happily—"a fellow that's not
above putting poultices on cattle and drawing a tooth for a
cow now and again when he's needed, that simple old fellow
comes up with the answer. They'll have a spasm," he said
with deep pleasure.

"You see," he said, turning to Elizabeth at last, with
glittering eye, "I knew that there must have been a reason
that damned limb didn't heal properly. For the shell was
removed, there was no infection, he ought to have been, at
least, free of pain. But though I racked my brain, I couldn't
account for it either. But I knew there was an answer.

"Now," he said, looking at Elizabeth, but not seeing her,
"when that young cawker put a bullet deep in his thigh—"

Elizabeth could not restrain a gasp. The doctor looked at
her as if seeing her for the first time. "Ah, in his limb, I
meant," he said quickly. "Sorry, my girl, though I didn't
think you so missish," and then went on, "I sharpened up
my knife and went in after it. I made the incision good and
deep to get at it, and wide as well, for there's no telling what
infection will result if you don't clear the whole area. That
much I do know. I got at the ball quick and neat as you
please, and then when I went to feel the wound to make sure
it was clear before I closed the whole, I felt it. I felt it," he
cried in exultation.

"Only the tip of it, the sharp tip, for the rest, the bulk of
it, was way down near the top of his old scar on his knee. A
fragment, my dear. A long splinter, a fragment of the shell

that had crippled him in Spain. One that those fools at the hospital had missed. Though I do say," he said magnanimously, "that I can see how they did. Things must have been a fine mess during battle, and it was down snug against the bone, that I will give them. But there it lay, and that is why the poor devil had the pain. It took me the better part of my time to get it out at last, it was so firmly in. But get it I did. Now," he said, wagging his finger in front of her nose, "I shan't say he'll ever be ready for the corps de ballet. Nor that he'll be waltzing at Almack's with you. But he'll have no more pain. And one can never tell, can one?"

Dr. Woods closed his eyes as if in supplication. Then he opened them and grinned hugely. "But their faces, their faces when they read my paper. For they missed it entirely. It's true," he said with satisfaction, "that there's no way a man can see through flesh and blood. But they ought to have known something was amiss. For I did."

"I'm sure," Elizabeth said, giddy with relief.

"I'll get to it tonight, see if I don't. At least ten pages," the doctor said again, "and I'll be back here in the morning. He'll have some fever, to be sure. But he's got the luck of the angels. If that young cousin of yours had aimed just some inches higher, his lordship would truly have needed to name an heir, for he would never have been able to . . ." But here the doctor seemed to recollect himself and his audience and he stopped and glowered at Elizabeth.

"Why are you waiting here?" he demanded. "I told you his lordship wants to see you. You'd best hurry, before the sleeping draught I gave him takes hold."

Elizabeth fairly flew up the stairs, not even pausing to argue with the doctor.

When she reached the bedchamber, she knocked softly and Lord Beverly opened the door for her. But she had eyes for no one save the Earl, who lay unnaturally still, and so pale that her heart sank. She went to his bedside and saw that he was watching her with a smile upon his lips.

"Forgiven, Elizabeth?" he asked slowly.

She could only nod.

"Good, good," he sighed, closing his eyes, "for it was only for your own good, you know."

"What can I do?" Elizabeth asked Lord Beverly frantically. "What I can do for him?"

"Why, stay, Elizabeth," the Earl said softly. "Stay with me."

Elizabeth stayed. She stayed till the day three carriages arrived, one to bear off a weeping Lady Isabel to London, another to take Lord Kingston off on the first leg of his enforced and permanent journey to the Continent, and yet another to carry an excited bespectacled Owen off to his new boarding school. She remained until the first tints of autumn touched the margins of the trees and a cool wind began to spring up around her when she took her daily walks in the garden. But she took those walks only while Morgan had no need of her, when she was not at his side reading to him, talking with him, or watching as he made his first strides across his room.

Now she waited for lunch with him, as he was closeted with Cousin Richard. Cousin Richard had returned shortly after the "accident," as they now called it, and had remained at Lyonshall as well. But he was, at last, to leave today. Anthony and Lord Beverly were off on one of their frequent jaunts, and Elizabeth put down the book she had been reading, and wondered how long it would be before her own homeward journey began. For though she had been in the Earl's constant company, and they had laughed at many a jest and shared many comfortable moments, there had been nothing loverlike in his attitude. He had looked at her, she knew, for now and again she had inadvertently caught him at it. His eyes had rested upon her, she thought, but there had been no other sign of preferment, and certainly nothing in word or deed, like that she had experienced with him before Anthony's rash action.

She had thought that this would be enough for her, this closeness and camaraderie. But, she discovered, it was not. To be able only to look at his strong features, to see his easy smile, to hear his deep rich voice, was in itself a torment. She would be better off, she told herself, to be away at last. She could not be his sister. And would not, she corrected herself, for as the summer drew to a close, so did every reason for staying. Now he could walk. Still with his stick, of course, but with greater ease. Now he could be off to the wide world again, and she to her own family and occupations.

As he had arranged (with only a little arm twisting, now that he was the lad's legal guardian, he had grinned) for Owen to be taken from his mother's care and put in a boarding school to pursue his studies with other lads his age, so he had arranged for Anthony's future. With the autumn, Anthony would be gone as well, but to university. "He has the makings of a politician," the Earl had said, with Lord Beverly agreeing by nodding at his every word. And when Elizabeth had protested that Anthony was a trifle revolutionary for that position, the Earl had thrown back his head and laughed. "Of course, but temper that with knowledge and maturity, and we may well have a patriot." He had chuckled. "Or at least a prime minister."

Their futures were set, Elizabeth thought; she ought to be happy. Uncle would receive assistance, and so she need not return to Miss Scott to the manufacture of bonnets. But she would, she thought, laying her book down, or else go mad with loneliness during the long days at home again.

Cousin Richard came from the study with a dazed and dreamy air. He paused when he saw Elizabeth stand to greet him. "I'm off," he said, "and I wish you the very best, Elizabeth. I don't know when I shall return, but I wish you every happiness. Lord knows," he added with a smile that quite transformed his long and dour face, "I am happy enough, and wish the whole world to share in my joy."

"She has reconsidered?" Elizabeth gasped.

"She?" Cousin Richard asked in confusion. Then his face cleared and he laughed. "Oh, Caroline. Oh, no. In fact, I think I shall dance at her wedding to the poor Baron before I leave. No, no, Elizabeth, much better than that. I have my independence at last, I have my future. And I don't think some fickle chit from London figures in it. Thank God," he breathed. "But my wits are addled. Morgan wishes to see you. Good-bye, Elizabeth"—he smiled—"and the greatest good fortune to you."

He bowed and left whistling softly under his breath.

Elizabeth entered the study to see the Earl standing there gazing out of the window.

"Cousin Richard is in alt," she said, walking toward him. "What did you say to him? If I may know," she put in quickly as he turned to her.

"Of course," he said. "It is only that I had a letter from my man of business reminding me that I had some time past purchased a tract of land in the United States—Virginia, it is—and reminding me that I wished at that time to begin horse farming there. But I never did, as I had no one to do it for me. I only asked Cousin Richard if he would take it in hand for me, as a favor. And told him that as he was to live there, he might as well take half the land in payment. But the gudgeon insisted that I wait until five years had passed, and then, if I were pleased with his work, he would take it from me. Well, of course, my back was to the wall," he sighed, "so I agreed."

Elizabeth laughed. "Some time past, is it, Morgan? I'll wager the ink is yet wet upon the deed."

"Why, Elizabeth"—he smiled—"what a wicked mind you have."

She only chuckled in reply, and began to ask him if he was ready to lunch with her, when he cut her off and came closer to her, bearing only a light weight upon his stick.

"As you are here," he said, "in the room where I do all my dire business, there is a thing I wished to say to you. If you have the time, that is, and can bear to let your soup grow cold?"

Elizabeth grew chilled at the seriousness in his voice, but concealing it as well as she could, agreed.

"There's still the matter of my heir," he began, standing close to her. "I have not named one as yet. No, that decision I spoke of was, you know, only a ploy to remove you and Anthony from Harry and Isabel's sphere. I have not, never did, name an heir. I wanted you to know . . ." he said impatiently. "No, I waited till I could stand upon my own two feet to let you know that I have decided not to name one. That is to say,'' he went on, with none of the cool aplomb he had begun with, "I don't want to name one by myself. I have decided,'' he said with a grin, "not to choose one, but rather to do it myself, in the more natural way. Although,'' he went on, looking down at her wickedly, "not quite by myself, of course.

"Devil take it, Elizabeth''—he said looking at her with embarrassment—"I am making a botch of this. When I was young, I declared myself in love like a silver-tongued orator. But now that I know what that emotion truly is, I am a tongue-tied boy. I want you to be my wife.''

Elizabeth, disbelieving, only gazed back at him.

"I know that I am not a great prize,'' he went on a little desperately, "for you do not judge me by my title or fortune. And I am older than you by a decade, and I do limp. Although Bev assured me a long while ago that it would not be noticed by the right female, still I fear I shall never partner you in the dance. But I do wish to partner you, Elizabeth, aged and infirm as I am.

"You know, at least, that I of all men will be a faithful partner. Ah, Elizabeth, you have been my heart's surgeon, for I think that I no longer bear so much as a scratch upon that organ, or at least so I think when I am with you. Do not desert your patient now. How else can I say it? Elizabeth, will you be my wife?''

"But,'' Elizabeth said in a very small voice, "why should you wish me, when you have all the world to choose from?''

"Where in the world shall I find such another as you,'' he asked, "with such courage, such wit, such integrity? You will note,'' he said, smiling, "that I wish to put it to you reasonably, and I do not mention your eyes, nor your hair, nor your lips, nor form. But, Elizabeth, there is another matter that has preyed upon my mind most onerously, and I have only waited until I was sure I was in health enough to prove to you that I am not a liar.''

"A liar?'' she asked incredulously.

"Yes,'' he said, taking her into his arms, "for I did tell you I suffered from no incapacity other than my leg, and,

Elizabeth, you have no idea of how I ache to prove that to you. How," he said, before he covered her lips so she could not answer, "I long to demonstrate that to you."

Elizabeth stayed deep in his embrace, responding to him without words, lost to all save his warm mouth and the feel of his strong frame against her own. It was only the sound of a loud expostulation that recalled her wits, as he dragged his lips away from her.

"Morgan!" Lord Beverly cried indignantly. "This is not at all the thing. Elizabeth is a guest in your house. I leave for but an hour, and see what transpires. What is the meaning of this?" he demanded with feeling.

"Elizabeth . . . ?" was all that Anthony said as he stood wide-eyed by his friend and stared at the Earl, and particularly at the Earl's hand, which remained firmly about his cousin's waist.

"Elizabeth," the Earl begged, his eyes dancing with light, "please, before Anthony takes aim again, tell me your answer."

"But I have no fortune," she said, her lips cold and numb without the sweet pressure of his. "I am not worldly-wise."

"You are all the world to me," he said simply, "and wiser than anyone I have ever known. You will be my fortune. Now, Elizabeth, do not compromise me further, please."

A world of words spun before her, but Elizabeth tried to be as wise as he thought her. "Yes," she said.

"Oh, good," Lord Beverly spoke, rubbing his hands together. "Now, as to the makeup of the wedding party, Morgan—"

"Later," the Earl said with decision, ushering his friend from the room. "Much later."

It was several days later that Elizabeth and the Earl stood at the base of the great white steps to Lyonshall and prepared to see Anthony and Lord Beverly off. Lord Beverly was fussing with the baggage and coaches as though he were going to London itself, instead of Tuxford, the Earl joked.

"Devil take you, Morgan, I'm going to meet Anthony's family. I have to see things right. I have to see to the second coach for the ladies as well as the one for the gentlemen. If they are to journey right back here with us, they have to be comfortable.''

When at last all was in order, Anthony bowed and happily took his seat in the carriage. ''We'll be there faster than the letter, and won't Uncle be pleased. See you next week for the wedding.'' He grinned.

But Lord Beverly paused, and he watched narrowly as his friend Morgan slipped his arm about Elizabeth again, and noted with dismay how she leaned in closer to her fiancé.

''By the by,'' Lord Beverly said, stepping down from the coach steps and walking over to the pair, who seemed to have already forgotten his presence. ''A word with you. Out of young Anthony's hearing. There is no longer any chaperone at Lyonshall, not that Isabel ever was one, of course, or at least not a proper one. But now that I am going and taking Anthony away for the entire week, there will be no one. I think it would not be at all proper for you to remain here without a chaperone, Elizabeth. I think you should take your old room at the Rose and Bear and only have Morgan visit during the day, or for tea, or dinner, or such. It will not do for you two to remain here alone for the week before the wedding. Not at all the thing, Morgan,'' he said, growing ruddy at the look he inadvertently intercepted that passed between the two of them.

''Of course,'' the Earl said smoothly, never taking his eyes from Elizabeth's lips.

''Naturally,'' Elizabeth sighed, ''I shall leave until the wedding.''

''Very good,'' Lord Beverly said abruptly, and turned on his heel and left. But the last thing he saw as he turned his worried eyes back toward the couple as his coach pulled away, was the sight of them still standing closely together gazing into each other's eyes as though the world had gone away along with him.

But that is exactly what did transpire. Elizabeth left Lyonshall not ten minutes after her cousin and Lord Beverly's dust had died down. She took a room at the inn, and stayed there, seeing the Earl only at teatimes, until her wedding the following Sunday.

At least that is what they told Lord Beverly when he returned. And that is what they told Simon Beverly Anthony Courtney, who was born the following spring, when he grew older. And that is what he, the eighth Earl of Auden, always told his grandchildren when they begged again to hear the thrilling story of the search for the heir to their great house of Auden. But it should be noted that as he remembered his parents and the long years they had together, he always grinned when he came to that part of the tale.

About the Author

Edith Layton has been writing since she was ten years old. She has worked as a freelance writer for newspapers and magazines, but has always been fascinated by English history, most particularly by the Regency period. She lives on Long Island with her physician husband and three children, and collects antiques and large dogs. Her previous title, *The Duke's Wager,* is available in a Signet edition.

ROMANTIC INTERLUDES